MEMORY REBORN

LIVING MEMORY SERIES
BOOK 3

DAVID WALTON

CONTENTS

for Emmanuel
our last little hatchling

CHAPTER ONE

Distant Rain Sweeping Towards Home as Night Falls woke yet again in her bare, odorless cell, wishing she could die.

It wouldn't be that hard to accomplish. Rain knew how to use her own chemicals to alter her body. The changes she could make were limited—she couldn't, for example, turn into a snake and slide through a small hole to freedom. But altering her glands to produce a chemical that would kill her? That she could do. It would be painless. She would simply fall asleep and never wake up.

She wasn't ready to actually do it, though, not yet. Partly because she didn't want to die until she understood what had happened to her and to the world she knew. Partly because she didn't want to die until she had taken her revenge.

She still knew almost nothing about the creatures who entered her cell twice a day, with their wire nooses and sticks that delivered jolts of lightning from their tips. They could force her to sleep with chemicals pumped into her cell, but usually, they chose not to. Instead, they burst through the doors without warning, driving her back with shocks whether she fought them or not, and lashed her neck and legs with their nooses. They forced her down and harvested the chemicals from her scent glands, chemicals that, when threatened, she instinctively tailored toward dominance and control.

She supposed that was why they didn't put her to sleep. The chemicals they drew out of her were more potent because of the violence. Once, she had given them scents that prompted pity instead, but when they discovered the change, they returned. They held her down and jabbed her again and again with their lightning sticks, shocking her face and neck and genitals, until in her rage she gave them what they wanted.

She had never smelled them, not once. They wore suits that completely covered them and blocked the smell of their bodies entirely. The suits were cleaned with caustic chemicals both before and after they entered her cell, removing all trace of their scent and destroying any scent she deposited there for them to smell later.

But she could be patient, and the rage never left her. Somehow, she would break through, and then they would pay.

Through careful trial and error, Rain began to search for a scent that would survive the caustic cleaning of the creatures' suits. The chemical required a covering of its own, a delivery package for each molecule that could withstand the cleaning but then decay over time to release the scent within. The scent would have a simple effect: forgetfulness, confusion, claustrophobia. Forgetfulness of security procedures, confusion about the consequences, claustrophobia at the thought of wearing a suit. All working together to create a desire to enter her cell without their suits on. If successful, she could take it from there.

It took a long time and many attempts. Finally, without warning, it worked. A team of five creatures entered her cell without their suits, wearing only soft coverings that did nothing to block their scents. These were the same creatures that had hurt her again and again. Distant Rain wanted to tear them to ribbons right then, but she held back. Their scents told her much about them: that they were mammals, which she had suspected; that they ate a complex variety of meat and plants; that they were not the ones in charge; that they were terrified of her.

Instead of killing them, she flooded their awareness with her memories. Not her distant memories, but her experiences in this cell. She forced them to feel the helplessness and violation and pain, to know what it was like to be electrocuted and held down and opened up and sucked dry. It wasn't so much that she wanted to be understood. She just wanted to hurt them as she'd been hurt.

The way they screamed and writhed, she was sure they were getting the message. She had chosen a memory in which these specific individuals had been her tormentors, so they would see their own hands inflicting the pain, even as they felt it from her point of view. But just as she started to leave the cell, more of them came with their suits and lightning sticks and shocked her until she could barely breathe. They took away the others and she never saw them again.

Rain cursed herself. She had been foolish. They had been hers to control, at least for the moment. She could have used them to help facilitate her escape instead of hurting them. She had reached first for revenge, and that had cost her the opportunity.

She still had no idea what lay outside her cell—maybe more cells, maybe thousands of creatures with lightning sticks. Or maybe wide open space, and freedom, and connection once more with her people. Though, if she were honest with herself, she knew that was unlikely. She had gone down into the pit knowing that the world would be different when she woke. In fact, it was more radically different than she had thought possible, with creatures she'd never seen and devices she'd never imagined. How long had she slept? Who were these creatures, and where had they come from?

She needed to be more clever if she ever hoped to get out. She tried a different strategy. This time, she developed a chemical caustic enough to eat through the skin of the suits they wore. It burned her own skin, too, but that was a small price to pay. When the next team came in, tiny traces of the chemical wafted through the air and stuck to their suits. The holes it made were too small to see. No longer airtight, however, the suits admitted the scents she flooded the room with, and she dominated them.

This time she was more subtle. She let them continue with their extraction, painful as it was, and leave unaware of her intervention. She required only one thing of them: that they not lock the cell on their way out. When night fell, she eased it open a crack, allowing the air from outside to filter in without drawing attention to herself. She smelled her captors, then: a musky, mammal smell, mixed with odd chemicals she couldn't identify. Judging by the intensity, some were not far away.

As much as she wanted to escape immediately, she knew that without knowledge of her surroundings, she wouldn't get far. She needed information before she could risk leaving, or they would just capture her again and adjust their methods. They could chain her permanently to the wall, or cripple her, or blind her, and still get what they wanted from her. She couldn't take the chance until she knew she had a good chance to succeed.

So she gathered her captor's scents, learned what she could from them, and waited.

CHAPTER TWO

As soon as she reached the facility exit, Li Ling knew something had gone wrong. A long line of employees stood at the exit, waiting while security guards comprehensively searched them and their belongings before letting them leave. Before today, there had been occasional, random searches, and those only half-hearted. Li Ling sighed. She would be home late.

Li Ling was not cleared to whatever went on in the part of the facility built deep into the caves. She was a research zoologist by training, but so far this job had shown no sign of requiring the skills for which she'd been hired. She was doing grunt chemistry work, refining a chemical with no idea of its origin or purpose. Every day, she donned protective gear, performed the same chemical process over and over without deviation, and went home, with no idea what it was all for. Given the protective gear and the secrecy, she suspected a chemical weapon, and though that disturbed her, no one was going to give her any more information.

It was all so frustrating. She'd been thrilled when she was accepted to the State Key Laboratory of Genetic Resources and Evolution, a top research lab associated with the China

Academy of Sciences. But instead of the lab at Jiaochang Donglu, she'd been assigned here, to this remote military facility far to the south in Yunnan province, with no explanation. She didn't even know what they were studying.

She wanted to quit, but government-sponsored science labs represented a large percentage of available research jobs, and a black mark from this one could cost her a lot of future opportunities. She sighed. She was still young. She would give it a little longer.

As she slowly approached the security checkpoint, she wondered what had happened. Perhaps someone had been caught selling secrets to the Americans? If so, the security team would be humiliated. They would want to show that they were in control and handling the situation. Best not to ask any questions or complain about the delay. Just do as you're told and get out of there. Maybe she should quit this job after all. Research zoology wasn't exactly a hot field, but there had to be options better than this.

When she reached the gate, she surrendered her bag to an angry looking man who dumped its contents out onto the table. Wallet, eye drops, lip balm, gum, planner, receipts, and a dozen other random items went spilling out and were stirred around by the guard. He handed her planner over his shoulder to another guard, who paged through it carefully, to her annoyance. That was her private life. When the first man picked up her set of three feng shui coins tied together with red string, she blushed. Her mother always insisted she carry them for good fortune. It was pure superstition, but it was a hard habit to break. Finally, they pushed her things across the table to her, and she hastily threw them in her bag, feeling invaded.

As she walked through the door, thinking she was free, a young man in a suit and tie stepped in front of her, blocking her exit. "Doctor Li? Please come with me."

What now? It wasn't like she had anyone waiting for her at home, but she always texted Keju after work on her way. He would be wondering what had happened to her. She hadn't been able to retrieve her phone from the tiny lockers at the gate yet, so she hadn't been able to let him know.

Li Ling stalked after the young man, angry but also a little scared. No one ahead of her had been stopped. She'd seen them retrieve their phones and then walk out into the sunlight. Had they found something suspicious in her belongings? She couldn't imagine what. But if not, why were they detaining her?

She followed the young man into a side room. It was small, consisting of a few cubicles with monitors showing views of the security line and the outside of the facility. A security office, then.

"Have a seat," the young man said, pointing to a chair. She sat.

A moment later, a tall, gray-haired man entered. She would have recognized him at once, even without the ribbons on his uniform, because his framed picture was mounted at regular intervals in the hallways. It was the site commander, Colonel Zhanwei. Startled, she started to rise, but he waved her back to her seat.

"*Li xiaojie, ni hao*," Zhanwei said.

Ling flared. He had called her 'Miss Li', but using an old-fashioned term, *xiaojie*, that in modern usage implied prostitution. He was an old man, and had almost certainly meant it in its older, formal sense, but she wasn't in the mood to give him the benefit of the doubt. She had earned her title, and he could damn well recognize it.

"*Li yisheng*," she snarled at him. *Doctor Li*.

He stared at her for a moment, taken aback, then he started to laugh. "Doctor Li, then." He turned to the young man who had led her there. "Yes, I think she will do."

"What is this about?" Ling asked.

"Li *yisheng*," he said, emphasizing the "doctor" this time

with a nod. "Graduate with honors from Kunming University of Science and Technology, post-graduate work at Kunming Institute of Zoology. Dissertation on odor-based pheromone communication among hynobiid salamanders." He looked at her questioningly.

"Yes," she said. "That's me."

"How are you enjoying your work here?"

She hesitated, but only for a moment. "Boring as hell, sir."

"You think the work here is beneath you?"

Ling winced. She'd played that badly. "It's not what I trained for, sir. I could do more."

"And so you shall. Do you know of any reason you should not be trusted with the secrets of the government of China?"

There was only one answer to that. "No, sir."

"Well then, Li *yisheng*, your work is about to get a lot more interesting."

FOUR HOURS LATER, LING FINALLY BOARDED THE LONG TRAIN ride from the facility to her apartment. She opened WeChat on her phone and texted Keju to apologize for being out of contact.

'Are you there?'

Li Ling's hands shook as she took her seat on the train. She held them together in her lap, clutching her bag, but she couldn't stop the grin from breaking out on her face. She could hardly believe it. *More interesting*, indeed. It was a dream, an impossibility, the most incredible zoological study that could possibly be happening anywhere in the world. She had been ready to quit, but that would have been the worst mistake she could have made, though she never would have known it. Whatever had happened that put security on high alert, she couldn't help but be glad for it, if it had opened up this new position for her.

After an endless round of paperwork, Colonel Zhanwei had led her past the vault-like doors that protected the high-security wing of the facility, built directly into a cave system on the side of the mountain. She had imagined a few small, cramped rooms, perhaps with stone walls sweating moisture and a persistent dripping sound. Instead, she found a vast complex, easily larger than the part of the facility she knew, all of it newly constructed, with fresh white paint and bright LED lighting. He led her past well-equipped labs and passed her off to none other than Sun Guo-Dong, one of the world's foremost molecular paleobiologists. A bit starstruck—she hadn't even known Sun was working at the facility—she barely even stopped to consider why when he instructed her to don hazmat gear. She was more worried about saying something stupid. Whatever she was going to see, it was obviously more interesting than what she'd been doing, if it attracted someone like Dr. Sun.

On the train, everyone wore masks and sat as far away from others as possible, afraid of the Julian virus. Several provinces in the north had been quarantined already to prevent the virus from spreading any further. It hadn't yet reached Yunnan, but things didn't look good. So far, worldwide attempts to contain the virus had failed.

Worries for another day. It was all she could do not to tell the sour faced woman what she had seen that afternoon. If not for the dire national security warnings, she probably would have.

Her phone chimed. It was a text from Keju: *Hey little phoenix.*

Ling and Keju were *lóng fèng tāi*, or 'dragon phoenix twins': a pair of twins with one male and female child, dragon for a boy, and phoenix for a girl. Keju often called her *fèng*, his little phoenix.

Long day today, she sent.

Everything okay?

Yes. Just had to stay late.

The phone rang in her hand, making her jump. She answered. It was Keju.

"You know I can tell when you're lying to me," he said.

Li Ling laughed nervously. It was both a blessing and a curse to have a twin. In the village where they'd grown up, none of the other children had a brother or sister at all. As twins, they'd been an exception to China's one child policy, a unique and curious relationship in a society that had no siblings. It had kept them close. It also meant she had trouble keeping secrets from him. But this time she had to.

She hadn't been prepared for what Dr. Sun showed her, not even a little bit. Who could have been? He'd led her down a metal corridor and into an airlock that hissed as the air they had come in with was replaced. Labs often operated under positive air pressure to help keep contaminants out, but this was something different. What were they replacing the air with? Was it a different atmosphere? All the science fiction books she had read as a child had raced into her mind in that moment, and she thought: *aliens*. Looking back, she hadn't been entirely wrong.

The door had opened, and she'd found herself face to face with a *living dinosaur*. Bigger than her, with powerful jaws and alert eyes, it was covered with simple feathers like spines that shimmered in the harsh lights as it moved. She'd seen dinosaurs in movies before, and even in skeletally-accurate paleoart, but it was a completely different experience in real life. She could see the intelligence in its eyes, the calculation. If there hadn't been a sheet of glass between them, she would have been terrified.

"I can't tell you," she told her brother. "I really can't. It's classified."

"But you're upset."

He was right. She had hardly even admitted it to herself yet. Without a chance to process what she'd seen, she hadn't yet put words to her discomfort. The idea of getting to work with a live dinosaur was so overwhelmingly exciting that her mind had so far focused on that, without acknowledging her underlying uneasiness.

Just what were they doing with it? She'd seen the dinosaur, but she'd also seen where it was being kept: the concrete walls and floor, the small space, the chains. Zookeeping had come a long way since the days when elephants were kept in bare pens with iron manacles clamped to their legs. Why was the zoological miracle of the century being kept in the equivalent of a medieval dungeon? She hadn't asked, not wanting to offend the famous scientist or jeopardize her chance to be a part of the project. She'd been focused more on the incredible impossibility of the dinosaur's existence.

Now, though, with time to think, she worried about its abysmal living conditions. Perhaps it had only been in that room temporarily, while its real habitat was being cleaned or prepared. Maybe it had needed veterinary care, requiring a small compartment to pump gas in to anesthetize it. It wasn't like they could walk in and put a mask over its face. She was certain that in time, she would understand the choices they had made and why. And if not? Well, maybe she would be in a position to influence them. The grin crept over her face again.

"Everything's okay," she told Keju. "Really. There was some kind of security breach. They never told us what, but they wouldn't let anyone leave until they'd tracked it down. Just annoying bureaucracy stuff."

She could tell from his voice that he wasn't buying it, but he didn't press. She was grateful for that. She asked about their parents, whom Keju was taking most of the responsibility to care for. After Li Ling had left to attend university in the big city, her parents had been forcibly relocated from their village to make room for a new shopping mall and a water recreation park. It was a common experience, but the only work her father knew was farming. He hadn't found a job, and the money the government had paid them for their house was all but spent. The stipend they continued to receive as recompense wasn't nearly enough.

Keju had a good job in construction and took care of them. Li Ling felt bad that she wasn't doing more, but her parents wouldn't have wanted her to give up her place for their sake. When she'd scored high enough in the college entrance exam to go to university, it had been their proudest moment. They were so pleased with her job as a government scientist, and bragged about her to all their neighbors. As Keju had said many times, the best way for her to care for them was by not disappointing them. She knew he was right, but she still felt guilty about it.

It was dark by the time she reached her stop. She made her way to her apartment building, exhausted, and fumbled in her bag for her key card. A man stood in the light of the neon sign of a corner teahouse, facing away from her. His silhouette looked somehow familiar. As she held her card in front of the reader, she studied him. *No—it couldn't be.* An acid taste filled her mouth and her heart pounded. Just as she opened the door, he turned, and she saw his face clearly in the neon light. Lao Zhou. A face she'd thought never to see again. He recognized her, too, but before he could speak or step forward, she stepped into the apartment building and slammed the door hard behind her.

CHAPTER THREE

In public, as Queen Sirindhorn of the Chakri dynasty, Mai was always serene and composed, as if nothing could overwhelm her or take her by surprise. In private, however, with only Kit and Arinya to hear her, she raged.

"Three hundred kilometers!" she said. "That's practically on our doorstep! An entire Chinese carrier strike group camped a stone's throw from Samut Prakan." She brandished a piece of paper at them, the report handed her by the Defense Secretary. She read aloud from it, striking the paper for emphasis. "The aircraft carrier *Liaoning*, cruiser *Anshan*, destroyer *Chengdu*, frigate *Zhaozhuang*, fast combat support ship *Hulunhu*, and cruiser *Wuxi*, plus I'm sure some submarines we can't see. Along with their complement of attack helicopters, fighter jets, and cruise missiles. That's enough firepower to obliterate our entire armed forces several times over. They could shut down our ports and ground our aircraft, and there isn't anything we could do about it." Mai glared at them. "So? What are we going to do about it?"

Kit and Arinya looked at each other. They were the only other people in the room, not counting Mongkut, her personal bodyguard, standing like a marble statue in the corner by the door. Mai trusted Kit and Arinya more than anyone else in her government, which was often a good thing. At times like this, when she wanted them to solve impossible problems, it didn't feel like it.

Only Kit and Arinya knew all the secrets of how Mai had come to power. Only the two of them had been by her side every step along the way, as she had used the domination chemical they had brought her to take over the largest crime syndicate in the country, leveraged her popularity into ousting the coup leader who had killed her family, and taken the throne. A year ago, Kit had been a paleontologist and Arinya a museum lab director. Now Kit was Brigadier General and Minister of Science and Technology, while Arinya was a high-ranking member of the Privy Council and a royal lady of the court. More than titles, though, they were the queen's closest confidantes, the advisors to whom she revealed weakness and fear and talked through the problems she didn't know how to fix.

Mai paced across the plush carpet. She was a tiny woman, barely five feet tall, but she radiated power and authority. They stood in one of the many lavishly decorated rooms of the palace, a room that Mai favored for the broad beams of sunlight that illuminated it during much of the day. The walls were covered with complicated patterns of red velvet, mosaics, and gold. A row of identical two-inch high carved demons with lion faces ran along the intricately carved crown molding against the ceiling, guarding the room against spiritual attack. The ceiling pitched toward a high point at the center, from which hung a massive chandelier stacked like a rounded pyramid. Kit and Arinya stood by the window as Mai alternately paced away from them and then turned on her heel to march toward them, her eyes blazing.

"Well?" she said, stopping in front of them. "Are we helpless? A month ago, they enslaved me and tried to take over our country through mind control and deceit. Are they just going to finish the job now with their military power?"

They had enslaved Arinya, too, but neither Kit nor Arinya pointed that out. "Have the Americans responded?" Arinya asked instead.

"Always the damn Americans!" Mai shouted. Arinya winced, but she didn't step back. They both knew berating them was part of Mai's thinking process. "Are we always going to go running to the Americans to rescue us? Should we skip the pleasantries and just apply for American statehood now? Or no, they wouldn't give us that status. We could just be one of their *territories*, convenient for staging military power. No. I will not rely on any foreign power to liberate us. That's just trading one master for another."

"They may be able to help in more subtle ways. That CIA agent, Smith, has been calling—"

"Smith." Mai scowled. "Don't even say his name. I never want to see that *farang kee nok* again."

Smith—if that was even his real name—had been instrumental in Mai regaining her throne from the Chinese, but she had always resented him for it. From her perspective, he had provided far less than the strength of American power he had at his disposal, but expected her gratitude and concessions for his government that far exceeded the service he'd rendered. Like a foreign tourist rich enough to pay who expects to get things for free anyway. Smith had been to the palace at least weekly, badgering Mai with requests for an American presence in Thailand, both overt offerings like radar and comms installations and more covert spy network arrangements. He presented all of these things as great opportunities for Thailand to benefit from increased intelligence about their neighbors, especially China, as if the United States would pay for such things in the spirit of national philanthropy. He also implied that the only reason she had her throne was because of him and American support, which—true or not—was an approach guaranteed to put Mai in a bad mood. Whenever she refused him, he slunk away looking aggrieved and offended.

Kit loved her for it. He enjoyed seeing her send the American agent away, his tail between his legs. Kit liked to think that at least in small part, he had influenced this foreign policy. Thailand alone for Thailand, and no one else. China and the United States were the giants here, engaged in a struggle for world domination. After China's attempted takeover, it would have been easy to think of the United States as the good guys and align themselves accordingly. But the United States government didn't care about Thailand. Taking sides in that struggle would only lead to Thailand being used up and thrown aside. They had to learn how to protect their own borders, whether through might or diplomacy, or they would never truly be a sovereign nation.

"We can't fight them with ships and planes," he said. Thailand had nothing close to the power of an aircraft carrier battle group, and their aging fleet of F-16s were no match for China's fifth generation Chengdu J-20 fighters. Add to that China's premier space capabilities, able to observe, coordinate, and precisely guide all units in a battle, and the Thai forces, despite the billions of baht spent on them, would be like waving a feather at a hurricane. "The only way for us to win is to get them not to fight."

"And do you have an idea how we might accomplish that?"

Kit gave a tentative smile. "I might."

KIT HOPED PAK COULD HANDLE THIS. THE EX-FARMER VISIBLY trembled in the queen's presence, probably made worse by such an intimate setting, a palace room with only her two closest advisors and bodyguard present. Pak had no such trepidation talking to Kit, with whom he had once plotted an invasion of this very palace to rescue Mai from Chinese control. But Mai was royalty, and to Pak, that wasn't far off from divine. Kit understood. Despite his daily experience with her as a human being, he felt much the same.

Pak prostrated himself before Mai, his face pressed into the carpet, showing the classic reverence of a Thai citizen to his monarch. Mai reached out an elegant hand. "Rise," she said. She knew how to play the part. Pak stood, but he kept his eyes firmly fixed on the floor in front of her feet.

"General Chongsuttanamanee tells me that you have a secret of value to our great country, known only to you."

Pak lifted his head slightly, though he didn't meet her gaze. "General who?"

Mai rolled her eyes. "Brigadier General Kittipoom Chongsuttanamanee, my advisor here."

"Oh! Kit!" Pak said. "Right. Yeah, I do. I mean, yes, your Majesty. I do have a secret."

"And will you share this secret with your queen?"

"Of course! That is, it involves a crime. If I tell you…"

"Pakasit Paknikorn, your service to the nation and to my person is so great that I gladly pardon you of any crime short of treason. You may speak freely, without fear of punishment."

Pak swallowed visibly. "Well, um, depending on how you think of it…"

"Just tell me."

He dropped his gaze even further, pressing his chin into his chest and staring at his feet. "I found a fossil."

"On your farm?"

"Yes. No. Not really. It was in the hills past my cassava plot. I was trying to route more water to my crops, and while I was digging, I saw this thing, you know? Sticking up, like a bone. I knew people would pay good money for some fossils, so I dug it up."

"By yourself? Did you tell anyone else?"

"Only Nikorn," Pak mumbled.

"Speak up."

"Just my brother-in-law, Nikorn. I needed him to help me. It was too heavy for me to manage by myself."

"So just one other person knows the location of this site?"

Pak let out a little wail and tugged on his collar.

"What's wrong? Did you tell other people?"

"I killed him. I killed Nikorn."

"You killed your brother-in-law? Over the fossil?" Mai traded a glance with Kit.

Kit already knew the story. "Just tell her the truth," he said. So Pak told how he had seen a vision of a dinosaur that had terrified him, and how he had fired his shotgun at the beast, only to find that it was Nikorn he had killed instead. He explained how he had fled from Khai Nun, leaving the fossil behind, and went to work for Ukrit in Tachileik, until the day Mai herself had walked into the camp and had taken control.

"That fossil was the same one the police found by Nikorn's body and asked me to examine," Kit said. "The one where I first discovered the chemical and what it could do."

"And no one else knows the location of the site where you found the fossil?" Mai asked. "You haven't told anyone else?"

"No one," Pak said. Only Nikorn, and he's gone."

"Could Nikorn have told anyone else?"

"I don't think so. He was a simple man, but not stupid. He knew we had to keep it secret."

"Did you see any other fossils while you were digging there?"

Pak shrugged. "No. I'm no expert, though. Plenty of rock there I didn't look at."

"And do you think you could find that place again? Could you lead others there?"

He nodded eagerly, risking a quick glance up. "Yes, ma'am. I mean, your Majesty. I know exactly where it is."

"Your Majesty," Kit said. "Allow me to mount an expedition to this hillside. "It is a mere ten kilometers from the site that was destroyed. The site that my team—the American team—found such a wealth of preserved fossils, as well as the dinosaur they were able to revive. It stands to reason that the location Pak discovered is the site of another modification pit, similar to the first. It could hold huge quantities of the raw chemical used for domination, or even another hibernating dinosaur, waiting to be revived. It could give us the power we need to resist the Chinese."

"Or it could give us another tempting prize for them to try to steal," Mai pointed out.

"We have that already. We have the land from which these fossils have been uncovered. China will assume there are more to be found. The only defense we have is to find them first and use them."

Mai nodded, thoughtful. "Then go. And find them first."

CHAPTER FOUR

Samira knew it wouldn't last. Their living arrangement on the Waters Ranch in Oregon was perfect in so many ways. The big house had room enough for Samira and Beth and their parents, Gabby and Arun, Alex, and even Wallace, her red-and-green macaw. The acres of land gave Charlie room to run, and no one else lived for miles in any direction. Their host, Brook Waters, was delighted to have them, and didn't even mind all the money he was losing on the cattle Charlie ate. He'd accepted Charlie as a thinking person more easily than anyone, and the two of them had formed a special bond. But it was just the illusion of safety. They had stolen one of the most powerful and secret weapons of the US government. They would use all the resources at their disposal to hunt for them, and they wouldn't give up. Eventually, their little group of fugitives would be found.

She still held out some hope that the CIA, seeing the way Julian was spreading, would offer them an olive branch. Everson might hate her for stealing Charlie, but tens of thousands of people had died around the world, and even conservative projections showed millions dead within a few months if something didn't turn around. If he was smart, Everson would set aside the past and actually help them get to Thailand. But she didn't really think that would happen. The idea that a dinosaur could use ancient genetic technology to find a cure was too outlandish for the intelligence community. Much easier to operate from the more familiar playbook of hunting down traitors wanted for stealing a classified national asset.

"Look at this!" Beth said. She burst into the big kitchen, waving the tablet Brook had lent them to use the internet, though they were all careful not to access email or any other accounts that might identify them. If Brook had been under any kind of suspicion, the CIA would be here already, so they felt reasonably safe using his accounts to research and communicate.

Beth shoved the screen at Samira, who took it from her to see an FBI alert with all of their pictures staring out at her. All of them were included, even Mom and Dad.

The alert identified them all as dangerous bioterrorists connected to the Julian virus and urged people to call a hotline with information on their whereabouts. Samira felt her heart lurch. So much for holding out hope. She'd expected to be branded a criminal, but seeing her own face on the digital equivalent of a wanted poster brought it home a bit more keenly. To everyone else in the US, they were terrorists now. She hated that she'd dragged her parents into this mess as well. On the other hand, she was glad they weren't at home seeing this news and believing the worst.

Samira passed the tablet over to Arun, and the others gathered around to see.

"We can't stay here anymore," Beth said. "We have to leave the country."

"Staying is a risk, sure," Gabby said. "But leaving is, too. Leaving means custom checks and passports and security, not to mention trying to smuggle a live dinosaur out of the country. None of us are criminal masterminds; we don't even know how to get fake IDs. They've got the whole United States to hunt through for us, and they don't even know for sure we're here. I say we stay."

"For how long?" Beth asked. "Because eventually, they will find us. One of Brook's ranch hands will spot Charlie one day, no matter how well he hides. Or someone will visit unexpectedly and recognize one of us."

"We should only stay long enough to formulate a workable plan," Gabby said. "Long enough so maybe they're not looking for us quite so intensely."

"We're not making plans, though," Beths said. "We're just sitting around waiting to get caught."

Samira knew her sister was right. The moment Everson discovered where they were, it would be too late. The CIA would descend on this place from every direction, with soldiers and helicopters and nets and guns, with no hope of escape. Nowhere in the United States could be safe, at least not for long.

"Let's talk about it then," she said. "Beth's right, it's past time we made plans." She held up her hand as Gabby started to object. "Even if we decide to keep laying low for a while, we still need an emergency plan if we think we've been compromised. Every option is dangerous. It doesn't hurt to talk it through."

"The obvious place to head is Thailand," Arun said. Gabby shot him a glare, but he shrugged and ignored her. "What other country is there where we know a guy who knows the ruler? We could have the direct protection of the queen there, and with Kit's power and influence, we'd have at least some expectation that the government wouldn't just use Charlie the same way the US wants to. They have large areas of open jungle more comparable to the tropical climate he was born into. Kit could, I don't know, designate a wildlife preserve, and we could keep Charlie there indefinitely."

"And you don't think China and the US will try to capture him again?" Gabby said.

"We'd keep him secret, same as here, but with the help of our host government. It's got to be better than trying to do it on our own. Besides, a place like that might provide a more permanent solution for Charlie. A place for him to live."

"He has a place to live," Gabby said, spreading her arms to indicate the ranch. "Brook has made it clear we're welcome to stay. He *wants* us to stay. As far as I can tell, he thinks our showing up with Charlie was the best thing that ever happened to him. What we should be doing is figuring out how to correct the narrative. Tell the world the truth about Charlie and about us. Work toward clearing our names while we're still free and can have a voice, not land ourselves in prison with a doomed escape attempt." She tapped the tablet. "If we're caught, this is the only narrative anyone will ever hear."

"You're forgetting one thing." Samira's mother spoke up quietly from a small table by the window where she'd been working on a jigsaw puzzle. "I understand your point, Gabriela, and it is dangerous. But from my husband's perspective, staying here is a death sentence."

Everyone knew what she meant. Samira's father had the disease, but thanks to Charlie, it was dormant, not making a significant impact on his health, and not spreading to the rest of them. Charlie had warned them that it wouldn't last, though. It wasn't a cure, just a slowing of a process that would eventually kill him.

"It's not just him, either," her mother went on. "It's easy to forget in our little slice of paradise here, but all over the world, people are dying. We can't stop it if we stay here, but if we get Charlie back to his modification pits, he might just be able to figure it out."

"We don't even know if there are modification pits left," Samira said. "We could dig in the same region, but it might take years to find anything, if there's even anything to find."

"Even so," her mom said. "It's better odds than here."

When Brook joined them after work that evening, they were still talking about it. Arun and Gabby had taken meal prep that day, and they'd made a simple rice and beans dish from Gabby's childhood, spiced up with the liberal application of ginger and garlic from Arun's Bangladeshi upbringing. Alex fanned his mouth and took a big gulp of water when he tasted it, but to Samira, raised on Ethiopian food, it was simply delicious.

"We should charter a boat," Beth said. "It's the safest option. Plenty of room to move around, and we can board in secret."

The eight of them crowded around Brook's big oak kitchen table, passing the food and piling it up on their plates.

"Takes a lot of people to drive a boat big enough to carry us all the way across the Pacific," said Arun. "Charlie can dominate people, or give us the chemical to do so, but it takes weeks to sail across an ocean. A lot could happen in that time, and we'd have no options. A plane would get us there in a day."

"But how could we take a plane?" Beth asked. "Planes mean airports and crowds of people and cameras and security. With a boat, we could leave from anywhere."

"Could we charter one?" Gabby asked. "Take off from some private airfield?"

Beth raised her hands. "If we had the money, I guess. But it takes a big plane to cross the Pacific, too, not some hobbyist's little puddle jumper. We'd need a major airport, and that means people and security and registering a flight plan. Planes get tracked by radar and directed by traffic control."

"I know Jerry over at Wagontire," Brook said. "He'd let us use his, no questions asked."

"What's Wagontire?" Alex asked.

"It's a little strip maybe ten miles north of here. Jerry owns some property; he's got a gas station, a little restaurant, an RV park, and on the other side of the road, a dirt airstrip. Private pilots land there and fuel up, get a bite to eat."

"Could an airplane big enough to cross the Pacific land there?"

"Land there? Sure, probably. But not take off again. The bigger the plane, the longer the airstrip you need to get off the ground."

"So how does that help us?"

Brook scratched the stubble on his cheek. "Well, I figured you could take a small plane from there over to Rogue International. If you're switching from one private plane to another, you probably won't need to go through all the ticketing and security checkpoints." He grinned. "Walking down a crowded concourse to your gate would be a bit awkward with a dinosaur."

"We need two planes, then," Beth said. "And at least one pilot."

"What if Charlie dominated a pilot? He can do that, right?" Arun asked.

"Yeah, but are we okay with that?" Samira asked. "Are we comfortable with the ethical step of taking over some innocent man's mind? It's like stealing his plane at gunpoint, only worse. We'd be forcing him to take risks he doesn't even understand. Even if we got away with it and the CIA found out afterward, they could treat him as an accomplice, ruin his life."

"So we need a volunteer," her dad said.

Samira gave a short laugh. "You have someone in mind?"

He shrugged. "We know pilots. Folks who've flown in and out of some pretty dicey situations before."

Samira knew he was talking about pilots for missionary and international aid organizations. "You really know someone who might be willing? Someone we could trust enough not to report us to the authorities?"

"I think so." He looked at her mom. "What do you think about Rod?"

Mom scoffed. "He's a risk-taker, a loudmouth, and a brute."

"But can he get us to Thailand?"

"And he smells bad."

Dad just looked at her.

"Yes, yes, I can't think of anyone better. He'll get it done, and he'll keep his mouth shut about it, too. I don't like him, though. He makes me uncomfortable."

"So that's a pilot. Maybe," Gabby said. "Does this pilot have a plane? One that can get seven people and a dinosaur across the Pacific Ocean?"

"We don't need to bring everyone," Samira objected.

"I can requisition a plane through Compassion," Mom said. She worked as one of Compassion International's regional directors. "Rod can pick it up from Colorado Springs and fly it to an international airport here. We work with planes that size all the time."

"They let you just do that?" Beth asked.

Mom grinned. "Being a director comes with a certain amount of trust."

"Everyone doesn't have to come," Samira repeated. "It was Alex and I who stole him; we're the ones who have to go. The rest of you could stay."

"I'm going," Beth said. "No way you're leaving me behind on this."

"We just got the band back together," Gabby said, and Arun took her hand. "Let's go find Kit and make it a five-some again."

"And of course we're coming," Dad said.

Samira gaped. "What? No. Mom, Dad, you're—"

"What? Too old? I'm not going to just sit around here worrying if you're still alive," Mom said.

Dad crossed his arms. "And I'm not sitting around waiting to die of the virus."

"Besides, it's my plane," Mom said. "Discussion over."

"It might get pretty rough," Samira said. "You really don't have to do this."

Dad raised his eyebrows. "Young lady, I've been traveling through war-torn third-world countries since before you were born. I've flown into a jungle on a two-seat Cessna and hiked over mountains with a pack on my back to bring eye care to rural people who couldn't understand a word I said. I've learned more languages than you've had dinosaur expeditions, so don't tell me what I can't do."

"Okay, okay," Samira said, laughing and raising her hands in surrender. "It's a party."

CHAPTER FIVE

In one day, Ling had moved from work so boring she was planning to quit to the most fascinating work of her life. Possibly of any zoologist's life, ever. Dr. Sun and the other scientists working with the maniraptor treated her with respect, even though her doctorate was so new the ink had barely dried. They answered her neverending questions about where the maniraptor had come from and how it lived, and enjoyed her astonishment and enthusiasm.

She even felt like she brought something new to the team. This maniraptor species had communicated via scent, and her work on scent communication among salamanders gave her insights into the mechanisms and experiments to try. Unfortunately, since they had only one maniraptor, there was no way to see that communication first hand, but she had unique experience in the area that she hoped would be useful to the team.

Her first day in the lab felt like it lasted a week. She didn't interact with the maniraptor directly, but she saw it again, just once, hunkered in the corner of its enclosure. She knew Dr. Sun and others went inside with it sometimes, but she didn't yet know why. She wasn't eager to try that herself. The thing was a killer. She might enjoy studying a tiger, but she didn't want to spend time in its cage.

Even so, she felt sorry for it. She hadn't been brave enough yet to ask why its habitat was so harsh. Perhaps it was just a matter of expense, though there seemed to be plenty of money flowing through this place. Eventually she would ask. She didn't like seeing an intelligent creature trapped, with no escape. She knew too well what that felt like.

When she retrieved her phone at the end of the day, she had dozens of messages waiting for her. One was from Keju, but all of the rest were from Lao Zhou, the young man she had seen standing outside her apartment. She had changed her number after college, but he had apparently gotten her new number somehow anyway. She wondered which of her friends had given it to him. Lao Zhou had always been good at charming people when he wanted to.

'*Where are you?*' his messages said, and '*Please don't ignore me*' and '*I just want to talk.*' She deleted them all.

I saw Lao Zhou last night, she sent to Keju, once she was on the train.

His response was immediate. *No! Why? Stay away from him.*

I didn't talk to him. He was standing in front of my apartment building.

Do you want me to come?

She did want that. It had been two months since she'd seen Keju, and she missed him. But he would have to take off from work to come, and that would cost him.

No. I can handle it.

When she got home, Lao Zhou was standing in front of the door to her apartment. He was dressed formally, in black pants and a black tang jacket. He was blocking the card reader.

"What are you doing here?" she asked coldly.

"My father died. I was at his funeral."

That startled her. She had never met his father, but of course he had one.

"I'm sorry," she said.

He narrowed his eyes, as if finding her wanting. "That's my Ling. Always thinking everything is about you."

She flared. "I'm not your Ling. And I was asking what you're doing in front of my apartment."

"I wanted to talk to you while I was nearby. Is that a crime?"

"That time is over," she said. "We have nothing more to say to each other."

He held up his hands. His nails were neatly manicured, she noticed, and his hairstyle perfectly set. He had always been careful with his appearance.

"Please," he said. "People can change. I'm going back home tonight. I just want to talk."

"Fine. Talk."

"Can I come in?"

She folded her arms. "No."

His look was aggrieved, as if she was hurting him with her unreasonableness. He'd worn the same look when she'd left the apartment they'd shared for over a year.

"At least let me buy you some tea," he said, indicating the teahouse on the corner.

She supposed she could give him that much. "Fine," she said. "But not for long. I'm tired, and I need to go to work again tomorrow."

The soothing scent of freshly brewed tea greeted them at the door. The place was small and inexpensive, with plastic seating instead of wood, paper lanterns hanging from the ceiling, and stock nature photos on the walls. Still, it was a peaceful place, and the dim lighting and gentle instrumental music made up for what was lacking in decor.

Lao Zhou ordered two cups of dark oolong and a plate of dim sum. "I've missed you," he said. His voice was too loud, disturbing the ambience. "Why did we ever break up? We were good together. Everyone said so."

She was too tired to argue with him. "What did you want to talk about?"

"I have a good job now," he said. "I work for Pinduoduo."

It was a good job. Pinduoduo had been started by a former Google engineer to help farmers connect to consumers. Small, traditional farmers could sell directly through their app, avoiding the large markups charged by middlemen. It had been very successful, with the added benefit that it helped China's traditional farmers survive financially.

"I was thinking I might be able to find a job for your father," Lao Zhou said.

Li Ling's eyebrows rose. "What sort of job?"

"We have programs where we invest in young farmers who want to follow traditional farming practices."

"My father is not young."

"I know. But not all the young men have fathers to show them how to do it well. We send older men with experience out to help them get started. It's a good program."

Li Ling sipped her tea, trying to hide her excitement. This was not what she had expected. What Lao Zhou described would be perfect for her father. She imagined him with dirt under his fingernails again, picking up a basket of produce and smelling it the way she remembered him doing when she was a child.

But no. This was Lao Zhou, she reminded herself. This was what he always did. These moments of kindness, of apparent insight and compassion, were only the honey that led you into doing what he wanted. Somehow he would never get around to fulfilling his promise for her father, but in the meantime, he would have her dancing from his strings.

"What exactly is your job with Pinduoduo?" she asked.

"I write software. But I know the director of this program.

He owes me money, in fact. I can get your father the job, trust me."

"Great," she said. "Do it."

"Maybe we could go together," he said. "I haven't seen your father for a while. He might not remember me. We could take a weekend, I could tell him what the job would entail, and then we could go meet my friend the director."

So reasonable. But Li Ling knew better now. She could feel the trap closing in.

"That won't be possible," she said. "I have work."

"Surely you could take off for a day or two."

"No, I'm sorry. It's a new job, and I can't jeopardize it."

Lao Zhou scowled. "Not even for your father? Really, what else are you doing for him? You're not exactly a good daughter."

She felt the wash of guilt he'd intended her to feel, but she knew his game now. He had kept her like this for over a year, pinballing between hope and guilt. Even toward the end, when he'd actually struck her, he'd been able to make her feel like it was her fault, like if only she behaved like a good Chinese girl should, they could have a happy future together. It had been Keju who had broken her out of his spell, who had made her realize how ridiculous it all was. Lao Zhou had tried to isolate her from him, but it hadn't worked. They were dragon phoenix twins, and inseparable.

She would not step into that prison again. "I think you should go," she said.

"Li Ling," he said, his tone scolding. His expression said that she was a foolish, petty little girl. A girl too selfish to care for her own parents in their old age.

"I don't have to explain myself to you," she said. "I told you when I left that I never wanted to see you again. I meant it."

He stood, hurt. "I thought you might want to help your father. Here in the city with your big government job, I thought you might at least do this little thing. But you won't, just because of some old argument. I forgot how selfish you are."

She stared at her tea, cold now, not trusting herself to look at him. "I'm sorry about your father. You'll have to leave me to care for mine the way I see best."

"Not care for him at all, you mean," Lao Zhou said. He turned on his heel and stalked out.

It was only after he was gone that she realized he had left her to pay the bill.

CHAPTER SIX

Kit's paleontology team descended on Khai Nun like a swarm of locusts. Besides the small army of scientists, students, and hired diggers that doubled the population of the village on their own, the surrounding land was overrun by nearly a thousand soldiers from the Royal Thai Army, entrenched in a perimeter with their trucks, artillery, mobile comms, and radar installations. They transformed the cassava fields around Khai Nun into a mud-tracked tent city. Any crops the local farmers had planted that year were unlikely to grow, thoroughly trampled by boots and off-road vehicles.

Despite the disruption to their agriculture, the farmers and their villages had welcomed them with open arms. Perhaps that was because Kit had paid each of them five times what their cassava crops could have earned them in a year of good harvest. And with so many customers, the village's trade in craft goods and herbal remedies grew substantially.

Kit and Arinya had disagreed about the size of the expedition. Kit had originally wanted a small team, a secret mission with strict need-to-know rules to prevent China from finding out about it. Arinya had argued that secrecy was impossible.

There would be too many people involved, and China would be specifically looking for that kind of activity. Better to assume their enemies knew everything and apply every possible resource toward developing the site and protecting what they found. Eventually, she had convinced him. More importantly, she had convinced Mai.

Pak was now a local hero. The fact that he had fled the village the previous year, leaving his brother-in-law dead, had apparently been forgiven in light of his return with more wealth than the village had ever seen. Kit had often spotted him walking through the village with his daughter, showing off her new school uniform to the important people of the village, basking in the respect of the other village men. His story had changed to fit the latest situation, and no one seemed too caught up in the details. Pak was the man of the hour, the local boy who had gone out into the world and come back with the rich city folk, who would find riches of untold value buried underneath their humble farmland.

There was only one problem. They hadn't found anything.

Kit had reached out to every professional he could think of with adjacent skills. Thailand didn't have much of a paleontology program beyond himself and his students, but they had geologists and anthropologists. Organizing the disparate professions and the hired labor to understand the goals had been difficult, but the task was clear: dig carefully, layer by layer, and report anything you find.

He'd been enthusiastic at first. The dig now covered acres, centered around the spot where Pak's fossil had originally been found. It was the largest paleontology expedition he'd ever heard of. Surely they would find more of the maniraptor fossils, and find them fast. But days turned into weeks, and all they found was rock.

In some areas, the Cretaceous rock was right at the surface; in others, several layers had to be removed to get down past the K-Pg boundary. As days turned into weeks, however, it became increasingly clear that this was not the site of a maniraptor modification pit. Kit grilled Pak multiple times, thinking that the farmer had led them to the wrong location, but Pak was insistent, and Kit didn't really doubt him. He'd seen the spot where amateur hands had hacked something out of the ground.

Kit couldn't sleep. Three weeks they'd been there, with nothing to show for it. He climbed out of his tent and wandered the site, ignoring the chill that came fast on this arid plateau once the sun sank below the horizon.

Even alone, in the middle of the night, he wore tight-fitting noseplugs that blocked all sense of smell, just in case. There had been no way to keep an expedition of this size secret. The dig stretched over an area of almost half an acre, larger than any paleontological dig Kit had ever heard of. He'd hired all of his former students and some archeologists as well, scouring the country to find enough people skilled at this sort of work. It didn't seem possible that China and the United States, given their intelligence networks, money, and focus on fossil digs in Thailand, could be unaware of the work. They would surely try something to take over or disrupt their efforts; either by slipping a spy in among them or compromising one of their workers. To prevent that, at least by chemical means, the team insisted on strict noseplug discipline, no matter the circumstances. Of course, either nation might take out their dig site with missiles or mount an invading force that overwhelmed their defenses, but at least Kit wouldn't make it easy for them.

String crisscrossed the ground on wooden stakes, gridding the site, a tripping hazard even during the day. The moon shone bright enough to walk by, though, and Kit knew the terrain. He'd been staring at it for weeks now. He followed the paths from plot to plot without a flashlight, going by memory and moonlight.

Nearly an acre of hilly terrain painstakingly chipped down

to Cretaceous sandstone, with nothing to show for it. Exposed like this, he could imagine it the way it must have looked then: a verdant tropical paradise, carpeted with ferns and dotted with monkey puzzle trees. He imagined them digging the pits as he'd seen in their stored memories, filling it with liquid, rushing to it to escape their doom. But if it had been here, what had happened to it?

The most obvious answer was that it had been destroyed. Sixty-six million years was an incredibly long time, more than enough to eradicate any trace. The fossils that did manage to survive from ancient eras were always something of a miracle. Only the tiniest fraction of the animals that died did so with the perfect conditions to preserve their skeletons across the ages.

His eyes traced the uneven ground, the grid of string, the neat tags fluttering from them indicating their coordinates. Underneath lay the ground that the maniraptors had walked when Thailand had belonged to them. In places, the K-Pg boundary line glinted in the light. The boundary was a line of sediment, found around the world, where the debris from the asteroid impact that annihilated the dinosaurs had settled. In the daytime, it was a thin gray line, barely noticeable, but notable for its high iridium content. At night, the light reflected differently from it than the underlying rock, catching his eye.

Something caught his attention, tugging at his memories. He studied the path the boundary line took as it snaked its way across the surface. It would have fallen from the sky as ash or burning debris while animals fled and died. Which meant that except where tectonic activity had warped it, its basic shape should follow the terrain as it had appeared on the day the asteroid fell. And it looked familiar.

It wasn't possible. Was it?

Not believing his own mind, he walked a little farther, examining the barely glinting line of sediment. It wasn't a continuous line. In most places, it had been cleared away to reach the Cretaceous layer underneath. Wherever the terrain rose or fell, however, he could see the edge of it, and it formed a pattern. In places, the layer of sediment was horizontal. At others it dropped slightly, then continued horizontal again. It wasn't perfect—nothing survived the pressures of a geologic age without some shifting—but he knew what it was, because he'd seen it before. It was a staircase.

A long, low staircase, with a slower rise over a longer distance than those designed for human feet. The maniraptor culture hadn't created very much that could stand the test of time; no temples or monuments or statues. A simple staircase like this, even to the extent that it lasted, would have been overlooked by human explorers. He would have overlooked it himself, except for one thing: he recognized it.

The memories he had experienced from smelling the maniraptors' chemicals were burned into his brain, more vivid in some ways than his own memories. The vague shape of the staircase sparked one of these memories, and suddenly his mind's eye was filled with maniraptors running in terror as the ground lurched underneath them. The black sky filled with roiling clouds. They were headed for the modification pits.

He remembered the ravine, filled with shining green liquid. But it wasn't here. Kit could see the direction the maniraptors were running, farther down the slope. The pits weren't here. They were digging in the wrong place.

The maniraptors in his memory ran downhill, but in his present version of the world, the ground sloped up. As so often happened, the shifting of the Earth over the eons had altered the terrain, eroding away hills and pushing new ones up to replace them. In his mind, Kit tried to rotate the landscape to match his borrowed memories.

As if in a dream, Kit followed the path the maniraptors had followed towards the hope of salvation. He scrambled up the hillside, seeing two scenes simultaneously: the cool Thailand night, quiet and moonlit, and the chaos of the scene sixty-six million years earlier, filled with the smell of sulfur and the shrieks of frightened maniraptors trying to reach their only hope for survival, however small. Kit followed them, navigating a doubled terrain until he stood above the edge of the green pool. At least, he stood where the pool should be, several meters below him.

As day approached and the sky turned orange-pink in the east, Kit started shouting. He didn't dare leave the spot, in case he couldn't find it again. His bewildered teammates crawled out of their tents, blinking and wondering who was making such an early morning ruckus.

"It's here!" Kit shouted at them. "I found it! We have to dig here!"

CHAPTER SEVEN

Samira tapped impatiently on the coffee maker as coffee dribbled slowly into her mug. Since they'd talked about leaving, she'd felt increasingly stir crazy hanging around here. She felt like there was a target on her back, as if they were all standing in the open where they would be spotted at any moment.

"Good news," her mom said, taking Brook's phone away from her ear. "We've got a plane. It's still in Colorado at the moment, but it's ours to use as soon as Rod can fly it here."

"Where's Rod?"

"Still in transit. He's driving in from Arizona. Didn't want to take a flight because of the risk of Julian."

Samira had just taken a first sip of her coffee when they heard the engine growl of a vehicle moving fast. She lifted the curtain slightly and peered outside.

It was Brook, roaring up the drive toward the house in his pickup. He hit the brakes hard enough to send a plume of dust swirling into the air and leaped out without even turning off the engine. He crashed through the front door with his shoulder and burst into the kitchen. "Strangers in town," he gasped, out of breath. "Showing your pictures around. They know you're here."

"What? How did they find us?"

"Doesn't matter," Samira said. "Are they right behind you? Do they know which ranch?"

"Not yet, unless they saw me panic," Brook said. "I don't know how they tracked you, but it's no coincidence. You've got to get out of here. Now."

"We were too slow," her mom said. "Another two days, and we would have been gone."

"Doesn't matter now," Samira said, abandoning her coffee. "Leave everything and get to the truck."

"The plane isn't here yet. Where do we even go?"

"Go straight to Rogue International," she said. "Wagontire is no good now, not without a plane. At Rogue, maybe we can charter one."

"Bring Charlie into a crowded airport terminal? That's crazy!"

"Let me know when you've got a better idea. In the meantime, get everyone to the truck."

Brook took the stairs two at a time to go tell the others. "Don't forget the masks!" Samira called after him. She grabbed an N95 mask herself from their emergency stash. If Everson was coming, it would be with the domination chemical. If he got close enough for it to work, he would have enough guns with him that it probably wouldn't matter, but at least he wouldn't control them that way. Mask in place, Samira ran outside to get Charlie.

The sun was blinding after the dim interior of the house. She held up a hand to block the light and ran toward the wooded area of the property, calling Charlie's name.

How had they been found? Had a ranch hand seen something and reported it? Had they been spotted from a spy satellite? Or maybe Everson and his team had just systematically investigated every person Samira had ever known until they finally got down the list to Brook Waters and his Oregon ranch. It didn't ultimately make any difference. What mattered was that they were here.

By the time she reached the trees, she was breathing hard, and there was no sign of Charlie. At almost a thousand acres, Brook's property was far too large for her to search on foot. This narrow stretch of forest was his favorite place to be, though, and was where he generally spent his time during the day, coming back to the house only at night, when no one else was around.

She plunged into the woods. "Charlie!"

Why hadn't they thought of this? They could have fitted him with a walkie-talkie, or insisted that he always tell them where he would be. She had wanted to give him his freedom, something that had been in short supply during the months he was trapped in the underground facility. Despite knowing that the CIA could show up on their doorstep at any time, she hadn't really imagined this scenario properly or planned for it. How could she have been so stupid?

"Charlie!"

The woods stretched in a narrow strip running roughly east to west, following the meandering path of a tiny stream. Samira ran down the bank, jumped between two rocks to cross the water, and stumbled back up the other side. Dinosaur footprints ran along the muddy bank, but they didn't look fresh. She pushed through some undergrowth and out of the woods on the north side, where another vast field of grass stretched flat and unbroken into the distance.

"Char—"

She broke off mid-yell. In the distance, at the edge of the next field, dark shapes moved in her direction. They were just blotches at this range, five or six of them, camouflaged to blend in with the tawny scrub grass. They were moving. Samira had no doubt they were soldiers, armed and masked, coming to subdue Charlie and take all of them captive.

She ran back into the woods and leaped back across the water. She had to warn the others. By this time, they might be surrounded. She started across the field toward the house, but her breath came in ragged gasps. She wasn't used to this much running, and the fear closed her throat. The sky toward the south roiled with dark clouds. A storm was coming.

She heard galloping behind her. Were they chasing her with horses? She turned and saw Charlie, racing out of the woods farther to the east and gaining on her fast. He thundered to a halt beside her. "The CIA is here," she gasped.

"I saw," he said in his screeching voice. "Climb on."

"What?" None of them had ever dared to climb on his back. He was built like a bird, not a horse, and weighed no more than she did.

"Climb on. Carry you."

No time to argue. She awkwardly threw one leg over his back and clung to his neck, digging her fingers into the rough protofeathers for purchase. He shot forward, and she nearly slid right off, but squeezed her knees together and just managed to keep her balance. She could feel his powerful muscles propelling them along, apparently unfazed by her extra weight.

Despite her terror, she marveled as they sprinted across the field. She was riding a dinosaur. No human being in the history of the world had ever done such a thing. She remembered a series of fantasy novels whose covers featured medieval knights riding to battle astride roaring tyrannosaurs. She probably looked less magnificent, knocked about with every step and just barely clinging on, but still. She couldn't help but revel in the moment.

The others had thrown the tarp off of the battered Isuzu box truck and were hurriedly climbing in. Samira had planned to climb in the back with Charlie, just as they'd driven here to begin with, but Charlie had stamina and speed on foot, and could go places vehicles couldn't easily follow. It was Charlie the CIA wanted most. Maybe if they traveled separately, it would give the people in the truck a better chance to get away.

"Meet up outside Stacy's," she said. They had worked here for a season on an ichthyosaur dig, and Stacy's had been their favorite spot for a drink after a long day in the sun. It was a bit of a drive to get there, but then, nothing was close to anything else out here. Beth and Gabby and Arun would know exactly where she meant.

"Wait," her mom said. "Where are you—"

Charlie took off again, heading southwest. "Meet us there!" Samira shouted over her shoulder.

The wind buffeted Samira's hair, and she felt the jolt of each impact with the ground. She had ridden horses before, but not at a gallop, and Charlie's back was not as conveniently horizontal as a horse's. They had clocked him at 30 mph running on open terrain. Carrying her weight, he couldn't be making that speed, but he was *fast*. A herd of mule deer caught sight of them and sprinted away toward the woods.

As they flew across the endless brown grass, the dark clouds in the south converged and raced toward them. A minute later, they were running through a steady rain. The stinging drops hurt her face, but she was glad for them. Rain meant poor visibility. On the flat Oregon grasslands, a clear day meant you could see for miles. A woman riding a dinosaur and kicking up a plume of dust would have been easy to follow.

Soldiers on foot had no chance of catching up to them. She risked a look back, and saw two black sedans jouncing wildly across the uneven terrain towards her. She grinned. They were leading cars away from the truck, and she didn't think they'd be able to catch her on this open ground. As long as they didn't have any all-terrain vehicles—or a helicopter—Charlie should be able to lose them.

She worried for the others. Only so many roads crisscrossed these ranchlands, and the Isuzu would have as much trouble crossing the fields as those sedans. She looked back again, and saw the sedans falling farther behind. It wasn't working. She and Charlie might get away, but if they didn't draw off enough pursuit, everyone else would be captured for certain.

A gunshot echoed across the plain. At first she thought someone was firing at her, maybe with a long range rifle, but the black sedans were out of sight, and there was nowhere for anyone with a rifle to hide.

"It's the others," she said. "Charlie, we have to go back!"

But Charlie was already turning around.

As they thundered back the way they had come, Samira could make out a cluster of Jeeps and black sedans on the road that led to the county highway. It looked like the truck was surrounded by government vehicles. She couldn't see what was happening, but it couldn't be good.

Charlie swerved away from the vehicles, toward the strip of woods. "That way!" Samira shouted, pointing. "We have to draw them off, give the others a chance!"

Charlie ignored her, still racing towards the woods. They plunged into the undergrowth. The rain pattered against the leaves above them, but it was quieter here. Samira shivered and clutched Charlie's wet neck.

The mule deer they had seen earlier, maybe half a dozen of them, sheltered among the trees. They stood frozen in shock, poised to scatter, but they didn't run, not even as Charlie trotted right up to them. Samira realized Charlie was dominating them. With a sudden dash, he sprinted away again, bursting out the far side of the woods. The deer bounded along after them, keeping pace.

They raced along the line of woods like a herd of deer with Charlie as the alpha buck. What was he doing? They hadn't heard any more gunshots, but somewhere beyond those trees, Samira's family and friends were being captured or hurt.

The idea had been to draw them off, but Charlie wasn't doing anything like that. Samira certainly couldn't control where he was going; she could barely hold on. Thunder boomed to the south, and the rain fell harder. "What are you doing?" she shouted. "We have to help them!" But she couldn't tell if he even heard.

A quarter mile down, Charlie suddenly swerved into the trees again, the deer following. They leaped the stream once again and crossed over to the south side of the woods. They broke out again next to the cattle pens, fifty head of red Angus cattle in wooden enclosures. As soon as Charlie approached, they lowed and rolled their eyes in fear. They pushed up against the gates, trying to get out.

Suddenly, Samira realized what Charlie was trying to do. "I'll get the gates," she said. She slid off his back and landed with a smack on the muddy ground. She ran through the rain and unlatched each gate in turn, pulling them wide. The cattle surged out. Samira ran back to Charlie and clambered up again, slipping on his wet feathers at first, but finally getting a hold. As soon as she did, Charlie charged forward, and the cattle bolted in terror.

It wasn't simply the terror of a predator. Charlie was dominating them, controlling their fear and using it for his own purposes. The cattle thundered across the plain, their hooves churning up the dirt and sending clods of mud flying into the air behind them. They galloped in formation, like a living freight train aimed directly at the cluster of Jeeps and black sedans surrounding the truck. The deer bounded in a wider arc, coming at the cars from a different angle, like a cavalry unit flanking the enemy while they faced the main infantry charge.

The soldiers, who had been surrounding the truck, now turned to face the oncoming attack. Behind them, Samira could see her parents and Beth and Arun and Gabby, out of the van, their hands still in the air. Brook was there, too;

apparently he had decided to run with them rather than stay at his ranch to be arrested and questioned. The soldiers waited, then opened fire, raking the cattle with automatic weapons. It wasn't enough.

Several cattle went down, flipping and plowing into the mud. The others dodged around them or leaped clear, but didn't slow down. They closed the gap quickly. Samira saw the wide eyes of the soldiers as they tried to run, too late. Fifty thousand pounds of stampeding cattle slammed into them, trampling men, smashing vehicles aside or flipping them over, unstoppable. The deer flew in from the west, kicking and screaming, shattering windshields, the bucks swinging their antlers from side to side. Charlie himself charged into the fray, his claws and teeth rending. The sounds of gunfire turned into the sounds of screaming, then finally into a terrible silence.

The rain stopped. A breeze blew across the plain. Charlie stood still, breathing hard, his chest heaving. Samira slid down from his back and looked around in horror. A circle of carnage surrounded them, the crushed and torn bodies of soldiers and animals scattered among the wrecked vehicles. Only the center, where Samira's family and friends stood, was untouched. Outside that circle, no human remained alive. Samira scanned the dead. No one she recognized, but all of them young men, no doubt told they were confronting terrorists and traitors. Cattle milled, some limping or bleeding from bullet wounds. A cow with broken legs rolled and screamed by an overturned car. Brook picked up a dropped gun and shot it, once, through the head.

Samira turned slowly to look at Charlie. His muzzle was smeared with blood. "What have you done?" she whispered.

"Men had guns," Charlie said. "Guns to kill."

She wanted to say, *they wouldn't have used them*. But that would only have been true if they had surrendered without a fight. For her and Beth and the others, surrender meant imprisonment. For Charlie, surrender meant physical violation, torture, and probably death. It wasn't fair for her to say he should have done differently. But did killing humans mean the same to him as it did to her? Did it have any moral weight? Or was it just something that had to be done, like putting down a dangerous animal?

"We can never go back now," Beth said. "We'll all be held responsible for this. We have to get to the plane."

"That was true already," Gabby pointed out.

"Whoa, hang on." Samira's father waved his hands as if to stop them, though no one had yet moved for the truck. "What about these men? We have to bury them. We can't just…" He trailed off, looking helplessly at the torn and broken bodies.

"I'm sorry, Dad," Samira said. "I'm sorry I got you into this. I should have left you and Mom in Colorado, organizing aid relief and trucking food and medical supplies to communities impacted by the virus. But we can't stop. We can't bury them. More men will come after them, and soon."

"Back into the truck, then," her mom said, tears on her face. "Let's go."

Charlie stepped forward, but he stumbled, and nearly fell down. For the first time, Samira noticed just how much blood matted the feathers on his stomach.

"You're hurt!" she cried.

"Gun," Charlie said.

She rushed to him, gingerly pulling back the feathers to see a gaping hole, wet with blood. "No, no, no. He's been shot. What do we do?"

"I have first aid supplies in the house," Brook said.

Samira shook her head. "There's no time. We can't go back; these men weren't alone. More will be here any moment. We have to leave now."

"Here." Alex pulled off his sweatshirt. "Get in the truck and press this into the wound. They'll have first aid at the airport. That will have to do."

"But he needs more than first aid! He probably needs surgery. If there's a bullet in there…"

"I know. But we have to go."

He was right. She knew he was right. It was a terrible solution, but they didn't have any better ones. They clambered into the truck. Brook insisted on caring for Charlie in the back, saying he had experience with injured steers, so Samira took the wheel, Alex next to her in the passenger seat, and Beth tucked into the tiny seat behind. The rest of them piled into the dark metal box in back. With a jolt, they took off toward the county highway, leaving the dead behind them.

CHAPTER EIGHT

Prey lay on the cold metal floor in the dark as the truck roared on to their next destination. He had only ever traveled like this, blinded in the dark, surrounded by the smells of burning gasoline, hot metal, tarmac, and fear. He had no sense of direction, no concept of the terrain they traveled through. How far was this airport? How long would he be trapped in this box with these terrified mammals?

That was his own fear talking. They were not just mammals; they were people. They were his friends. They were all in danger because they had rescued him from captivity. And the truck, though confining, was not a cage. He had entered it willingly, and it was a step toward freedom. All the same, he wondered if it would ever be possible, in this world of humans, for him to truly be free. To make his own choices and come and go as he pleased. He thought probably not.

They were afraid of him now. He had killed some of their kind. He had killed enemies, true, violent men armed with the weapons that threw death from a distance, men who had been intent on capturing him and taking what they wanted from him by force. He was not sorry to have killed them. But he could tell that the others saw him differently now. He smelled it in their wary fear. They were afraid of being caught, yes, but now they were also afraid of him. Even Samira feared him now.

His side burned where the gunfire had struck him. Brook's steady pressure hurt, but he said it was necessary to stop him from losing too much blood. The box was hot and rank with too many people breathing at once. Prey produced a calming scent, meant to relax everyone and put them more at ease.

He couldn't see them, but he could differentiate them by smell. Brook, smelling of dirt and animals, his weight pressing on Prey's wound. Gabby and Arun, holding each other in the corner. Samira's parents together at the far end, near the door. Her father spoke softly and continuously, and Prey understood that he was praying. The man's belief in a God he had never smelled or seen intrigued Prey. He had always understood the world to have been intentionally made by an extremely powerful being—it was too perfectly balanced and exquisitely constructed to be otherwise—but the idea that you could *talk* to that being was completely alien. He supposed it was logical that a being that powerful could hear words spoken anywhere, or even read thoughts, but how would you know he was listening? Or that he cared?

Samira's father had told him all about the Book that God wrote, and about how everyone couldn't stop doing evil things called sin, and that they needed to be rescued. But if that were true, why had God told these things only to humans and not to his own species? Maybe his species didn't have the sin problem. But that didn't sound right—in his limited experience, humans and maniraptors had the same tendencies to selfishness, violence, and hate. Maybe God *had* revealed himself, but to some other Roost, and the news hadn't reached him before the end. Or maybe Samira's father didn't know what he was talking about.

Prey took a deep breath and let it out slowly, wincing at the pain. He needed something to take his mind away from it.

He tried to slow his breathing and concentrate on the things he could sense around him. The interior of the truck was almost completely black, but sight had never been his primary sense anyway. He focused his mind on the smells filling the air around him, reaching past the obvious, dominant scents toward the subtler chemicals among them.

He could still detect the Julian virus lurking in Samira's father. The changes he'd made to slow the symptoms were fraying at the edges, as the man's cells reverted to their normal genetic makeup. He studied the virus again, comprehending its structure and turning it about in his mind. Its mechanism for hijacking the human body was not too different from the way Prey could manipulate chemicals and build them up to his liking. He wondered if that was a coincidence. Rain had once told him the earliest changes his people had made to their genome weren't even remembered anymore. Was this how they had done it? Had an ancient maniraptor generation incorporated a virus into their genetic makeup? Or had the merging of a virus with their own genetics given them their ability to reshape scents in the first place?

So then, a cure. He wanted Samira and Beth and their parents and Alex and Gabby and Arun and Brook to survive. He had grown to know them and care about them. A human had once given her life to save him; surely he could return the favor and save some of them. This planet didn't belong to his people anymore. Their civilization would never exist again. Humans were the new rulers of this planet, and he wanted them—most of them, anyway—to survive.

He started to modify the virus, samples of which Samira's father had shed all over the truck. It wasn't easy. It was a complex chemical with many layers of functionality. Fully understanding it would take more expertise and resources than he had, but he was making progress, breaking down the pieces and understanding it a little better. After a while, he thought he had discovered a way to slow its progress a little more, but he still fell far short of a cure. That would take a more radical step, one he wouldn't be able to manage without access to a modification pit and more of the memories of his people. Even then, he wasn't sure he could do it, not without the help of an expert. But as far as he knew, all the experts were dead.

It made him think of the mysterious second maniraptor, supposedly out there under the control of a rival human roost. A female, at least according to Samira's friend's description. Prey understood that Samira had not seen the other maniraptor, and that Samira's friend had not seen her either. It was a story told from person to person. Did she really exist? If she did, then she was in human captivity just as he had been, or maybe worse. If not for Samira, he would probably be dead now. Would the other maniraptor die before they had even met?

Wherever you are, stay strong, he thought. *You will win your freedom yet.*

CHAPTER NINE

Li Ling barely went home anymore. She told herself it was because the work was just too fascinating, and there was so much to do. That was true, but it wasn't the only reason. The other was Lao Zhou.

She hadn't actually seen him since the night in the tea shop, but he had seen her. He kept leaving her texts, telling her how much he missed her, making what almost sounded like reasonable requests to get together for old times' sake. Twice, he had told her how attractive she looked in the clothes she was wearing that day, commenting specifically on the color of her shirt or jacket. He was stalking her.

She hadn't told Keju. She knew she should, but she didn't like the idea that she needed her brother's protection to live her life. He would overreact, take time off of work, come stay with her. And then what? Would he beat up Lao Zhou? That wouldn't solve anything.

Instead, she did the easy thing: she worked. Lao Zhou couldn't reach her inside the government facility, and so when she was there, she was safe.

And there was plenty of work for her to do. The pheromone they extracted from the maniraptor was extraordinary. She'd never seen such an enormous, complex molecule, almost two micrometers long, with a fractal, repeating pattern that looked more like machinery than organics. It looked like it could encode an incredible amount of information. But for what purpose?

Dr. Sun had been cagey about that question, and she suspected he knew more than he was telling her. She knew they extracted far more of the pheromone than remained in this lab for study. Were they sending it to other labs around the country? Or—this was a military facility after all—did it have a military purpose? If so, what?

There must be some reason for all of this secrecy. Dr. Sun had explained to her where the maniraptor had come from. Like the team in Massachusetts working to bring back a woolly mammoth, they had injected maniraptor DNA from a well-preserved protofeather fossil into a modern ostrich embryo and carefully allowed the DNA to guide its development. If it was true, then it was the biggest scientific coup of the century, leapfrogging far over similar efforts elsewhere in the world. So why had their success never been published?

Li Ling suspected that it was not true. She had no other explanation for how there could be a living dinosaur in a cage in the next room over, but there was clearly more to this story. Sun had deflected her questions about the details. She had excitedly asked what percentage of the original DNA had been recoverable, how they had filled the holes when no extant species was a close relative, what DNA editing techniques they had used. Sun's answers were vague, and he had changed the subject when she persisted.

She worked twelve hours a day, six days a week, an infamous Chinese 996 work schedule that no one had forced on her, yet everyone else in the lab seemed to follow as well. There was a sense of excitement here, the discovery of things that no one had known before, at a tremendous rate of speed. There was a shared feeling, too, that the work was important, that they were in some way making China greater by their discoveries. Li Ling didn't know why that would be, but she felt caught up in the excitement of it all.

One Sunday, she woke early, and a text from Lao Zhou was waiting for her: '*I'm in town today for your day off. We should get together, have some fun.*'

The idea of anxiously sitting in her apartment all day jumping at noises was unbearable.

'*Have to work*' she sent back. She dressed in minutes and was out the door to the train.

The facility was almost deserted, but her card let her in, and the guards nodded at her as she passed. Back in the lab, Dr. Sun was there, working as hard as ever. She wondered if he ever went home.

"Ah, Li Ling, good," he said. "You can help me with something."

She kept calm outwardly, but she felt a buzz of excitement. She knew they hadn't told her everything that was going on. She was new to the project, and also the only woman. Maybe her work ethic had proved to Dr. Sun that she was a worthy colleague, someone who could be trusted with the full picture. There were mysteries here, and she wanted to understand what was really going on.

He led her back to the area where the maniraptor was kept. They entered through a metal vault door, which Dr. Sun securely locked behind them. The maniraptor stared at them from behind a thick sheet of glass. It had been sleeping on the bare floor, its head tucked under its feathery arm like a bird, but the moment they walked in, it sprang to its feet, wary and alert. It was beautiful. Though she could see places where its feathers had fallen out, and it looked in poor health.

"How is it doing? she asked. "It doesn't look very good."

Sun made a wry, sad expression. "Its very existence is a miracle," he said. "But it lives to serve the state, just as we do."

She puzzled over this statement, wondering whether to

press. She didn't want to irritate him, but she didn't know what he was talking about.

Sun handed her a bright yellow bundle: a hazmat suit. "I can't do this by myself," he said. "At least, it isn't wise."

He put his own suit on, and she mimicked him. He helped her check the seals.

"I will control the animal," he said, his voice crackling through a speaker in her suit. "You will collect the sample."

"I've never done that," she said.

"I know." He handed her a small suction pump and a handful of thermal desorption tubes, the absorbent resin inside already prepared. "The scent glands at the neck are the easiest to collect from. Press firmly just behind its jaw. That will express a small amount of liquid, which you will then collect in the tubes. It's a volatile substance, so you'll have to be quick."

She eyed the creature in the cage, crouched as if to attack. Its legs were fastened to the wall with leather straps on a short leash, but it looked deadly and alert. "Are we going to sedate it first?"

"No, it has to be awake. It has to be frightened and angry to produce the chemical we want. Do you understand?"

She didn't understand, but she nodded anyway.

Sun swiped his card against the magnetic lock on the cage, and the light flashed from red to green. He hefted the long rod he carried in one hand and a metal noose in the other. "Let's get this done," he said.

She followed him into an airlock with a decontamination shower. The door closed with the suction of an airtight seal, and she heard the sound of air recyclers. Finally, the door to the cage opened, and she stood in the same space as a living dinosaur.

As soon as they stepped inside, the maniraptor ran towards them. It reached only two steps before its bonds kept it back. It snapped its jaws and screamed at them. Dr. Sun strode forward confidently and struck it with the long metal rod. Blue lightning cracked from the end, and the maniraptor shrieked in pain. Sun struck it again and again, driving it back. It lunged forward with its terrible jaws, but Sun stood far enough back that it couldn't reach. Finally, he looped the wire noose expertly around its neck and dragged it to the ground. He held the noose tightly, drawing the maniraptor's body taut against the ground between the noose around its neck and the straps around its legs. Its agile hands scrabbled at the wire, but to no effect. It seemed to be suffocating.

"Now!" Sun called.

Ling rushed forward. She fumbled to connect the first tube to the pump.

"Tell me when you're ready," Sun said.

She got the two attached. "Ready."

Sun drove the electric prod into the creature's throat. It screamed and thrashed. "Do it now!" he shouted.

Ling pressed on the creature's neck as she'd been told. She could barely see what she was doing through tears that she couldn't wipe away. Dr. Sun continued to brutally electrocute the maniraptor as she collected one, two, three, four tubes of liquid. The last took the longest; there wasn't much left to collect.

"Done," she said.

"Good. Get out of here. I'll be right behind."

She rushed out through the door. She was hyperventilating, barely trusting herself to stay upright. Sun came behind her and closed the interior door. As soon as the seal was shut, the shower activated, spraying their suits with a caustic chemical to remove any organic trace. Li Ling raised her hands and turned slowly in the spray, sobbing uncontrollably, the tears and snot covering her face behind the glass.

Finally, the cleaning cycle finished, and the outer door opened. She stumbled into the room, tearing the helmet off of her head and struggling out of the rest of the suit. She fell to the floor, still sobbing. In the cage, the maniraptor still lay on the floor, shuddering and twitching.

Ling took a shaky breath. Someone stood over her. It was Dr. Sun, holding out a neatly folded pocket handkerchief with a flower embroidered in the corner. Hesitantly, she took it from him and wiped her face. She folded it so the worst of the mess was inside, and he took it back from her without a word and tucked it into his pocket.

"I should have prepared you better," he said. "I forgot you were a woman."

She glared at him. Was that what he told himself? That what he had just done was not brutal and vile; that she was just faint of heart because she was a woman?

"That was torture," she rasped. "That wasn't science. I *trusted* you. I thought there must be an explanation for how it was kept, for its terrible living conditions. But you just hurt it for no reason at all. You could have sedated it to get that sample. You could have trained it and earned its trust. You could have followed decades of research for the care of dangerous animals. Instead, you resorted to violence and cruelty. No creature should be treated that way."

Sun nodded sadly. "You're right. No creature should be treated that way. And yet we do. And we must."

She stared at him, incredulous. "Why?"

"Come," he said. "Share a cup of tea with me."

Dazed, she followed him. He brought her to his office and helped her to sit. She watched as he prepared tea with a dark clay tea set that looked expensive. He went through the ritual serenely, unhurried, pouring the water and arranging the cups on a bamboo tray.

Finally, he set the tray on his desk in front of her and offered her a cup. She took it gladly, the hot surface and warm smell settling her nerves. He took one himself and breathed deeply.

"This is not a science institution," he said. "At least not

foremost. The science we do serves a larger goal. The safety of our people, the might of China. Our mission is paramount, and that mission is to supply our great nation's most powerful and valuable asset."

She raised her eyebrows. "The dinosaur is China's most valuable asset?"

He nodded soberly. "To you and I, it is a scientific treasure. A unique and irreplaceable source of knowledge. But to the nation, it is so much more. This pheromone, when refined, works on the human psyche in a powerful way. It can compel others to act against their own wishes. The nation that controls it can control the world. The nation that does not will find itself quickly overcome by its enemies.

"The creature in that cage produces that pheromone in large quantities only when frightened and in pain. We are studying how to replicate it, and when we do, there will be no more reason to harm the creature. They have promised me I can then keep it in comfort, study it, learn from it. But first, the state will have its due."

Ling thought about that. She started to realize just how deep this evil might go, and how thoroughly trapped she might be. She took a sip of tea. It was hot and strong and calmed her nerves. "You didn't bring this creature to life from DNA, did you?"

Sun shook his head. "It was found. From what we can tell, it was preserved, intentionally, through a chemical and genetic capability that exceeds our own. This maniraptor actually lived during the Cretaceous, a member of a technological civilization destroyed by the asteroid that killed so many. It survived in hibernation to the current day."

Ling stared at him, her mouth open. The stress that had been building up in her threatened to break out in laughter. She had been imagining a grand conspiracy, right up to the paramount leader himself, with prison for her if she didn't go along. Now it seemed she was just dealing with a lunatic. An animal hibernating for sixty-six million years? Part of an ancient civilization never before glimpsed? Ridiculous. She took another sip of tea to hide her reaction, which was mostly relief. Sun had been a great scientist once. Was it Alzheimer's? Dementia? Surely others must know. They would have to take steps to remove him. It was sad, but he couldn't stay here, not when he did things like she had just witnessed.

She noticed he was watching her intently, a gentle smile on his lips. "I'm not crazy," he said.

She blushed. "I didn't think—"

"Of course you did. I almost think so too sometimes. But the other scientists in the lab will confirm my story. I can show you the details of the site where it was uncovered. The geneticists and doctors involved in reviving and stabilizing it are also available, should you wish to talk to them."

"You're telling me that the maniraptor in that cage was alive during the Cretaceous period? Not just its species, but that very one? And that it's a sentient being? Part of a civilization like ours, all evidence of which was somehow lost?" She almost expected him to start laughing and reveal it was all a joke. But Dr. Sun only looked sad.

"It has language," he said. "It thinks and communicates in symbols. It tells stories."

"You can *talk* with it?"

"No, I'm afraid its language is beyond us."

"Then how do you know—"

"Take a moment. Drink your tea. I think that's enough revelation to digest for the time being."

She obeyed. The tea had cooled a bit, but it was still excellent. She wondered what blend it was.

Despite the insanity of his claims, she believed him. She had been asked to accept the impossible the moment she saw a living dinosaur in this facility. This was just a little more.

The problem was, believing him meant that the truth was even worse than she'd feared. She'd thought a man was hurting an animal out of convenience, as the easiest way to get the sample he wanted. Instead, the government of a nation was torturing a sentient being, a *person*, in order to gain a weapon that could hurt countless others. It was evil, pure and simple. And she couldn't be a part of it.

"It's a lot to take in," she said.

Sun smiled like an indulgent father. "It takes some time to get used to," he said. "But you're a smart girl. Think how fortunate you are to get a posting like this, so important to our nation! If you do well here, you could go a long way in your career."

She nodded and attempted a smile. "I understand. It's an honor, and I hope to make you proud."

His smile widened. "I'm sure you will. Your work so far has been impeccable. Your experience with pheromones brings a lot to the team."

"Thank you." She stood. "And thank you for the excellent tea."

"Do you like it? I have a special seller I always use; I can give you his name."

"You are too kind."

Li Ling returned the tea cup, made a slight bow, and left the office, hoping he couldn't see her hands shaking.

She felt like a coward. But she knew the stakes. She wasn't foolish enough to think she could morally object and be allowed to return to her apartment or find another job. Dr. Sun would make a call, and security would stop her at the gate. She would disappear. A liability to the state who could not be allowed to walk free. Her friends and family would never know what happened to her.

She had known a girl in college who had spread unsanctioned information on her blog. She'd downloaded an app that allowed her to subvert internet censorship and access articles about events in China from outside journalists. She posted these on her blog and social media and hung posters around campus with slogans about government lies and the right of the people to know the truth. Then one day, she was gone. Ling didn't know if she'd been imprisoned or just removed from campus, but no one was willing to talk about her anymore. Her blog had been shut down. It was like she'd ceased to exist.

Li Ling didn't leave the lab after talking to Dr. Sun. She went straight back to her station to work, analyzing the pheromone in her microscope and devising experiments to understand how it was constructed. She could hardly concentrate, but she didn't want it to seem like she was running away. Besides, she didn't want to go home, where Lao Zhou might be watching or waiting for her.

The lab had seemed like a sanctuary before. Now nowhere felt safe.

SHE SPENT THE NIGHT THERE. DR. SUN SENT HER A LINK TO A shared directory containing a wealth of information on what they knew about the maniraptor. For a while, she read descriptions of an ancient civilization, from its biological technology and chemical language to its matriarchal government, social structures, and public institutions for mating and group child rearing. It was fascinating reading, despite the dry, academic style, but how could they possibly know all this? Dr. Sun had said they didn't understand the language.

Finally, she found the papers describing how the pheromones could store memories, and her mind exploded with connections. She had seen those constructs in the chemical itself. She hadn't understood what they were for, couldn't conceive of a purpose for such elaborate molecular mechanisms, but here was the explanation. She understood now why the samples were all sealed. She had thought it was just a volatile substance that would break down if exposed to the air.

Reading wasn't enough. She wanted to see one of these memories for herself.

Despite her misgivings, she went to ask Dr. Sun, and was surprised to discover he had left for the day. When she checked the time, she understood why. Five hours had gone by while she read. It was well past her usual dinner time, and she hadn't even noticed. It was like she was back in college, cramming for an exam and forgetting to eat.

She was alone in the lab. She didn't discount the possibility that she was being recorded by hidden cameras, but she didn't care. She examined one of the sample slides. It contained only a tiny amount of chemical, thinly spread on the glass surface and sealed with a clear plastic coating. A sample number was written in black permanent marker in the corner. She bent it slightly in her hands, studying the slight green tint of the liquid inside, considering. Then she took a pair of crucible tongs, set the slide facedown on the table, and brought the tongs down as hard as she could on the glass.

The glass didn't shatter like she imagined it might, but it did crack. As soon as it did, she leaned in close, breathing deeply. A strong smell like petroleum assaulted her nose, crawling up her sinuses and stabbing painfully into her head. When she straightened up, she froze, her heart hammering in sudden terror. The maniraptor was *right there* in the lab. It had escaped! She tried to take a slow step backwards, but her body wouldn't obey her. The creature loomed toward her, becoming impossibly large. She screamed and fell backwards. She never felt herself hit the floor.

Fourteen days until impact.

Distant Rain Sweeping Towards Home as Night Falls looked out over the hibernation pits. They had cut broad stairs out of the rock to make the job of hauling dirt out more manageable. Mist hovered over the pits, glistening in the early morning sun. How many more mornings like this would she see? Despite all their frantic work, it was hard to believe she really might have only fourteen more days to live.

Don't get sentimental, *she told herself.* There's work to do.

She and Prey had continued to work side by side, day after day, racing against time to get the pits dug and filled before the apocalypse. Her mind drifted to the night before and their laughing, sprawling, passionate sex in the pits after dusk when everyone else had gone. She felt a warm flush spread over her skin. An accident, almost, if such a thing could ever be called accidental. Certainly not what she'd had on her mind during the day as she worked past the point of exhaustion.

And yet, she didn't regret it, not even a little. Her mother would have been appalled at her mating with a scrawny intellectual, especially such a low caste runt from the Ocean Roost. Most females she knew only thought about a male's strength and size when they visited the breeding grounds to choose a mate to dominate for the evening. What she had shared with Prey was so much more. They were partners in their work, and they had been partners that night, each sharing and giving to the other.

Rain knew she was pregnant. As attuned to scent and the chemicals of their bodies as they were, females knew immediately if they started producing the hormones that meant an egg had been fertilized. If she got too close to another female, they would smell it, too. Calcium was beginning to leach from her bones to produce the shell, and if she didn't stop the process, she would eventually lay and it would develop into a child. Hers and Prey's.

She could *stop the process, if she wanted to. Her control over her body's chemicals also meant that she could turn off those hormones, effectively halting the growth of the new life inside her. Most thought females had always been able to do this, but Rain knew it wasn't true. It was an intentional modification to their species, like many made before it. Females in her society wouldn't believe her if she told them, and would in fact be offended by the very suggestion. But the idea of the unmodified genetic "purity" of females was a recent notion, based more on politics than fact. It was those same politics that prevented most of them from accepting the only solution to their present danger that had any hope of success.*

The tiny maniraptor starting to grow in that egg could never survive. She knew that. Even if she laid tomorrow, it would need to develop inside the egg for three weeks before it would hatch. But in only two weeks, almost everyone she knew, if not everything living on the planet, would be dead. Within hours of the asteroid's impact, debris would plow through the atmosphere, turning the air into a furnace hotter than anything could withstand and setting fire to the trees. The world would burn.

The only possible hope she had of surviving it herself was the hibernation pits. But no egg could survive there. The baby could never live. She should stop its development immediately, before the process weakened her bones, and the energy she desperately needed to finish creating the pits was rerouted towards its growth.

The problem was, she didn't want to. If not for the coming asteroid, she would gladly raise it. She wanted to have a child that would share genetic characteristics with Prey: if not size, then intelligence, kindness, and dedication to a cause. They weren't animals fighting for food and survival in the wild anymore. Why did size matter?

But this child would not live. Could not live. Rain had never been one for sentimentality. She acted based on how things were, not on how she wished them to be. She had let this go on long enough. But despite the exhaustion she felt, despite knowing that it would only get worse, she couldn't bring herself to terminate it. Not yet.

Li Ling sat up with a shout, confused at first about her surroundings. Where was she? She had been at the hibernation pits, and now…

Slowly, realization filtered back into her mind. She saw the lab, the broken slide, the chemical. It had all seemed so real! It wasn't like having a dream; it had taken over her mind and senses entirely. She had been there, fully awake. She had been a maniraptor.

She dragged herself to her feet. There was, of course, no maniraptor in the lab. That had simply been the beginning of the memory experience. Perhaps it was a tag of sorts that indicated to others whose memory it was, or maybe just her own brain's first thrashing attempts to make meaning out of the inputs from the chemical and connect it to what her own eyes could see.

She wasn't in the memory anymore, but she still remembered the experience as if it had been her own. She felt grief for her child, soon to be lost.

She shook her head to clear it. She didn't have a child. It wasn't her memory. But she still felt that sense of loss.

Ling walked carefully across the lab, awkward in her own body. She made her way down the hallway and into the room where she could see the maniraptor through a thick sheet of glass. It tensed and stood when she approached. But this was no 'it'. Ling could see that now. She was a person, terrified and alone. She had a name, though not a spoken one, something like the scent of a rainstorm. She was a person, and no person should be treated like this. She had somehow survived for millions of years when the rest of her species had died, and for what? To be tortured and used for the chemicals her body could produce?

Ling rested her forehead against the glass, watching her. The maniraptor watched her back.

Rain, Ling thought. *Your name is Rain.*

CHAPTER TEN

The drive to Rogue International took four hours. It didn't look far on a map of Oregon, but with a target on their backs, the road felt endless. Nothing to do but dwell on the images of soldiers trampled to death, crushed under vehicles, or gored by dinosaur claws, and to wonder about the intelligent creature she had started to think of as a friend.

Those soldiers were human beings, just doing their jobs. They probably had families. And yet, they had come to take Charlie away into slavery and torture. Charlie had done what he had to do. If Samira had the ability to drive fifty head of cattle and half a dozen mule deer into the soldiers holding her family and friends, wouldn't she have done so, too? But the deaths bothered her. Did they bother him? How readily might he kill again?

Finally, she reached the airport and pulled onto Terminal Loop. The place was a lot smaller than she thought. Compared to Denver, it looked insubstantial, just a collection of low buildings with little to see in any direction. She wouldn't have guessed it offered international flights.

She pulled into the International Departures drop-off

point and shifted into park. "You all sit tight," she said. "I'll see what I can do."

She stepped out of the truck, and the enormity of what she was going to try to do hit her. This was insane. The chemical was powerful, yes, but she was about to try to march a living dinosaur through a crowded airport to catch a flight, without creating a stir. How did she possibly think they could get away with it? She ransacked her brain yet again for other options, and came up blank. There would be no safety in the US, just waiting for the next raid, and probably not escaping it next time. And there were no other countries she could expect to shelter them. Only Thailand. Unfortunately, that meant crossing the very inconvenient ocean in between.

She sprayed herself liberally with some scent that Charlie had provided and pushed through the revolving doors into the international terminal. It would be enough to dominate any ticket seller or security guard, but she doubted she could control everyone in the airport at once. She had to minimize the number of people who saw Charlie, even keep it at zero if possible. If Everson got word they were here, he would have all the security and police after them in a moment.

Everyone was wearing masks, afraid of catching the Julian virus. Most of the masks wouldn't stop Charlie's scent from getting through, but those wearing N95 masks would be effectively immune. The domination chemical was a large molecule, definitely among those filtered out by the mask. Those people would see Charlie and see what was happening. They might sound the alarm.

Why were so many people here anyway? She had hoped people would stay away from the airport for fear of contracting Julian, but it was crowded. Maybe they were trying to escape it. Maybe the spreading disease had come too close for comfort, and they were flying to places they'd heard were safe. And possibly spreading the virus to those places in the process.

The line for the ticket desk was long. If she jumped the line and dominated the ticket seller, though, everyone in line behind her would raise a hue and cry. Besides, she needed more than just tickets. It wasn't like Charlie could board a passenger jet and sit down in business class. She needed a plane.

She thought of the Compassion International plane currently in Colorado Springs, and their pilot en route from Arizona. Maybe they should have driven there instead? But it was a 17 hour trip. They'd done it once before, with the help of some carefully laid misdirection, and managed to evade capture, but she didn't lay high odds against pulling that off a second time. Besides, Charlie was injured. They were going to need medical attention for him, which meant getting to Thailand as quickly as possible. There were no good solutions. She had to stop second-guessing this one and do the best she could.

A security guard stood on his own toward a corner of the room, wearing an ordinary blue surgical mask. Samira approached him.

"Excuse me," she said. She waited a moment before going on, giving the scent plenty of time to make its way around his mask. "I need to speak to the person who has the highest authority in this section of the airport. Someone with the power to bypass security and get me and my friends on a private jet."

The guard looked like he was about to object, but then his expression changed and he quailed. "Right away, ma'am," he said.

He picked up his radio, but she pushed it down. "Take me in person, please."

The docile guard led her through a back door and into a maze of corridors. She felt guilty for taking advantage of him. He was going to break rules and maybe get himself in trouble for leaving his post, simply because she told him to. The rationalization that the end justified the means didn't sit well with her, but she did it anyway. The fact was that in this situation, she *did* feel like her actions were justified. She wasn't just trying to save those she loved; she was trying to save Charlie, who just might find a way to save the whole human race in return.

The guard led her to an office with a door that read "Marilyn Gayle, Director of Operations." Samira opened it without knocking. A middle-aged white woman in a gray skirt and jacket looked up from behind her desk, surprised at the intrusion. She wore no mask. "May I help you?" she asked in a chilly voice.

Samira smiled. "I need a plane."

AT DIRECTOR GAYLE'S INSTRUCTION, SECURITY OPENED A PAIR of locked gates, allowing Alex to drive the Isuzu directly onto the runway. A private Gulfstream G550, fueled and ready to fly, stood on the tarmac where Gayle had ordered it at Samira's direction. Samira wondered what multi-millionaire CEO was going to miss his flight today.

Alex parked the truck by the rolling stairway that allowed access to the plane. Samira walked toward it with Director Gayle still in tow. "Both pilots are already on board," Gayle said in a clipped, businesslike tone. "You're fully fueled, and I've cleared your takeoff with the tower."

Samira thanked the woman. She knew that shortly after they left, Gayle would regain command of herself and probably report this as theft. Hopefully her confusion about why she had gone along with the plan would delay her at least long enough for them to take off. They had to be in the air before anyone could stop them.

Alex climbed out of the truck and headed for the back of

the trailer. By the time Samira noticed anything was wrong, it was too late to turn back.

Dan Everson stepped out from behind the rolling stairway, a semi-automatic pistol in his hand. At his signal, a dozen soldiers in fatigues emerged from behind runway maintenance and transport vehicles and approached at a run, rifles at the ready. Alex put his hands up, and reluctantly, Samira did the same.

"Let's try this again," Everson said. "This time, no one needs to die."

PREY WAS HURTING. HIS SIDE THROBBED WHERE HE'D BEEN shot, each agonizing jolt of the truck stabbing jolts of pain through his body. His breath came in ragged gasps. With all the humans stuffed in the back of the truck with him, the air felt close and too warm.

He wished he could see out. After an endless drive, they stopped. He could hear loud engine sounds and the sharp smell of oil and machinery. Still, the door didn't open. He had to trust Samira, but it terrified him to think of the vast human world around him, full of alien beings and incomprehensible technology. He could smell the terror of his friends. Despite their kind, hopeful words, he could tell they didn't expect to escape.

The truck's engine roared to life again and started to move. Prey moaned, both from the pain and the endless fearful waiting. Had Samira failed? Would they take another endless drive now, trying to find a place they could be safe?

He heard strange sounds, ratcheting and roaring and repeated tones. What was happening out there?

Suddenly, he smelled the metal-and-oil tang of human guns.

"Guns," he screeched, panicked. "Guns!"

But it was too late. The rolling door opened, blinding them all in the sudden sunlight. He smelled gasoline and hot tar and smoke. He smelled the guns, too, but then all of the smells were washed away by a powerful scent he never thought he would smell again. A wonderful scent, glorious and perfect, the scent he had longed to smell ever since he woke trapped in the humans' cage. A scent against which he had no defense.

An unfamiliar voice said, "You can all come out now."

SAMIRA KEPT HER HANDS UP AND WATCHED EVERSON WARILY. Neither he nor any of his soldiers were wearing masks or noseplugs. That was odd. Were they blocking scent in some way she couldn't see?

"Stand down," she said in her most commanding voice. "Put your guns on the ground."

None of them moved. "That's not going to work, I'm afraid," Everson said. He holstered his gun and walked forward. He lifted the trailer door on the back of the truck. "You can all come out now."

Samira was baffled. Why didn't the soldiers respond to the chemical? Had the government surgically cut the olfactory nerve leading to their brains, permanently removing their senses of smell?

Gabby and Arun and Brook and Samira's parents all climbed down, their hands in the air. Charlie followed, and Samira could see immediately that he was in pain. Blood soaked the feathers on one side, and he walked awkwardly. He leaped down from the truck, causing the trailer to bounce up on its shocks, and almost fell over when he hit the tarmac.

"Dan, listen," Samira said. "Charlie can cure the Julian virus. We just need to get him to Thailand. Please."

Everson gave a short, incredulous laugh. "Get him to

Thailand? Is that all? You just want to deliver a unique and irreplaceable weapon to our enemy's backdoor? If he can really cure Julian, then let's do it. Tell us what needs to be done. Don't sneak him out in the middle of the night." He turned to his men. "Get the creature under control, and let's get him out of here."

"Thank you, Dan, I'll take things from here," said a female voice in a clipped British accent.

Everson's assistant, Michelle, stepped forward. "Ms. Shannon, I do have to thank you for this opportunity," she said. "I never could have done this without your help."

"Michelle? What are you talking about?" Everson demanded.

"Sorry, no time to chat," Michelle said. "Do be quiet and step out of the way."

Samira turned to Charlie, hoping maybe he could dominate them directly where she had failed. To her surprise, he had flattened himself to the ground in what looked like a submissive posture. What was he doing? Why couldn't he control the soldiers?

"I'm afraid we can't stay," Michelle said. "You call him Charlie, I believe? How very American of you. Charlie, get in the plane."

Charlie obediently backed toward the stairs leading up to the plane, keeping his body low and scraping his feathered face along the ground.

Samira watched, astonished. What was happening? Michelle was Everson's assistant, but she was giving him orders, and Charlie was submissively doing everything she said. Finally, Samira caught on. "You're not CIA, are you? You're Chinese."

Michelle gave a slight nod. "I'm both, as it happens. You didn't think we'd be seeding every government in South East Asia with loyalists and not have agents in the United States? But you're right, my dear, I was born in China, not Taiwan, as my employer has for so long believed." She patted Everson on the cheek. "Samira, my dear. I've been trying to find a way to accomplish what you've done here for so long. But then you went and did it for me! I do appreciate it."

"Charlie, don't go with her!" Samira called. "She's trying to kidnap you. Tell her to go away."

Michelle gave her a patronizing smile. "He can't do that, of course. His scent is generally quite effective on humans, I have no doubt. But he's only a male, after all."

"Charlie, tell the soldiers to aim their weapons at her," Samira said.

"Ooh, not very nice," Michelle said. "But you don't understand. Charlie's mine now. He's only going to obey me. He's a male, as I said, and the scent I'm using is all female. If you don't want me to tell him to rip your throat out, I suggest you try not to interfere."

Charlie hung his head. He awkwardly climbed the stairs and disappeared into the hatch.

"Thank you for providing me with a plane," Michelle said. "You will all stand here perfectly still until I get away. I'm tempted to tell the soldiers to kill you all, but that seems uncharitable. I have what I want, after all. Goodbye."

She climbed the stairs. The hatch closed, and the plane began taxiing away.

Samira tried to move, but found that she couldn't. She didn't even want to. She stood motionless with everyone else while the plane took its place on the runway, and then finally took off. When it disappeared into the clouds, and control of her body finally did return, she still couldn't move very much, because a dozen US soldiers were pointing rifles at her.

Everson sucked in breaths of air as if he were drowning, his eyes wide in shock. "No," he whispered. "No, no, no."

"They're still in US airspace," Samira said. "Can't you turn her around?"

After a pause, Everson seemed to come back like a man

surfacing from underwater. "Yes," he said. "Yes, you're right. If we act fast enough." Suddenly animated, he yanked a phone from his pocket and pressed a button. "This is Everson. We lost him. No, listen. There's a Gulfstream G550 taking off from Rogue Valley International *right now*. Scramble two F-35s out of Edwards and force it down. I don't care about the chain of command; call the director if you have to, but get it done. Force them down. If they do not comply, you are cleared for lethal force to prevent them from leaving US airspace."

"What?" Samira ran toward him, but a soldier stepped in her way. "Charlie's on that plane," she shouted over the soldier. "You can't just shoot him down."

"You should have thought about that before you stole him," Everson said.

"You're the one who brought a Chinese spy along! If you'd just left us alone—"

Everson waved her away. "It doesn't matter now. We can't risk China having two." Then into the phone: "That's right. I don't care if it's a private aircraft or who the pilots are. Those are enemy combatants stealing a weapon crucial to the war effort. Shoot it down!"

CHAPTER ELEVEN

In the morning, Ling told the others she had dropped the glass slide accidentally, releasing the chemical into the air. They listened, fascinated, as she described what she'd seen. They had all experienced a maniraptor memory before, so they knew what it was like. Ling got the impression some of them were jealous. The chemical was so precious, they weren't allowed to use their few samples that way, but she could tell they wanted to.

"They don't let us keep enough for experimentation," one of them said. "Imagine how much more we could learn about their civilization!"

Dr. Sun shook his head. "Our country needs it more than we do," he said. "If we succeed in isolating the effect and synthesizing it, then we will be able to keep the true samples for ourselves and learn from its memories. Until then, we keep working!"

The other scientists murmured their assent, but their hearts weren't in it. Ling wondered how many of them recognized the evil in what they were doing. She couldn't very well ask. Like her, they were compelled to continue the work or lose everything. None of them would admit to ethical qualms, even if they had them. And if she confessed her concerns to the wrong person, they might report her. Better to stay quiet.

By noon, she was so tired, she was falling asleep standing up. Dr. Sun sent her home.

"Your dedication is exemplary," he said. "But you can't expect to work all night and get no sleep at all. Please, go home and rest. The work will still be here when you get back."

Ling retrieved her phone and purse and drifted out of the facility in a daze. She boarded a train, less crowded in the middle of the day than it was when she generally rode it home in the evening. She found a window seat with no one in the spot next to it and sat gratefully, resting her head against the cushion.

The train started, and she watched the city rush by. What was she going to do? In only a few weeks, her life had transformed. She felt like the dinosaur in its cage, trapped and frightened. She couldn't leave her job, couldn't tell anyone what they were doing to Rain, and she was afraid to go home. Maybe she could just leave. Take a plane to America and don't come back.

But that was ridiculous. She didn't know anyone in America. She could read in English, but she barely spoke the language. Besides, now that she was cleared to China's most valuable asset, they probably wouldn't let her leave. They were probably watching her. They would track her to the airport, and large men in sunglasses would intercept her at the gate. She would never be seen again.

The blur of city sights through the window was mesmerizing. Despite her fears, she relaxed and closed her eyes.

THE SCREECH OF BRAKES AT A TRAIN STOP WOKE HER. SHE SAT forward, disoriented. How long had she slept? The seat next to her was occupied now. She glanced over and saw that it was Lao Zhou.

Her mind cleared and she came instantly awake. “You can’t be here,” she said. Where had he come from? He must have been watching the facility entrance, waiting for her to come out so he could follow her home. She realized he had probably taken the train with her on other occasions, watching her from a distance. But she had spent all night at the lab. Had he spent the night in the street, watching for her?

“This is a public train,” Lao Zhou said. “My taxes pay for it as much as yours.”

“What taxes? You don’t actually have a job. Or does Pinduoduo pay you to stalk young women?”

“I only planned to stay in town one night,” he said sourly. “But you refused to see me.”

“I did see you. I went to a tea house with you. You’re the one who walked out.”

“I can tell when I’m not wanted.”

“Can you?”

He switched from wounded to angry in a moment. “You're a cruel and ungrateful girl,” he snarled.

“Ungrateful?”

“Yes. I’m willing to give up anything for you. And you treat me like trash. I stay in the city for you, probably losing my job, and you won’t even respond to my texts. You wear clothes you know I like, just teasing me, but you won’t see me.” He leaned forward, trapping her in her seat. “You can tell I’m devoted to you. What do you think, some better man is going to come along? You’re not that pretty. No one else would give you a second look.”

The train slowed, approaching another stop. She shoved him. “Let me go!”

She thought he might hold her there or block the way, but too many people were watching. He leaned back, reluctantly, a mutinous expression on his face. "I'm not going away," he said. "I love you."

She stumbled off of the train, half blinded by tears. It wasn't her stop, but it didn't matter. She thought he might follow her, but the train pulled away, and he didn't get off. She sat on a bench to wait for the next one, shaking. She texted her brother.

Lao Zhou cornered me on the train today. I'm afraid.

She waited for the phone to ring, but it didn't. No response to her text. Of course—Keju would be working. He might not see her text for hours.

When the next train arrived, she boarded it and rode the rest of the way home. She was terrified that Lao Zhou would be outside her apartment building, waiting for her, but the street was empty. She let herself in, closed the door, and locked it. Then she finally let herself cry.

Ten minutes later, her phone rang. Keju.

"Call the police," he said.

She sat on her bed, sighing. "What are they going to do? They can't guard me. And they can't arrest Lao Zhou. He's done nothing wrong. Nothing illegal, I mean."

"You can get a personal safety protection order taken out against him."

"You need a lawyer for that," she said. She knew because she'd looked it up. "And you need a record of abuse. Evidence. All he's done is talk to me."

"He's stalking you. Maybe if the police just spoke to him, he'd leave you alone. He's a coward at heart."

Li Ling lay back against her pillows. "I'll call," she said. She knew it wouldn't do any good.

"I'm coming," Keju said. "If the police won't chase him away, I will."

"You don't have to," she said. "I work sixteen hours a day. If you come, you won't even see me."

"I'll see him. And I'll ride the train with you. I mean it,

little phoenix, we have to do something. He's a cowardly little weasel, but that doesn't mean he won't get violent with you. I don't want to think what would happen if he managed to get into your apartment."

The thought chilled her. She climbed out of bed and double-checked that the door was locked. What if he was watching from the street? She didn't see him from the windows, but she pulled the blinds anyway. She felt like a prisoner in her own house.

"Okay," she said.

"Okay?"

"Okay, you can come."

"I wasn't asking permission," Keju said. "I'm already packing my bag."

She felt a flash of anger. Why didn't any of the men in her life care what *she* wanted? They just did what they thought was best for her without regard for her opinion.

But that wasn't fair. Keju did care what she thought. And she had made the choice to text him, knowing he would come. She had wanted him to come. No point complaining about it now.

"I'll be there in two hours," he said.

She smiled. "Thank you, big dragon."

"See you soon, little phoenix."

KEJU ARRIVED AS PROMISED AND SPENT THE NIGHT IN HER apartment. In the morning, he woke with her and took the train. She had to admit, she felt better with him there, and there was no sign of Lao Zhou. He walked her right to the gate of the facility. She hugged him there.

"I won't finish until the evening. What will you do?"

He shrugged. "Go shopping maybe."

Ling had never known her brother to enjoy shopping. "Just stay out of trouble."

"Of course." He grinned. "You, too."

Li Ling worked for several hours before she saw Dr. Sun walk through the lab from his office. He motioned to another scientist, a man named Shen Bo, who stopped his work and followed. Ling knew where they were going.

She kept working. It wasn't her problem. They were going to shock and terrify Rain again, but she couldn't stop them. She tried to look at a sample in the microscope, but her vision blurred and she couldn't concentrate. She imagined the shock stick driving into Rain's body, the pain and scorched flesh, the screams.

Almost involuntarily, she pushed her stool back from the table and straightened her back. What did she think she was doing? Was she going to demand that Dr. Sun stop? Threaten to tell the world? Better to stay at her station than to go witness something she was powerless to prevent.

Even so, her legs took her out of the lab and down the hallway toward the maniraptor cage. The outer metal door was locked, but she knew the combination now. She took her time and opened it on the first try.

Inside, the scene was just as she had expected. Dr. Sun and Shen Bo were behind the glass, dressed in hazmat suits. Shen Bo held Rain down with a wire noose around her neck while Sun shocked her again and again with his stick. Rain screamed and thrashed, but she couldn't get away.

Ling couldn't help herself. She didn't even bother with the hazmat suit. She slapped her badge against the magnetic lock. The light flipped to green. The door buzzed when she opened it, but the noise of screaming and electric discharge was so loud the two men didn't notice. She burst through the other side of the airlock and into the cage.

"Stop!" she shouted at them. "Stop this!"

Shen Bo looked up and saw her, his expression startled, but Dr. Sun kept swinging the shock stick. He lifted it high to bring it down again, but Ling grabbed his arm and tried to pull it away. The stick came down on Shen Bo instead. He shrieked and fell, losing hold of the noose. Rain rose up in the same moment and sank her teeth into Dr. Sun's arm.

Sun shouted and pulled his arm away, tearing open a gash in the hazmat suit. Rain lashed out with a clawed foot, surgically this time, and tore Shen Bo's suit as well.

Scent flooded the room, like rotten fruit and gasoline. Ling hadn't been scared before; she'd been too amped up on anger and adrenaline. With that smell, terror gripped her, and she couldn't shout, couldn't run, could only look into the eyes of the maniraptor and know that it controlled her utterly. She was going to die, and she couldn't do a thing to stop it.

Rain looked into the eyes of the female human who had just apparently tried to rescue her. She recognized her; this same female had assisted once before in the violence done to her body. For weeks now, Rain had been producing a chemical that eroded the integrity of the yellow suits they wore. They thought themselves proof against her control, but they were not.

It had been hard to wait. Every day, they shocked her and took what they wanted from her. She could smell them all the time. She could have dominated them and killed them at any moment. But then the others would kill her in return.

She knew enough now to know there were many of them. The scents of many different individuals clung to their skin, so she knew she was surrounded by a whole roost full of humans.

Escape would not be as simple as killing the ones she could see and running away. She had to be clever. She had to understand. But gaining new knowledge just based on the scents of those who entered her cage was difficult. She couldn't devise a map from those scents. She couldn't know which way might be safe to run. She couldn't anticipate the obstacles she would face.

Worse, she had still detected not the smallest hint of any more of her own species. Either they were all dead, or she was isolated so far away from them that their scent couldn't travel that far.

Sometimes, she was tempted to kill the ones she could reach anyway, knowing it would mean her death. Death would be preferable to this.

The only thing that kept her going was curiosity. Rain had always been an explorer, an experimenter. Perhaps all this brave new world had for her was death. But she wouldn't be ready to die until she knew what was out there.

She had nearly despaired of learning enough from inside her cage, but then this female had come. Even as she had helped the leader of Rain's torturers to extract chemicals from her scent glands, she had felt compassion for Rain. She had been distressed by her pain. Rain knew how to smell emotion, and she could tell. The female could be an ally.

And now here she was, attacking Rain's torturers. It was too soon, though. They didn't have a plan. Even with the female's help, Rain didn't think they could get free, not yet. But the other humans would know the female had attacked them. They might punish or kill her. Rain knew what she needed to do.

She leaned close to the males on the floor. She fashioned a memory for them, a false one to replace their memory of what had happened here. It was easy to do. The adrenaline in their systems already heightened emotional memory and blurred factual memory. It would be simple to insert a different narrative this soon after the events, while memory consolidation was still happening in their brains.

She released control over the female and backed into the corner, giving her access to the other two. As intended, the female helped the one with the injured arm to his feet and supported him as he limped toward the exit. The other male followed quickly behind.

Soon, Rain thought. *Soon I will make my escape or die in the attempt.*

"SHE SAVED US BOTH!" DR. SUN CROONED. HE REGALED THE laboratory staff with the story of what had happened, a story which—to Li Ling's astonishment—bore little relation to the actual events that had just transpired. "Shen Bo's hold on the noose slipped," he said with a glare at Shen Bo, who looked at his shoes. "The creature got loose! It sank its teeth right into my arm!" Dr. Sun held up his forearm, now generously wrapped in bandages. "I thought that was it. It could have gone for my neck next. But then who comes through the door but Li Ling!"

He went on to describe a heroic and implausible rescue in which Li Ling kicked the dinosaur in the jaw, releasing its hold, and then dragged both Sun and Shen Bo clear, one in each arm. Ling thought he was mocking her at first. Her eyes stung. She knew she had acted foolishly—she had nearly gotten all three of them killed—but if he was displeased with her, he should just reprimand her, not make fun of her like this. Slowly she realized that he was not kidding. He believed the story. More, Shen Bo seemed to believe it, too. He nodded vigorously at the tale and shot grateful, affectionate looks at Li Ling.

What was going on? She had tried to stop them, and it had all gone wrong. But now, somehow, both scientists swore to an entirely fictional version of events.

Ling thought of the vision she had seen from Rain's perspective when she smashed the slide containing her pheromones. Was it possible Rain had generated this memory and inserted it into their minds? And for what purpose? Could she have understood the risk Ling had taken on her behalf and acted to protect her?

"There will be a commendation in it for you," Sun promised her. "And I have some good news for you. For all of us!"

He waited, letting the moment drag on, savoring the suspense.

"I have heard from the Intelligence Bureau," he said. "They have something incredible for us that will be arriving later today."

He waited again. "What is it?" Shen Bo asked.

Sun smiled. "They will be bringing us a second maniraptor."

CHAPTER TWELVE

Submission came easily to Prey. A lifetime of scraping and bowing settled back on his shoulders like an evening blanket, familiar and inescapable. The female scent his captor wore made resisting her impossible. The helplessness was infuriating, but inescapable.

Prey had smelled it the moment that the trailer door opened, but by then it was too late to warn anyone. Samira had told him there was another of his species who had survived, but not who. When he smelled her scent, though, he recognized her at once. It was Distant Rain. He knew it as clearly as if he had seen her face. She was alive.

Not only that, but they had been hurting her. The scent was one of pain and anguish and fury. It carried with it a desire to dominate and crush and kill. It was terrifying to Prey, but it was also enraging. They had hurt her, probably over and over again, just so they could take her fear scent and use it to control others. He had no doubt they would do it to him as well.

When the plane started its takeoff run, it was so loud Prey thought the world was ending again. Even if he hadn't been abducted and dominated, Prey would still have been terrified.

Then the plane lifted off the ground, and they were *flying in the air* in a vehicle even larger and heavier than the truck. They left the land and flew out over the water, giving him a dizzying view of the world from the perspective of a gliding pterosaur. But pterosaurs were lightweight creatures, hollow-boned, with wings of taut skin, not heavy monstrosities like the plane. How was it possible for this thing to fly?

He heard his kidnapper talking. "This is Michelle Jiankui. I have captured the dragon. I need military backup immediately." She continued with details of her location, heading, and situation.

Prey perched awkwardly on one of the large seats in the front of the plane, looking out the window. As time passed, he grew accustomed to the noise and started to calm down. The world was beautiful from up here. Wisps of clouds drifted past and birds flew by *underneath* them. The ride was much smoother than in the truck, like a bird soaring over water. It was marvelous.

Until a deafening roaring noise thundered past without warning, buffeting the airplane and tipping his balance. Prey shrieked and ducked his head. A voice from the front of the airplane said, "This is Captain Chavez of the United States Air Force. You are in violation of US law. Turn your aircraft around or you will be fired upon."

"Don't answer," Michelle told the pilots. "Hold your course."

Prey didn't know what "fired upon" meant, but it didn't sound good. The pilots flying the plane stank of terror, which scared Prey more than anything else. Through the windows, he could see that there were two other airplanes out there, though these were a different shape than those at the airport, made up of sharp points. They were much louder and faster, too. Could those threatening-looking planes hurt his plane? Could they make it crash?

"Come on, guys in the Gulfstream," the voice of Captain

Chavez said again. "It's going to be a real bad day for both of us if I have to shoot you down. You don't have any options here. Just turn—"

The voice went suddenly silent. Outside the window, one of the two planes suddenly exploded. There was no warning; Prey could see no attacker or explanation. What was left of it burned as it plummeted, then broke apart as it crashed into the ocean. Prey felt sick.

Michelle watched it fall. "Brilliant," she said.

The second plane swerved hard and turned sideways. It expelled hundreds of bright bits, which cascaded down, trailing smoke. This time, Prey saw a white streak fly through the clouds from directly above. The streaking object missed, flying through the sparkling distraction instead, but a second followed soon after, striking the plane and shattering its wing into a million shards. It spun in a fiery tumble into the ocean.

Michelle smiled. "Don't be afraid," she told the pilots of their plane. "Simply do as you are told and you will not be harmed. Please set a course for Luliang Airbase, Yunnan Province, China."

HOURS PASSED. PREY STUDIED THE WOMAN NAMED MICHELLE, sensing her moods through her smell. She swung wildly between terror and a kind of nervous elation. Prey understood that Michelle was risking a lot to abduct him, and that she still didn't know how it was going to turn out. What he didn't understand was why. If these Chinese humans already had Distant Rain, why did they need him?

He could tell something else that Michelle probably didn't know. She was infected with the Julian virus. It hadn't reproduced all that much in her body yet, so she likely wasn't experiencing any symptoms yet, but she would soon.

Over all those scents was the heady aroma of Distant

Rain, as clearly as when he had last seen her. Distant Rain in pain, furious and lashing out at her captors, and by doing so, giving them just what they wanted. The torture wasn't even necessary. They could have extracted the chemical while she was asleep, as his own captors had done. The resulting chemical wouldn't have been quite as powerful, but it would still have been enough.

He knew she had been awake when they extracted it, not just because of her pain and fury, but also because she had embedded messages in the scent. She didn't know how much time had passed; didn't know that their species was all but extinct, so she was sending messages about her captivity out to her people. Her messages were cries for help that only he could understand.

And now he was captured, too. Not that true freedom was a real possibility. They would always be the pawns of one group of humans or the other. The world he and Distant Rain had inhabited was gone. There was nowhere left for them to go.

Somehow, he had to get a message to her. His captors wouldn't be foolish enough to imprison him in the same cage. He would probably never see her. But he needed a way to tell her he was alive.

Prey resumed his study of the virus. He could have slowed the progress of the disease in Michelle, of course, but he didn't want to do that. Instead, he wanted to repurpose the virus she carried to do what he needed. After all, one of the virus's chief abilities was in communicating itself in a kind of chemical message-passing from person to person. It already had a mechanism to replicate and spread from host to host, which was just what Prey was looking for.

He began to form a chemical scent message that could be carried along with the virus. He wanted his version to be the one passed on, so he made it hardier and even more virulent than the current strain. Perhaps a few humans would die sooner as a result—or even a few thousand more—but it was worth the risk. If he could reach a modification pit and get it working again, he *might* be able to produce a permanent solution that could cure humanity entirely. And if he couldn't, the human race was doomed anyway.

He sent the new chemical into the air, infecting Michelle and the two pilots as well. When they landed, it would spread from person to person, eventually reaching someone who interacted with Distant Rain, and she would get the message. He hoped.

It might not succeed. If the Chinese were careful, they could prevent any organic chemical from entering or leaving her cell, and then nothing could reach her. All he could do was try.

Everson spent several minutes shouting into his phone before turning back to Samira and the others. He was about to speak when his phone rang again, and he snarled "What?" into the receiver.

His face went suddenly pale. "So this is it, then. Okay. I'll be back as soon as I can."

When he hung up, he looked beaten, like a man who has just heard a jury pronounce a verdict against him. He met Samira's eyes. "Do you remember when I told you the Chinese were developing the means to strike from space to any point on Earth?"

"Yes."

"Well, I was wrong. It's not in development; it's already fielded, much farther along than we realized. They must have been hiding them in other launches for some time. The planes that I sent to turn back Michelle and Charlie were just shot down less than a hundred miles off of our shoreline."

"Shot down?" Samira said. "You mean—"

"That's an act of war, which of course China knows. So moments after tungsten slugs tore those planes into scrap, a similar hail of metal fell on the USS Ronald Reagan off the coast of Taiwan, crippling her. There were five thousand US soldiers aboard. I don't know how many of them survived." His voice shook. "Chinese forces are heading to take Taiwan as we speak. We're about to start the biggest shooting war of the century."

Samira gaped at him. *Five thousand soldiers.* Were they all dead now? She wanted to reassure Everson that it wasn't his fault, that he couldn't have known Michelle was working with the Chinese, nor could he have resisted her dominance. But overwhelming her ability to speak was the understanding that her choices had also contributed to those deaths. The realization set her heart thudding and made it hard to breathe. "You're saying that, just to get Charlie, the Chinese—"

"We've been balanced on a knife point," he said. "The Chinese have wanted to claim Taiwan and expand into Southeast Asia for a century. Now, because of this stupid stunt—"

"I'm not the one who led a Chinese spy straight to Charlie!"

His shoulders slumped. "I don't know how I couldn't see it. I trusted her. She had access to everything."

His phone rang again. He glanced at the screen, then put it to his ear. "Everson. Yes, I understand, sir. Yes, right away."

He clicked the phone off and addressed his men. "Time to go."

"Wait!" Samira said. She ran in front of him, blocking his way. "Get me to Thailand. I have contacts there; we can try to find out where Charlie is going and get him back."

He sighed heavily and shook his head. "Get you to Thailand? Dr. Shannon, the South China Sea is a war zone. The Chinese just disabled the most powerful military asset we had stationed there, and in the minutes I've been standing here talking to you, they have probably launched similar attacks against our forces at Guam and Japan. The only thing going to Asia right now is our entire Pacific fleet, unless the President decides to skip the pleasantries and just send a few hundred nuclear warhead-tipped Minutemen flying into their eastern coast. You have no training in espionage, and at the moment—I'm sorry to say it, but your loyalty to this country is seriously suspect. Go home. Pray the virus doesn't get you, and let us take care of the Chinese."

"War with China," Mom said. "The Lord protect us."

Samira touched her arm. "Mom. I need to get to Thailand."

"You don't have to run anymore," her mom said. "He's letting you go."

"It doesn't matter. I have to get there. It's our only chance."

"We can't, darling, you heard him."

"I heard him, but come on. You know people all over the world. You guys have been to Chiang Mai for conferences, what, five or six times now? You've got to know someone who could help us."

Dad spoke up. "We know missionaries and aid workers. But Thailand's borders are closed. We don't know anyone who smuggles people in and out of countries."

Mom smirked. "Now that's not exactly true."

"I know who you're thinking of, and he doesn't smuggle," Dad said. "Country borders just aren't a big deal where he works."

"I bet he could help, though. The Laos airports are still open, or at least they were two days ago. We have six thousand sponsored children in Thailand, and with the airports closed, we've been working through Laos to reach them. A lot of the children are Hmong or Karen, and Chanchai can get things done in those regions."

"Chanchai is the guy?" Samira asked. "Who is he?"

"He's a missionary," Dad said. "He travels constantly, driving over mountains in a battered truck, fording rivers, navigating rickety bridges over flooded torrents, to visit these little churches scattered all over in rural villages. I met him thirty years ago, when he was fresh out of seminary, and he's still at it."

"He's brought lots of kids to our attention, and now he's helping us reach them when the usual supply routes are cut off," Mom said. "With this fighting, though, even he might not be able to get through."

"We could try, though, couldn't we? Can you put me in touch with him?"

Dad put a hand on her shoulder. "Samira? There's a war starting. A big one. It won't just impact China and the US; it'll range all over the world. Southeast Asia is going to be a dangerous mess, probably for years. What do you expect to accomplish, besides getting yourself stranded there and possibly killed?"

Samira looked at each of them, gauging their mood. They mostly looked scared. Not only had they just been held at gunpoint, but the world was plunging into a war with the potential to devastate civilizations and kill millions.

"I'm deep in this," she said. "This disease is killing everyone, and we're one of the few people on Earth who have some hope of doing something about it. We have contacts in the government of Thailand, and that's where the modification pits were. If we can get Charlie to a modification pit and buy him a little time, he might be able to produce a cure. I know it's a crazy long shot, but what else am I supposed to do? Go home? Wait for Dad to die, and the rest of us soon after? If we can't stop the virus, this war might not even matter. There might not be anyone left to fight it."

"Okay, then," Mom said. "What do you need?"

"I need a way to get to Thailand. It made more sense when Charlie was with us, but even so, it feels like our best option. I'm not sure what good I can do there, but I know there's nothing I can do here. Thailand is where the modification pit is. If Charlie manages to escape, that's where he'll try to go. So that's where I need to be."

"Our supply planes leave from SFO all the time," Mom said. "But we need to get there fast, before they shut down all flights to Asia."

"You don't all have to come," Samira said. "Just get me on the plane; I'll go myself."

"Let's not have that conversation again," Beth said. "We're all coming."

CHAPTER THIRTEEN

Samira couldn't sleep on the plane, at least not for long. For her, the ride became an increasingly fugue-like state in which the dreams of her brief drowses merged with the over-exhausted fears of her waking mind, until she couldn't tell reality from imagination. When at last she did fall into a semi-comfortable sleep, the wheels skidded against tarmac and the plane landed in Luang Prabang airport in Laos.

From there it was another flight to Hua Xai, a single white building with an airstrip right next to the Thai border, where Chanchai met them with an army of hard-worn trucks the same color as the dirt. Strong-looking men in loose pants and tight T-shirts loaded the supplies from Compassion International, and the eight Americans split up into different trucks.

Samira's driver didn't speak English, but Samira didn't care. She quickly fell asleep, with only a vague sense of traveling northwest into increasingly thick jungle and mountainous terrain.

They reached a village of grass-roofed huts that climbed the side of a hill. A crowd of colorfully-dressed women and children started emptying the supplies from the trucks. Samira climbed out and saw nothing but lumpy green mountains in every direction. She spotted her dad laughing with one of the drivers. Dad tried to say something in the man's language, and they both laughed again, the driver slapping him on the back. She smiled. That was how she remembered Dad from her childhood—friends with any stranger within minutes, and picking up new languages as easily as breathing.

She stretched her legs as the others came and joined her. "Are we in Thailand?" she asked.

"We didn't cross a big river, so I don't think so," Beth said. "We'd have to get over the Mekong to reach either Thailand or Myanmar from here."

Chanchai strode through the milling people, shouting at them goodnaturedly in a language Samira couldn't identify. When he passed nearby, Samira asked him what they were doing here.

He smiled hugely and replied in mangled but comprehensible English. "If we cross border, then guards stop us, supplies disappear. We go by hill paths now. Border means nothing in the hills. They are Hmong, Karen, Akha, Yao here—not care about government lines."

"They'll bring the supplies to the kids who need it?" Samira asked.

Chanchai grinned with a flash of white teeth. "Yes! Need it much. Thank to your blessed mother and her always working!"

At first, Samira thought he was making some reference to the Virgin Mary, but then she realized he meant her mom.

"How do we get south, across the border?" Mom asked, blushing.

Chanchai touched his chest. "I take you safe."

THEY SOON FOUND THEMSELVES IN A CRAMPED GATHERING IN one of the larger village huts. The women wore a wild array of bright cloth and hats with bangles and beads attached. Some carried babies strapped to their bodies. Most of the men were more subdued, wearing simpler hues, but a few stood out with a splash of bright color. Samira didn't understand a word that was said, but Chanchai explained that there was a black market highway of sorts among the various hill tribes that inhabited the region. They traded in all kinds of goods, including opium and sometimes methamphetamine, though Chanchai was quick to insist that none of the Christian converts trafficked drugs. The meeting was to determine where to distribute the new supplies—with little regard for the instructions of Compassion International—and who would take them there.

With the noise and Chanchai's accent, she couldn't follow everything he said, but she gathered that the hill tribes, although from varying ethnic groups and religions, were united by a fear and hatred of the nations around them, which had treated them poorly for centuries. All were displaced people groups, some without even a memory of their original homeland, forced to move again and again to make room for the progress of civilization. Their people lived in the hills of Myanmar, Laos, Thailand, and China, but didn't consider themselves part of any of those nations.

Chanchai told her a story of the man sitting next to him, whose sixteen-year-old son had been beaten and then imprisoned when he wouldn't give some policemen the methamphetamine they demanded, even though the boy had never been involved in the drug trade. He told her about pregnant women jailed for illegally working land that their families had farmed for generations. Governments took tribal land when it suited them, and the tribes involved were left to move on and fend for themselves. The Hmong had even been recruited and armed by the CIA to fight against communist Laos during the

Vietnam War, and many still felt abandoned by the United States, who had left them behind to fend for themselves when they pulled out of the country.

The moral of all these stories was that the hill tribes respected no laws but their own. Each tribe cared for their own people and, like strangers with a mutual enemy, they traded and helped each other as well. The Christian churches especially, with Chanchai acting as emissary and traveling preacher, gave of what they had to help those in greater need, even across tribal boundaries.

"I tell them you are here to stop the devil drug," Chanchai said. "They are very pleased."

"What's the devil drug?" Samira asked. "Wait, you mean the domination chemical? They know about that?"

Chanchai chuckled, though with little humor. "Of course they know. It is often their people controlled by it. The foreigners make them carry drugs, or spy on other groups, or they just take the women they please with no consequences. They would do much to see the devil drug gone."

Alex leaned in. "Do they know where it comes from?"

"How it is made, you mean?"

"We know how it's made. But it comes from a creature, a maniraptor, that can make it naturally. Have they ever seen such a thing?"

Samira raised an eyebrow at Alex so casually revealing that secret, but she supposed they were well past any concerns about sharing classified information with foreigners. It wasn't like they could get in any worse trouble with the United States government than they were already.

Chanchai looked confused. She guessed the word "maniraptor" wasn't in his English vocabulary.

"Dinosaurs," she said. "You know 'dinosaur'? China has two, and they torture them to get the devil drug."

Chanchai held up a finger. "Wait," he said. "Let me discuss."

He started talking to several of the tribesmen, and soon many others joined in a lively discussion, gesturing and talking over one another. Samira had no idea what they were saying.

Finally, Chanchai turned back to her. "They say yes, they know where it is. Many, many kilometers from here."

"Seriously?" Beth said. "They know where the Chinese are holding the dinosaurs?"

Chanchai waggled a hand back and forth. "Perhaps. They know the place the devil drug come from. They know it for long time."

Brook looked around at each of them, almost desperately. "Is that where we should go, then? Is that where they've taken Charlie?"

"It many long kilometers from here," Chanchai said. "And is in China. Not too far from jungle, but close to city. Many people. Fences and guards. You cannot go."

"But these people can get into China?" Alex said.

"In the south, no border, because no people go. Just jungle. These people go. But you not go. You very white."

"I'm not white at all!" Samira objected.

"You very American," Chanchai amended. "All of you, even him," he said, pointing to Arun, who was originally from Bangladesh. "Everyone notice. You cannot go."

"Is there any way your friends could look for us?" Brook asked. "See if Charlie is actually there?"

Alex shook his head. "It's not like the Chinese are letting the dinosaurs run around outside. Hill tribesmen aren't going to be able to look inside a classified Chinese government facility."

"Wait," Samira said. "I don't know what they can do to help, and maybe nothing. But if this is affecting them, they deserve to know what they're up against." She turned to Chanchai. "If I tell a story, can you translate for them?"

Chanchai shrugged. "I try."

Samira told them the story of Charlie. She tried to keep it

simple, without any scientific jargon that Chanchai wouldn't be able to translate and the people wouldn't be able to understand. She didn't treat them like children, though. These people might not have sophisticated technology, but they knew a lot more about this region and surviving in it than she did.

She told them Charlie was a kind of animal, very intelligent, that used to live in these hills long ago. She told them that Charlie was her friend, and how he had learned to speak English. She told them he had been hurt to get the devil drug, and that she and her friends had rescued him, but that he had been captured again in China, where there was another of his kind. She told them Charlie and the other dinosaur were not their enemies, but victims of the same oppressors.

Several of the people spoke. "They want to know how you will rescue Charlie," Chanchai said.

Samira shrugged. "I don't know how. We're not soldiers. I have no weapons. I plan to go to Thailand for help, but I don't know if they can do anything either."

Chanchai translated, prompting a prolonged and heated debate. Samira knew there were many people groups represented here, but she didn't know enough about the different groups to identify them. She didn't even know if they were all using a common language, or if they understood enough of each other's languages to make themselves understood.

Finally, Chanchai turned back to them. "They will help," he said.

"Help? How can they help?" Samira asked.

He shrugged. "I not know. Many tribes here, and politics, what would you say, hard to follow?"

"Complicated," Alex suggested.

"Yes. Complicated. Many more tribes than are here, yes? Many leaders. But they thank for your story and want to help."

"Great," Samira said. "I guess we need all the help we can get."

That night they slept on the ground around the embers of a fire. With no netting to put over them, the mosquitos were brutal, but Samira still slept, exhausted by all the stress of the previous few days.

IN THE MORNING, ALL EIGHT OF THEM PILED INTO CHANCHAI'S truck, a boxy ancient frame so covered with mud that Samira couldn't tell its make or model. It couldn't have been intended for more than five, but with a little creative seating, they made it work. Chanchai kicked the tires and tested the winch engine before climbing in. No sooner had they left when it started to rain.

The drive lasted for hours. Cramped, sweating, and jet-lagged, Samira found herself slipping in and out of a delirious half-sleep, and found it hard to distinguish dream from reality. Only her dad seemed energized, gazing out the window with interest at the mountainous rainforest and seeming not to mind the heat or close quarters.

For most of the trip, she didn't even know what country they were in. The track Chanchai followed seemed less like a path and more like a meandering route through slightly less dense undergrowth. They crossed several rivers on the way, sometimes on rickety bridges that looked made by hand. Occasionally, they passed thatch-roofed villages, but mostly they saw no sign of human habitation. Rain obscured the view, and white mist rose from the foliage all around them. Three times, they got stuck in deep mud and had to get out and push, twice with the help of the winch.

Finally, though, the deep undergrowth thinned and they came out on an actual dirt road, easily visible and moderately maintained. Twenty minutes later, they turned onto an asphalt road, pitted but serviceable, and several turns after that she saw actual houses, shops, and electrical wiring, and finally signs for Chiang Rai.

Thailand, at last. Samira remembered her fossils dashed to pieces by Colonel Zhanwei and his thugs, and felt the rage filling her once again. They were still hundreds of kilometers from their dig site in Khorat, but the emotions still hit her hard. They had destroyed her fossils and thrown her out of the country, but she was back. This time, no one would stop her.

Finally, they reached Chiang Rai, where they got some much-needed food, stretched their legs, and renewed their supplies. Khai Nun was still a thirteen hour drive away. While her dad looked into renting cars for them so Chanchai could return, Samira found an electronics shop and bought a burner cell phone to call Kit.

"Don't say your name or where you are," Kit said the moment she greeted him. "I guarantee you the Chinese are watching this site with all their fancy tricks. Which means that besides watching us from space, they're listening in on our cell phone conversations, and probably reading our minds if we think too loudly."

"You have armed guards, I assume?"

Kit laughed. "We have a battalion. The Royal Army has this place completely surrounded. They've built fences and walls and artillery emplacements."

"All of them with masks or noseplugs, I hope."

"It's rule number one. Of course, if the Chinese decide to drop a missile on us, we can't stop them. So far, they haven't, probably because they're expecting to take over the whole country and claim the site for themselves, and they don't want it destroyed."

"What if the Americans drop a missile on you to keep the site from the Chinese?"

Kit sighed. "Just as dead either way, I guess."

"Look, I'm not going to tell you where I am, but I called to tell you: I'm coming to you."

"What? How? No, don't answer that. You know there's a war on, right?"

"Don't worry about that. Just tell your battalion not to shoot us when we arrive."

She could almost hear Kit's smile. "You're coming. That's great. I've been so worried about you. And just wait until you see what we've found here. You won't believe it. And given what you've seen already, that's saying a lot."

"Kit. They took him."

"Who?"

"Charlie. Our maniraptor. The Chinese took him. Possibly to wherever they keep their other one. Do you know where that is?"

"No. Oh Samira, I'm sorry. Colonel Zhanwei told me it was in Yunnan Province, but not the actual location. That's a wide area."

"That's okay. It hardly matters anyway. The US will have to win this war to get him back, and with both maniraptors in China, I'm afraid that won't happen. Even if they did win, they'd never let me near him again. I don't…" Her voice wavered, and she took a deep breath. "I don't think I'll ever see him again."

"Just get here safe," Kit said. "Maybe there's something we can do."

"Against the Chinese? I don't see what."

"You haven't seen what we've found. I can't tell you on the phone. Just get here."

"As soon as I can."

CHAPTER FOURTEEN

The team rolled into Khai Nun the next day, sore and exhausted. They'd alternated driving the two rented Toyotas, but Samira hadn't been able to sleep when it wasn't her turn. She felt like her eyes had been sanded and her brain turned to mush. She snapped to alertness, though, when they crested a rise and saw the military encampment in what used to be cassava fields, with sandbag walls and barbed wire and a lot of guns pointed their way.

She rolled down the passenger window, and Alex slowed them to a crawl. As they approached, soldiers yelled at them to stop—Samira knew enough Thai to understand that much—and Alex pulled the parking brake.

The soldiers waved at them to turn around, but Samira shouted Kit's name out the window. Two of them approached. She was glad to see they wore gas masks. Not taking any chances.

"Turn around," he said in Thai. "This area is off limits."

"We're here to see Dr. Chongsuttanamanee," she said. "He told you to expect us."

"You are Samira Shannon?" the soldier asked, switching to an accented English.

She breathed a sigh of relief. "Yes."

"I am instructed to ask you for the names of your crows."

She laughed. "Cope and Marsh! How are they doing?"

She couldn't see the soldier's face behind the mask, but she didn't think he was smiling. "I don't have that information. You must leave your vehicles and all your belongings here. We will escort you inside."

After a thorough search of each of them and the two vehicles, the soldiers finally led them—grudgingly, Samira thought—past the barriers and inside the cordon. They walked through a tent city where the soldiers and dig workers slept. A grid dish on the back of an army truck rotated above them, presumably checking their surroundings with radar. Other camouflaged trucks held giant guns, and others what looked like batteries of missiles. Samira didn't know her military hardware, but it looked like a lot of weaponry. Armed men walked about everywhere. What had once been acres of farmers' fields was now churned to mud.

Finally, they reached the dig site, fenced off and additionally guarded, and entered a large tent nearby.

"Samira! Beth! Arun! Gabby!" Kit ran to them and hugged them each in turn. He bowed gravely to her parents, Alex, and Brook in turn as they were introduced, with his hands clasped in a *wai*. Each of them tried to return the gesture, with varying success. Her father did it gracefully, at just the right angle, while Alex looked more like he was going to stab Kit with his fingers.

"I'm so glad you are here," Kit said. "Though I'm sorry it's under these circumstances. I guess you've heard nothing more about your maniraptor?"

Beth shook her head. "They took him away on a plane. We're guessing he was taken to the same facility in Yunnan Province that the Colonel told you about, but we don't have any more information."

Kit shook his head. "What I wouldn't give to see something like that. A living Cretaceous dinosaur. I'm so jealous!"

Samira was quiet. "I'm sorry we took it from you, Kit. And I had no idea they were going to blow up the site."

"If you hadn't, the Chinese would have taken it. Which I guess is what happened anyway. I did hate you for it a little, at first. Wait until you see what we've got here, though."

"I'm ready. Let's see it."

Kit didn't move. "I need your promise first."

"What? That I'm not going to steal whatever you've found?"

"I need your promise that you're not working with the Americans. That you didn't lead them here."

"You know I'm not! We've been on the run; you helped us escape."

"I made a phone call for you. That's all. I only know what you told me."

Her mom spoke up, indignant. "She's not lying to you. They attacked us. We almost died."

Samira stepped forward. "Kit. I promise I'm not working with the Americans. But there's a good chance they already know what you're doing here. They have satellites, spies, they can hack cell phones and computer networks. Thai fossils have become one of the most valuable resources in the world. You know they're watching. The Chinese, too."

Kit sighed. "And it's not like we're being subtle here." He waved vaguely at the huge military presence around him. "We decided they would probably know anyway, so better to defend it as best we can. They could conquer the whole country if they wanted, though they may not want to spend the resources now that they're at war with the US. For days, I've been expecting to see planes or tanks or just to die from a missile strike in my sleep."

Samira hugged him, then pulled back and held his shoulders. "Show us what you've found."

THE DIG WAS VAST. THE FIELD OF CAREFULLY STRUNG gridlines stretched out for acres, each square uncovered layer by thin layer.

"At the right depth, there's memory liquid in all of it," Kit said. "Not in liquid form, like we found trapped in pockets around the skeletons before, but bonded to the sandstone. One of my colleagues, Arinya Tavaranan, has been perfecting a process to extract it from the rock and refine it. Even processed that way, it retains the same qualities. It stores individual memories along with the scent tags of the maniraptors who recorded them, which is of course its original purpose. The fact that it can also be used to dominate humans is incidental, just a side effect of the tags."

"You must have a lot of it by now," Beth said.

Kit shot her a suspicious glance.

"A treasure trove of knowledge about the Cretaceous," she amended. "Believe me, Kit, if I could keep the knowledge and destroy the power it gives people, I would do it in a second."

He relaxed and even smiled. "It's incredible. A library full of cultural and technological information about an ancient intelligent alien culture. I mean, can you imagine? It's not just the biggest paleontological find ever, it's the biggest archeological find, the biggest historical find, the biggest philosophical discovery. If we can actually preserve it long enough to study it, it will turn half of the disciplines we have on their heads."

They made their way slowly around the perimeter of the dig, surrounded by a serious-looking fence topped with loops of barbed wire, and beyond it, the military.

"We'd love to help," Samira said. "Most of us are pretty skilled paleontologists. But honestly, that's not why we're here. Not the main reason, anyway."

"You want to get your maniraptor back," Kit said.

Samira sighed. "Not for the chemicals he can produce.

And not even to study him. He can *talk*, Kit. He's a person. He's my friend. And—" she hesitated. "And because I think he just might be able to cure this virus."

Kit's eyebrows shot up. "Seriously?"

"I don't know. But his people had incredibly advanced chemical technology, and we thought, if we could just get him here, to one of their pits…"

Kit shrugged, his expression compassionate. "It doesn't matter. There's nothing I can do to get him back. Or even that the queen can do. She's just trying to hold the country together, and she's expecting to be conquered by China any day. There's no way she could mount an attack on the Chinese mainland, even if we knew where this Yunnan facility was."

"We just don't have anywhere else to go," Samira said. "If there was any possibility Charlie could escape, then I believe he would try to come here. Not that he knows the way, but he knows how to get humans to help him. I don't expect that, though. I just don't have any more options left."

"So stay here and help us," Kit said. "This chemical is the best chance we have to keep control of our country. Help us understand as much as we can about the maniraptors' culture and history, and then in some fashion, we keep them alive."

"That's not good enough," Samira said. "Charlie's not dead. He's still out there."

"I know," Kit said. "But that's all I've got."

As they turned back toward the tents, a woman walked toward them. Samira and Beth froze. "Who is that?" Beth asked.

Kit turned. "That's Arinya Tavaranan, my colleague and friend. She's the one I told you about, who—"

"She controlled me with the chemical," Samira said. "She pointed a gun at Beth and threatened to kill her."

"You were here with American soldiers to steal from us," Arinya said, close enough now to have heard the exchange. "Soldiers who *did* fire on Kit and I, I should add."

"We had a contract for the fossils from that site," Samira said. "Your government threw us out illegally."

"And that gives you the right to parachute in with soldiers and blow it up?" Arinya demanded. "I should have shot you all when I had the chance."

Kit held up his hands and stepped between them. "Stop, stop, stop!"

Samira seethed, but she held her tongue.

"We are on the same side," Kit said. "Samira, are you here on behalf of the American government?"

"No! I told you, we're on the run. If they found me, they'd capture or shoot me."

"Good," said Arinya.

"Stop!" Kit said again. "We all care about these fossils. Arinya, we need help, and my *friends* here are some of the best paleontologists in the world."

"We don't need any help," Arinya said.

"Yes, we do, and you know it. I know what they did. I was there. I choose to believe that it was the American government that blew up our site, not Samira and Beth. I know them. They love fossils as much as I do. They would never destroy them."

"That's true," Beth said. "We didn't even know they were going to do it."

"But you did come intending to steal the fossils," Arinya said.

Samira took a deep breath. "I did," she said. "And I'm sorry. Contract or not, this is your country. We had no right."

Arinya grimaced and shook her head from side to side before finally nodding and saying, "Fine. Apology accepted."

"I don't think we even have a country anymore," Beth said. "We're just here to help."

"I said okay," Arinya said. "Let's get to work."

For Samira, it was like sliding into a cool lake, a cleansing flood of data and research to wash away all the worries and frustrations of the world. Caught up in the delight of discovery, it was far too easy to forget about the war, forget about Charlie, forget about the fact that her father was still sick, and that without Charlie he—and millions or even billions of others—would die. And what was she supposed to do? Walk through hundreds of miles of jungle and break into a secret Chinese facility? She didn't even know where it was. So she immersed herself in the work instead, fifteen, sixteen, seventeen hours a day, anything to bury her growing sense of guilt.

She worked side-by-side with Thai university students and Thai anthropologists. Her grasp of the Thai language was put to the test, made more difficult by the ironclad law that everyone must wear masks all the time. It was inconvenient, but Samira knew how quickly they could lose control of this whole expedition if just one person were to come under the dominating control of a Chinese agent. Fortunately, many Thai scientific terms came from English, and the vocabulary needed to conduct a paleontology dig were the Thai words she knew best.

The team had developed a process to extract the tiniest amount of chemical needed to experience a memory, wrapping their eyes and plugging their ears before inhaling to limit the interference of their real world senses. The rest of the chemical for that memory could then be cataloged for later study. Arinya developed software to scan and compare key components of the molecular structure, allowing them to separate distinct memories out of the undifferentiated mass. Her approach meant they could avoid duplication, as well as correlate the written descriptions from each person experiencing the memory with the molecule itself.

Even so, they barely scratched the surface. Compared to the original site, Kit had uncovered the motherlode. Here, a cubic centimeter of chemical-infused sandstone might contain *millions* of distinct memories. There was more here than a hundred researchers could sift through in years of study. It was the historical record of an entire civilization.

The awe and wonder Samira felt doing the work, though, could not entirely mask her sense of guilt and foreboding. This was no research center where she could relax and enjoy the thrill of discovery. This was a temporary shelter in a war zone. Her friend was suffering unknown horrors in the hands of the Chinese, and any day the military on either side might decide to wipe their site off the face of the Earth, rather than let it fall into the hands of an adversary.

WHEN THE ATTACK FINALLY CAME, IT DIDN'T HAPPEN LIKE ANY of them expected. Early one morning, Arinya stormed into the tent where Samira and Beth slept and roughly shook Samira's shoulder to wake her.

Samira, who had only just managed to fall into a fitful sleep a few hours before, could have strangled her. "What is it?"

"Where is Kit?"

Samira yawned. "Left for Bangkok late last night."

"For Bangkok? Why?"

"I don't know." Samira propped herself up on her elbows, trying to blink the sleep out of her eyes. "He just said the queen had summoned him, and he had to go. Something important, I would guess."

"I just got off the phone with the queen," Arinya said, her voice like ice. "She did not summon him. In fact, she was quite unhappy that I couldn't locate him to speak to her."

All traces of sleepiness fled. Samira's hand flew to her mouth. "Oh, no."

"If not to Bangkok," Beth said, "then where has he gone?"

Arinya crossed her arms, glowering down at them as if it were their fault. "Exactly."

OUTSIDE THE TENT, THE SITUATION GREW EVEN WORSE. THE army was on the move.

The military camp was often busy, with groups of soldiers running drills in formation, others building more fences or barricades, erecting comms towers, and walking from tent to tent doing whatever it was they did. Now it was different. Now they were taking it all down.

Dozens of soldiers were striking tents with impressive efficiency, wrapping and stowing them in identical, tightly-wrapped bundles. Comms antennas were coming down. Men loaded military trucks with equipment, a few of which were already rumbling down the road away from Khai Nun.

Samira grabbed a passing soldier by the arm. "What's going on here?"

The man's voice was muddled through his mask, but not too much to understand. "We're moving out."

"*All* of you?"

"Yes, ma'am."

The others gathered around. "Why?" Gabby asked. "We're still working here. We have to protect this site."

The soldiers shrugged. "Orders. They don't tell me why."

"Who's in charge?" Alex asked.

The soldier scanned the area, then pointed. "There. Lieutenant Colonel Gajaseni."

Samira saw who he meant, a man with glasses and more decorations on his shoulders and chest than the others who seemed to be giving orders to the people around him. She marched up to him. "Colonel Gajaseni?"

He looked over his glasses at her. "Yes?"

"Why are you abandoning your post?"

Samira heard Beth sigh behind her, presumably because she was being adversarial again. She probably should have asked the question more diplomatically, but she didn't have time for niceties.

Gajaseni's face closed. "I do not answer to you. I follow the orders I am given."

"But how do you know those orders are authentic?"

He sighed. "They are delivered over encrypted comms using the right codes. Now if you don't mind—"

"Colonel?" Arinya said. She had caught up to them and addressed the lieutenant colonel in rapid Thai. "You know that our country's leadership was recently compromised by the Chinese. I was with the queen when it happened. What if it's happening again? What if your orders are actually coming from China? The Chinese desperately want to control this site. Isn't there a way you can authenticate your orders from another source? Just to make sure?"

Gajaseni glowered at her, but he murmured something to one of his captains, who raced off. "We will check," he said.

"Weren't you just on the phone with the queen?" Samira asked Arinya.

"I tried to get her back as soon as I realized the army was leaving," Arinya said. "I couldn't reach her. I couldn't reach anyone at the palace at all."

"That's not good."

"No. Even if they haven't gotten past her security, if they've infiltrated the army, she won't stay in power for long."

The captain returned with a chunky satphone, which Gajaseni held up to his ear. He rattled off a series of authentication codes and nodded, apparently satisfied. He requested order confirmation and listened again. Finally, he said, "Understood, sir. Thank you, sir." and passed the phone back to the captain.

"Sir?" the captain said.

"No change. We're moving out."

"That's a mistake," Arinya said. "Please, our work isn't finished. If you leave, the Chinese will be here tomorrow. We'll lose the only means to fight them we've got."

"I've heard enough from you," Gajaseni said. "Stay out of my way or I'll have my men restrain you."

He strode off, his captains following in his wake.

"This is bad," Beth said. "What are we going to do?"

"We need to get everything we've extracted as far away from here as possible," Arinya said. "Then—I don't know."

"We can't leave," Samira said.

"What about Kit?" Gabby said. "Where is he? Do you think they kidnapped him?"

"I don't know," Arinya said. "But I agree with Samira. I'm not leaving here, not until someone drags me away in handcuffs."

"It might come to that," Alex said. "Or worse. They might just kill us."

"We can't go home," Samira said. "There's nowhere that's safe, not anymore. The best thing we can do is stay here and work." She looked around for a reaction.

"We're with you," Beth said. She laughed quietly. "We're always with you."

CHAPTER FIFTEEN

Kit couldn't believe he had been so stupid. Mai said she needed him, and like a fool, he'd headed out with only a single soldier as a bodyguard. Despite everything that had happened, he hadn't thought to verify that it was really her. There were a dozen questions he could have asked that only she could have answered. Of course, that wouldn't have helped if they'd been dominating her. But if they were dominating her, then there was nothing left to fight for anyway.

Twenty miles from Khai Nun, his car had been surrounded by four other vehicles. They shot his bodyguard through the car window and then dragged Kit out. He hadn't recognized any of his captors, who wore masks and didn't speak. The masks told him a lot, though. Whoever they worked for knew about the chemical. They were also sophisticated enough to fake a call to him from Queen Mai over a supposedly encrypted line, which meant it was almost certainly China.

He was now locked in what looked like the concrete cellar of any of a million restaurants or retail stores. His hands were tied behind him around a metal beam. Two masked guards sat like statues against the wall opposite him and stared at him, almost without blinking.

It was hard not to be scared. China was not known for their fair treatment of military prisoners. For that matter, Thailand itself didn't have a great track record for humane incarceration. He had heard terrible stories of what went on in Bang Kwang Prison, where they packed thirty men into a cell with a bucket for their waste and forced them to sleep on the floor with the vermin and rats. There was a long war ahead which would only make conditions worse, and even if the Americans ousted the Chinese, there was no guarantee that would get him out of prison.

The door at the top of the stairs creaked open, and yellow light spilled down the stairs. Shiny black shoes tapped on the concrete steps, followed by black trousers and a black suit jacket with a peony in the lapel. A moment later, the head appeared, and a face turned toward him that Kit recognized all too well. It was Colonel Zhanwei.

The fluorescent light glinted off of his glasses and bald head. His eyes scanned the three of them and settled on Kit. His mouth widened into a broad smile.

"Ah," he said. "There you are, my friend. And aren't you looking very well indeed."

Kit looked away, though his heart hammered in his chest.

The colonel crouched in front of him. He leaned in close and leered, revealing misshapen teeth. Knowing what that poppy meant, Kit held his breath, but Zhanwei didn't even wait him out. He punched Kit in the stomach. As his breath rushed out, the familiar, sickly-sweet petroleum smell rushed in along with a feeling of awe and terror of this man. This man he must obey.

"That's better," Zhanwei said. "It must have felt good when you had me at your mercy. Didn't it? Did you enjoy that little episode? I'm sure you did. But you made a big mistake. You left me alive." He watched Kit, considering. "Don't let me interrupt you, though. You were trying to hold your breath. Go ahead. Hold it."

Eager to please, Kit drew in a deep breath and held it. The colonel watched him, holding his gaze. After a while, the lack of fresh air in his lungs became uncomfortable, then desperate. He needed air. His lungs burned in his chest. But Zhanwei had told him to hold his breath, and without permission, he couldn't do anything different. He thrashed, pulling against his bonds.

Zhanwei chuckled slowly. "You can breathe normally again," he said, almost wistfully.

Kit let out his breath in an explosive rush and sucked in a new one, panting hard. The bastard was enjoying this.

"I wonder if I could make you die like that, or if your body would eventually revolt?" Zhanwei said. He patted Kit gently on the cheek with a rough, dry hand. "Don't worry. I don't intend to kill you so easily."

"I won't help you," Kit said. "I won't betray Thailand, and I won't betray the queen."

"Brave words," Zhanwei said. "But you know how this works. I could tell you to chew your own fingers off, and do you know what? You'd do it."

He stood, stretching, and cracked his neck first on one side, then the other. "How devoted you are to your queen. It's touching, really. Very nineteenth century. Maybe, once I have her back under my control, I'll give her to you. The two of you could make a little porn film for me. The queen of Thailand, doing it on camera; I bet that would sell a mint. Honestly, I'm tempted."

"What do you want?" Kit growled.

Zhanwei's smile disappeared. "Want? I want to humiliate you, like you did to me. I want you to know what it feels like. I want to enjoy your pain."

When Kit didn't answer, Zhanwei kicked him in the face. Kit felt something break, and a hot stream of blood ran out of his nose and over his lips to drip on his lap. He couldn't do anything to wipe it away.

"You're a lucky man, though," Zhanwei said. "You see, I'm a loyal patriot. The needs of the state come first, and the state needs you. Just remember: they don't necessarily need you with all your fingers."

"What do you want me to do?" The question came partly from fear and partly from a desire to please this man. Kit hated the feeling, but he couldn't avoid it. Under the effects of the drug, Zhanwei seemed like a dark god, someone whose will must prevail, no matter how horrible.

"Oh, the usual," Zhanwei said. "You know what's going on at that dig site. You know what's been found and what it means. You know why there are Americans there, and you can probably tell me quite a bit about the defenses as well, though it's not your area of expertise. In short, you can help me attack it successfully and understand what I'm taking and how to use it." He crouched again, looking Kit in the eyes. "Start talking."

Kit had no choice. He told him everything. When he was done, Zhanwei patted him on the head. "There's a good pet," he said.

The colonel's shiny black shoes tapped their way back up the steps, leaving Kit shaking in terror and rage.

CHAPTER SIXTEEN

Distant Rain knew the moment that Prey was brought into the complex. In all the time since she had woken in this strange place, surrounded by these hairless mammals with their machines and their cruelty, she had caught not one whiff of her kind. She had sent out scent markers, attached to the suits and bodies of the creatures who came in and out, but with no reply. That meant either that her entire species was dead, or that the others who survived the asteroid were captured and contained or so far away that she couldn't sense them.

She had considered more than once the possibility that she was no longer on Earth. The idea seemed outlandish, but so did many of the creatures' materials and devices and the bizarre nature of the straight, reflective walls of her cell. Once she had contrived to open her cell door, however, enough familiar scents of air and water and grass came through that it seemed less likely.

Prey. Where had he been all this time? Had he been imprisoned next to her, sealed in to prevent any scent from passing? But no—his scent carried more than just his presence. He had discovered the scents she had scattered out using the creatures she had managed to dominate. Over time, she had arranged for them to intentionally spread the scent to others, without realizing they were being dominated to do so. So far, though, she had discovered little about the world outside. She still didn't know how many of the hairless mammals there were, or how many of her own people had survived the asteroid.

She had found small ways to break the seal to her cell and was able to track the comings and goings of various of her captors, whom she could identify by scent. Which meant that as soon as Prey was brought into the complex, they could speak together, trading chemical communication in the manner of their kind. It wasn't a fast way to communicate when they weren't in the same room, but a single chemical packet could hold a lot of information, both emotion and memory.

Prey's fear was sharp and acrid, and at first that overwhelmed everything, his messages more cries of anguish than any real information. He was hurt. He had been traveling for hours in great pain. Once he calmed enough to communicate, though, she found that he knew much more than she did about the world they now lived in. What he showed her was hard to accept.

The vast amount of time that had passed, the vast numbers of the hairless creatures that he claimed inhabited the world: it defied belief. But she did believe him. The memory pictures he sent her were vivid and clear. Until then, she had nursed the fantasy that her people might still be out there, their Desert Roost re-formed after the asteroid, and she might escape and kill her captors and return home.

But there was no home, not anymore. She could never kill enough of the hairless creatures to prevent the rest from recapturing her and torturing her all over again. Maybe the best she could do was to kill as many as possible before they killed her in return. But that would leave Prey all alone, the last of his kind, in the same imprisoned agony she had suffered. Maybe she should just kill them both.

But the memories he shared also showed that not all of the humans were as cruel as her captors. A few had helped him, taught him their language, and tried to rescue him, one at the cost of her life. But ultimately, they had failed, and here he was, captured yet again. Rain thought of her female captor, the one who seemed to have some conscience and might be prevailed upon to help them. Was there any real hope?

Whatever the result, now that Prey was here, she would delay no longer. She couldn't sit by while they held him down with their wire nooses and struck him with their lightning sticks until they tapped his rage for their own purposes. She would rescue him, and they would try to escape. If there was nowhere for them to go, then they would die together.

Prey was injured; she could tell. He had relieved some of his own pain and increased the rate of the healing process, but he still needed rest and time to recover. The humans wouldn't let him die, would they? They wanted the chemicals they could extract from him. He was valuable, if not as a person, then at least as a resource. They would treat his injuries before they tortured him, wouldn't they?

Quickly, before they could lock him away and seal his room, she returned a message of her own, simply urging him to stay calm. She would find a way to save them.

Li Ling could have wept. A *second* maniraptor, another survivor of a sixty-six million year hibernation and member of the only other sentient civilization ever to walk the Earth, had arrived at the facility. She was at the center of the greatest moment in the history of science, perhaps in the history of mankind: when two intelligent species could meet and communicate for the first time. Instead of a triumph, it was a horror. The human capacity to take anything beautiful and warp it into a tool for political power or financial gain had destroyed this moment before it could even begin. There would be no communication. No tentative meeting of equals, no years of careful knowledge trading and discovery to forge a mutual respect. This moment would start and end with slavery, torture, and death.

The new maniraptor was a male, smaller than Rain, with different markings around its eyes and on the feathers along its back. He was injured, but no one would tell her why. Despite the wound, he seemed in better health than Rain. His feathers were fuller, more lush, missing in places, but not plucked out as much as Rain's. He had thrashed and screamed as they brought him in, showing a good deal more energy and lithe grace than Rain ever showed. This maniraptor had been better cared for. At least until recently.

Where had he come from? When Dr. Sun had first announced it, she had assumed a second living maniraptor had been discovered at the same dig site and would be brought to them embedded in rock. She'd anticipated observing the careful revival process that her team had previously used to bring Rain to life. But this maniraptor was already alive. Who had revived him? Had another lab in China independently done the same work as this one? That didn't seem likely. Yet here it was.

She watched as they noosed his neck and limbs, holding him still while they cut away his feathers on one side and treated his wound. They extracted what looked like several *bullets* from his flesh, and then packed the wound with gauze and wrapped and taped it. Finally, while they had him immobilized, they drove their electrified shock sticks into his flesh. He thrashed and cried out, but he couldn't get away.

A first sample. There would be much to learn by comparing the pheromones from these two maniraptors, one male and one female. Much to gain for science. And for the glory of China.

After the ferocity of the shocks, the new maniraptor cowered on the floor, shuddering. Wherever it had come from, it couldn't have been worse than this. *Welcome to China,* Li Ling thought. *Welcome to Hell.*

At lunch time, Li Ling made her way back to the outer guard station so she could check her phone. She didn't feel much like eating anyway. She texted Keju.

Hey big dragon. Everything okay?

The response came quickly. *No problems. Everything good with you?*

How could she answer that? No, everything is not good; I'm complicit in the torture of a sapient species to extract a chemical weapon we can use to turn other humans into willing slaves.

Fine, she wrote instead. *Any run-ins with Lao Zhou?*

Haven't even seen him.

What have you been doing?

Just hanging out. Hoping to spot him, but no luck.

I feel silly with you wasting your time out there.

Don't worry about me. You go do great important secret things for our country.

Li Ling felt a stab of guilt. Great important secret things indeed. What she and her colleagues were doing to the two maniraptors was worse than anything Lao Zhou had done to her.

Okay, she wrote. *Stay safe. And thanks.*

Anything for you, little phoenix.

Li Ling made her slow way back inside, feeling trapped. She'd been a top student, with a promising career in science ahead of her. She'd never expected to make a lot of money, but she'd thought she might make a difference for good in the world. Instead, she was party to a horrible crime at work and afraid to go home to her own apartment at night. She didn't have any friends to ask for help, just her brother, who could barely spare the time he was taking from work. When had her life gone so wrong?

She felt like the maniraptors in their cages: no options, no allies, with nothing to look forward to in her life but pain and regret. Her parents had been so proud of her when she'd earned a place at university. What would they say if they saw her now?

As she badged through the lab doors, she stopped in the corridor. She knew what her father would say. He'd said it to her often enough growing up. *You were blessed with more luck than many and more brains than most. Don't give up just because it's hard.*

He was right. She wasn't in a cage, at least not yet. She had choices. They might be scary choices, but she didn't have to just do as she was told. She could choose to obey and participate in what she thought was wrong, or she could fight back. She had already fought back once, and here she was, unharmed. The maniraptors had incredible abilities, more than she expected. They were probably smarter than she expected, too.

Li Ling returned to her station, showing nothing. She worked hard all afternoon. Inside, though, she made a decision. It might end with her in a real cage, just like the maniraptors, where she would truly have no choices. She laughed quietly to herself at the thought: at least Lao Zhou couldn't get to her there! No matter what happened to her, though, she was resolved. What was being done to the maniraptors was wrong. She would see them freed or face prison trying.

When it came time for most of the workers to leave, she

made her way out to security like the rest. She retrieved her phone and texted Keju again.

I need you to rent a truck.

A truck?

A big one. Please. I'll pay.

I don't understand.

Please.

She sent him a map link for a parking lot on public land a few miles from the facility. Much of the land near the facility was old growth rainforest, trackless and untraveled except by a few Hani tribesmen. It had been built here intentionally, far from prying eyes, and except for a few military barracks, most of the people who worked there took long train rides home at night. In fact, anyone taking the train to the end of the line either worked at the facility or had missed their stop.

She put the phone back in the locker without waiting for a reply and headed back into the building, working her way through the levels of security to return to the lab. There she dove into her work again, though she could hardly concentrate over the beating of her heart. No one would think anything of her staying late. She did that most nights anyway.

Rain listened, watched, and smelled.

There was no sunlight in her cell, but the false lights that her captors controlled turned on and off in a daily pattern. At night, the building was quieter, and she thought the humans were either gone elsewhere or sleeping. Rain's plan was simple: spread her scent out through the compromised seals to her cage and compel any of the alien creatures in range to come and set her free. She had been waiting until she had enough knowledge of the outside to have some expectation of success, but now that Prey was here, she couldn't wait much longer.

As it turned out, she didn't have to. The human female who had helped Rain before opened the door for her anyway. She stood there alone, with no shock stick or noose, and without a suit to suppress her smell. Rain thought about dominating her, but perhaps she didn't need to. The human seemed willing to help her of her own free will.

The human made noises from her mouth and beckoned with one arm. Watching her carefully for a trick, Rain approached and stepped through the door. Rain could smell her terror, but the human held her ground, not backing away. As a prey animal, that probably took a special courage.

How had such weak creatures gained such technology and power? Rain would have thought only a predator species could evolve such dominance. A species used to holding other animals in thrall. These soft, nearly hairless creatures looked like they would be more at home cowering in a cave or burrow than in control of the world.

The door to her cage was designed so that the outer door could not open until the inner door was closed. The human closed the inner door with a click and worked a mechanism on the wall, causing a sudden rush of air. Rain understood: the air was being replaced in an attempt to prevent any airborne chemicals from passing in or out of the cage. She knew a caustic spray could be released from above, too, to scour their suits, but the human could apparently prevent that from happening. The outer door's lock released with a pop, and it swung open.

The rush of fresh air flooded Rain with new information, fuller and more complete than the little she'd managed to get inside her cell from chemical transfer. Her claws clacked on the unnaturally hard and flat floor as she made her way into the larger room. She was free, but this new room was just another cage, a perfect rectangle of four walls with a door Rain couldn't open. The human female pressed a flat object from around her neck to a raised part of the wall near the door. It made a noise, and the human opened it, allowing them to pass through… into another rectangular cage! How many layers did this prison have?

She needed to get to Prey. She was starting to realize that what she had imagined as a few small structures was instead an artificial labyrinth of unknown size. She couldn't guess how far the maze stretched or how to navigate it. She needed this alien creature to take her where she needed to go.

Fortunately, the alien seemed to have the same goal. Rain followed her through several more rooms. She could smell the residual scent of Prey; he had been here. Finally, they reached another room like hers, one with a row of yellow suits on hooks and a door leading to an interior cell. The human unlocked the door and went inside. Rain heard the locks cycling, then cycling again, and finally she emerged. And there he was behind her, after countless weeks and millions of years: another one of her kind.

Prey rushed forward and they collided in a tangle of claws and feathers and a glorious, heady rush of pheromones. She dominated him, just a little, and he showed his throat and crooned as she rested her jaws lightly around his neck. They scratched each other, releasing a cloud of skin particles and tufts of feather that drifted through the air. She ran the edge of her jaw against his, exulting in the familiar feel and smell of him. For the first time in weeks, she wanted to live.

The human watched them with growing anxiety. Rain was certain she was acting on her own. The other humans wanted to keep Rain and Prey imprisoned and separate. They wanted to keep torturing them and harvesting their pheromones. Only this one was willing to help. Was that because she was a friend? Or did she simply have conflicting motives—perhaps to deliver them into the hands of a rival group of humans? Either way, they had little choice but to trust her.

Rain released a chemical meant to calm the human. The

woman took a deep breath, then made more language noise with her mouth and beckoned them on.

They walked through a door into another room, and then another door into yet another room beyond that. Rain became lost, with no sense of how to return to her cell even if she wanted to, and even less idea how to get out of this ridiculous maze. She couldn't conceive of the amount of raw materials required to build this many walls with this kind of precision. Why did they do it? Was the outside world still inhospitable from the asteroid strike? That, she supposed, would make a kind of sense. Perhaps all of this building activity was to provide safe warrens to protect them from a poisonous atmosphere. Or maybe these mammals had originally been burrowing creatures, and this was just the kind of environment that made them feel safe.

When they entered yet another room, the human drew in a gasp of air and backed away. Inside, another human sat in front of a bright rectangle. Rain recognized it as one of the ones who had hurt her again and again. When he spun and saw her, his eyes flew wide. He opened his mouth to shout, but Rain dominated him and he fell silent.

She remembered this one striking her with his lightning stick in the most sensitive areas of her flesh, the sparking fire turning her very world into pain until she gave him what he wanted. She had waited before, but the time for waiting was over. At her desire, he stepped meekly forward, and with a quick strike of her jaws, she crushed his neck. He fell limply to the floor. His blood tasted sweet.

The human female who had helped them shrieked and covered her mouth with her hands. She backed away too quickly and tripped, knocking over a metal object with a terrible crash and falling to the floor herself.

Prey sent shock and dismay. *They're not beasts to be killed. They think and feel as we do.*

But she gave him her memories of what they had done to

her, day after day, harvesting her pheromones through unbearable pain. *This one deserved to die.*

The human female shrieked even more. Rain realized that in sending Prey her memory of torture, she had sent it to the human as well. She probably didn't have the mental capacity to compartmentalize the experience, examining it as a source of knowledge like Prey could. She was probably experiencing the torture as if it was happening to her right now.

Rain wasn't too sorry about that. The humans had done this to her; they deserved to feel what it was like. But this female had set her and Prey free, and they still needed her help. Rain stopped sending out the memory and allowed it to dissipate. The human lay on the floor, breathing hard and leaking water from her eyes.

Some are our enemies, Prey sent. *But some are friends.* He sent her again the memory of the human who had thrown herself in front of Prey to save his life and was killed by sticks that flashed fire and threw death. A human who had cared for Prey and treated him well.

Prey approached the female cowering on the floor. He sent her feelings of calm and friendship and trust. Then he opened his mouth and spoke to her.

CHAPTER SEVENTEEN

Li Ling realized she'd made a terrible, terrible mistake. She had released these creatures, and now Dr. Sun lay in a mangled, bleeding heap on the floor, his throat torn out, and it was all her fault. She was hyperventilating, but she felt like she couldn't get enough air. The room was closing in on her. What had she been thinking? These were predators, dangerous creatures that had been brutalized by her peers. What had she expected them to do?

She had planned to sneak them out while the facility was mostly quiet and load them into a truck before anyone could stop her. She hadn't really planned their escape beyond that. She'd just known she couldn't sit around while a second precious, beautiful maniraptor was tortured in front of her. But now she saw these beautiful maniraptors for what they were: killers. They would murder everyone they could find in the facility until soldiers came and shot them. And then what would Ling have accomplished? She wouldn't even be around to see it, because any moment now, she would be dead.

The male maniraptor approached her, and she braced herself for the strike. The female had killed Dr. Sun; now the male would kill her, and they both would feed. And why wouldn't they? Killing and feeding was what they were born to do. In their own time, they had probably killed and eaten her mammal ancestors on a regular basis.

Just as she expected to die, however, a sudden feeling of calm suffused her. Her muscles relaxed and her breathing slowed. She wasn't going to die. In fact, the maniraptors were her friends. She could trust them. She looked up at the male and knew he wouldn't hurt her.

And then, against all her wildest expectations, he *spoke*.

"Hello," he said in a screeching voice. "My name…is Charlie."

Li Ling's English wasn't great, but she could understand that much. She gaped at him, unable to formulate a response. Unable to accept the fact that a dinosaur had just *talked to her.* She felt a wild giggle bubbling up inside her and forced it down. *Get a grip, Ling.*

She took a deep breath and let it out slowly before trying to respond. "Hello. My name is Li Ling," she finally managed.

"Can we leave now?" the dinosaur said.

Despite herself, the giggle came bursting out. It was just so unexpected. She thought she might be finally going insane. "We can try," she said.

THEY MADE THEIR WAY ALONG HARD FLOORS AND ECHOING hallways. On several occasions, they encountered more humans. Rain still wanted to kill them, but Prey convinced her that the humans would have more usefulness if they dominated them. They could not work the humans' machinery, after all, and they would likely need to in order to escape.

Eventually, with the help of four dominated humans, they opened a huge wall that retracted up into the ceiling, allowing sunlight to stream through. Rain ran out into the light, whirling to take in the blue sky, the lush green of growing things, the smell of grass and trees and earth and water. For a moment, it felt like home, until the dozens of unfamiliar smells cut through her awareness. Humans, and the stink of fire and oil that clung to their machines, but also plants and animals she had never encountered before, and other smells she couldn't even categorize. This wasn't home. It was an alien world.

She soon recognized that although they were outside, they were not yet free of the human prison. The building they had escaped was only one of many, surrounded by multiple fences, guarded by more humans.

We can't dominate them all, Prey sent.

Maybe you *can't*, Distant Rain returned.

This was her moment. She took off running, stretching legs too long confined. They burned with the exertion, but she pushed on, reveling in the feeling of her muscles uncoiling. As she ran, she spread her scent, powerful and strong. The humans shouted and called to each other, but smell was such a superior communication tool. It moved more slowly than sound, but she could pack far more information into it, even given the humans' pitiful sense of smell. While sound waves merely moved the air, smell was *chemical*, with a much greater capacity to influence and change.

In moments, she had a dozen human bodyguards. They surrounded her and Prey, protecting them from the guns of the others. The other humans wouldn't shoot at their fellow soldiers, giving her scent time to work its way to them as well. The ranks of their bodyguards grew while those of their adversaries decreased. She could use the soldiers' knowledge of the facility to avoid dangers.

Then quite suddenly, it all went wrong.

PREY DIDN'T SEE THE SNIPER BEFORE THE BULLET SCREAMED past his head and hit a human behind him. He didn't know where it had come from, but Distant Rain must have seen, or else the soldiers themselves knew. At Rain's prompting, they fired a hail of bullets toward the top of a nearby building where a man had been crouching. The man tumbled over the edge and landed on the ground below.

At that, more rooftop soldiers began firing, and some of their bodyguards started to fall. Their peaceful escape turned into a bloody war. When the thundering reports finally fell silent, humans lay dead on every side. Blood soaked the ground.

Prey looked around in dismay. Some of these people had been cruel to Rain, he knew, but most were just guarding a building they'd been commanded to guard. Some of them probably hadn't even known he and Rain were there. He looked at the one nearest, his eyes open but unseeing. Prey could smell the fish he'd eaten that morning, and the scent of another human who had held him close not long before.

Get up, Distant Rain said, and Prey obeyed immediately, though whether out of habit or because of the authority her smell communicated, he couldn't say. *We should go before more of them come.*

This is awful, Prey sent back, indicating the dead humans around him.

We were lucky, she replied. *Nobody was hurt.*

She meant the two of them, Prey realized. The humans didn't count to her.

The female human who had rescued them crouched next to them, her eyes wide and her body shaking. She breathed in heaving gasps.

Then she stood unsteadily and pointed away from the setting sun. "This way."

Li Ling led the maniraptors toward the gate out of the facility. It was only two kilometers through a stretch of woods to the park where she had told Keju to meet her. She hoped he was there, or this rescue attempt would be over quickly.

She was committed now. People had died. She had never seen a dead body before today. In the last ten minutes, she'd seen people get shot and get their throats torn out, more blood and violence than she had ever imagined. And it was all her fault. All those people would still be alive if not for her betrayal.

The best she could expect was to spend the rest of her life in jail. More likely, though, she would be tried for treason and murder and then shot. Her parents and Keju might not even know what happened to her.

She thought about leading the maniraptors in a different direction, away from Keju. After all, if she met him, she would make him an accomplice. He would be just as guilty, a co-conspirator, even though he had no idea what was going on. They would both be charged with a bloody attack on a government facility in an attempt to steal a secret and valuable national asset.

But to give up now would be to doom the maniraptors to imprisonment and torture for the remainder of their lives. She'd come this far now. She had to try.

The maniraptors, big as they were, moved more gracefully through the woods than she did. In the growing darkness, she tripped over roots and walked headlong into sharp branches, but they seemed to have no difficulty. She wondered if their eyesight was better in low light than hers, or if they had some other way to navigate.

Two kilometers had seemed like a short distance when she'd looked at it on a map, but now, struggling through undergrowth, it seemed to take forever. At any moment, she expected to see flashlights approaching through the woods, searching for them, followed by rifles. They might just shoot all three of them on sight, without giving them a chance to surrender. The killing machines walking on either side of her had just murdered at least a dozen armed guards. They wouldn't take any chances.

Finally, the trees started to thin, and she could see light ahead. "Stay here," Li Ling said. "Let me go first."

The male maniraptor—Charlie—understood her, and must have communicated the message to Rain, because they stayed behind as she creeped ahead as steathily as she knew how. The light resolved itself into two powerful beams. Headlights. A little closer, and she could make out a large cargo truck. Good. Keju had done as she asked.

The lot was quiet. The park probably closed at sundown. "Keju?" she called softly.

No answer.

"Keju?" A little louder this time.

Then she heard her brother's voice. "Li Ling? Is that you?"

She breathed a sigh of relief. "It's me."

She walked out onto the asphalt, trying to make him out beyond the blinding headlights, when she saw not one person, but two. Had he brought someone along to help?

Then a flood of adrenaline hit her as the scene suddenly resolved. Lao Zhou stood behind her brother, holding a serious-looking knife against his throat.

"I'm sorry," Keju said. "I didn't realize he—"

"Shut up." Lao Zhou pressed the edge of the knife against Keju's throat.

Li Ling didn't dare move. "What are you doing, Lao Zhou?"

Lao Zhou made an incredulous noise. "What am I doing? I should ask the same of you. You've been sneaking around for weeks, clearly avoiding me, and now your *brother* shows up." He said the word with disdain.

"I have not been sneaking."

"Taking different trains, staying in that secret facility of yours late into the night? What am I supposed to think?"

"You're supposed to think that I don't want to see you! That I never want to see you, ever again! Why can't you just leave me alone?"

He looked mournful. "I told you. Because I love you."

"You *love* me? You're holding a knife to my brother's throat!"

Lao Zhou suddenly seemed to remember Keju was there. He shook him a little and renewed the pressure of the knife on his neck. "He's leading you into trouble, Ling. "Meeting you at night in a park with a rented truck? What has he gotten you into? Smuggling drugs? Weapons?"

"Nothing like that. You've gotten the wrong idea."

"Have I? He was never any good for you. Always hanging around, poisoning your mind about me. He never liked me. We could have been happy, if not for him."

"That's not true. Just let him go."

"If I kill him here, you and I can leave together. No one will ever know. We can go to Beijing or Hong Kong, make a new life together. Just like old times. We could be happy."

Li Ling took a shaky breath. He was truly crazy. How could she talk their way out of this? "Lao Zhou, if you kill him, I will never speak to you again. Not one word, not ever."

"You love him, don't you."

"He's my brother! Of course I love him."

"And you don't love me."

Her voice stuck in her throat. She should lie, reassure him, tell him that she'd go with him if only he'd let Keju go. But the words just wouldn't come. And then it was too late.

"I thought so," Lao Zhou said. "Then there's only one way to change that."

With a cry, he drew the knife violently across Keju's throat. Li Ling screamed as blood flooded out, but Keju had been faster. When he sensed Lao Zhou was going to attack, he'd thrown his arm up and managed to partially block the killing strike. Blood covered his neck and dripped onto his shirt, but he was still up on his feet and out of Lao Zhou's grasp.

Lao Zhou lunged at him again. Keju backed away, raising his arms to block, but he tripped and fell back hard against the asphalt. Lao Zhou turned the knife and moved in to finish the job.

"No!" Li Ling yelled and ran toward them, but she was too far away to do any good.

In a blur of movement, something drove itself into Lao Zhou's chest, sending him flying backwards and onto the pavement. The male maniraptor stood on his chest, jaws inches from his face. Lao Zhou thrashed and screamed, but he couldn't get away.

Li Ling ran to Keju. He was a mess of blood, but he was already sitting up. When he saw the maniraptor, he scrambled backward in terror, trying to get to his feet.

"Lay back," she told him. "You're hurt."

He stared at her like she was mad. "What is that thing?"

"He's a friend. At least, I think he is. This is why I needed the truck. But Keju, your neck!"

"Looks worse than it is," he said. "He just scratched me, really."

"You're covered in blood! That's not just a scratch."

The female maniraptor, Rain, joined them. Keju's eyes flew wide again, but he didn't try to run. Li Ling felt a sudden sense of awe and the desire to do anything she wanted. She knew Rain was causing her to feel that way, but she didn't mind. Lao Zhou stopped screaming.

Keju gingerly touched his neck and winced. His hand came away red. "I think there's a first aid box in the truck. In the driver's side door."

Li Ling rushed to get it. When she came back, he was lying down again. She pulled out gauze and bandages and tape and wrapped him up as best she could.

"You have to get to a hospital. You need stitches," she said.

He started to shake his head, then stopped with a grimace. "I'm fine. Li Ling, what's going on? What have you gotten yourself into?"

"I'll explain everything," she said. "But first we've got to go. It won't be long before they find us here. Are you sure you're okay?"

"It's just a cut. Look, it hasn't even soaked through the bandage yet. But go where? What's this all about?"

"I have a plan." Not much of one, she had to admit, but it was a start, at any rate.

She circled around Charlie to see whether Lao Zhou was still alive. She felt strangely detached, as if it didn't matter one way or the other. He was, however, still breathing. In fact, he seemed unhurt. He stared up at Charlie with obedient devotion.

"Should I kill him?" Charlie asked.

Li Ling looked down at Lao Zhou. It would be so easy. So many had died today already, and he deserved it. But she hadn't intended the others to die. It hadn't been her choice, even if her choices had led to it happening. She couldn't just order this death like a mafia boss, no matter who he was or how he'd hurt her.

Instead, she leaned down until her face was inches from Lao Zhou's. He continued to look at Charlie. She wanted to claw his eyes out. "Can he hear me?"

"Yes," Charlie said. "He will do whatever you tell him to do."

Whatever I tell him to do. A parade of brutal possibilities marched through her brain, but she swept them aside.

"You will leave here and never try to find me again," she said. "If you ever do see me, you will remember this day, wet your pants in fear, and run away. Then you will forget you ever saw anything. Do you understand me?"

Lao Zhou looked at her. He looked at the teeth of the monsters looming over him. He nodded fervently.

Li Ling knew he was a coward. She didn't know how effective the maniraptors' chemical influence would be over time, but she doubted he would bother her again, not after this. However, she could easily see him going straight to the authorities and reporting her.

"You will tell no one what you've seen here," she said. "You will go far away from here and never return."

"Yes, yes," he said. "Please."

She stared into his eyes. She wanted to hurt him, humiliate him, know that he was beaten. But this would have to be enough. "Go then," she said.

Lao Zhou scrambled away backwards on all fours, then turned and ran down the road away from them, not looking back. She hoped she would never see him again.

"Let's get out of here," she said.

Keju climbed to his feet. A little red had seeped through his bandage now, but he stood steadily enough.

Li Ling gathered up the first aid kit and walked back toward the truck, shielding her eyes against the still-blazing headlights. The space beyond the headlights was completely dark by contrast, which is why she didn't see the man standing there until she had almost run into him.

CHAPTER EIGHTEEN

Li Ling shrieked, startled and thinking it was Lao Zhou come back for further mischief.

But it was not Lao Zhou. It was a Hani man, a member of the hill tribes that lived in this part of Yunnan. Almost invisible, he stood like a statue, his indigo jacket blending into the night. His head was shaved except for a long top-knot hanging down his back. His wrinkled face showed no sign of his intentions. He carried a handmade hoe over his shoulder.

"Who are you?" she demanded. "What do you want?"

Keju came to her side and looked ready to jump to her defense.

"We watch you for a long time," said the man in accented but perfectly clear Mandarin. "We see you come out."

"We? You've been watching me?"

"Li Ling," Keju said. "Look."

She followed his line of sight to see another Hani man, and then another. They stepped silently out of the darkness, surrounding them.

"We look for the creatures who make the devil drug," said the first man. "Now we find them."

THE NEW HUMANS CAME OUT INTO THE FAILING LIGHT. THEY wore rough indigo clothing and a few had black cloth wrapped around their necks. They smelled like the earth, and Prey guessed they spent their time planting and caring for crops. They wore no masks or nose plugs, nor did they carry guns.

Rain dominated them immediately. The closest one approached and bowed low. When she put her jaws to the man's throat, Prey gently nudged her back.

These are people. They have done nothing to you.

Distant Rain turned to him in rage, dominating him ferociously. Prey groveled, scraping his face in the dirt and whimpering. She flooded his mind with her memories of her torture at the hands of her human captors. He felt the pain as she had felt it and cried out in terror and anguish. The humans felt it, too. They held their heads or fell on the ground and screamed.

When it was over, Distant Rain stood over them all, fierce and terrifying, her teeth bared and her breast heaving with exertion. Prey carefully, slowly, stood.

It wasn't them, he sent. *Humans differ as much as did our kind. Do not kill the good to punish the evil.*

The human man who had spoken stood carefully, his hands raised. "They tell me you speak English, yes?"

"Yes," Prey said, surprised.

"We are not Chinese army," the man said. "We are Hani. We never hurt you. The Chinese hurt us too, make us carry drugs, do work for them."

Prey translated into scent for Distant Rain. "I am sorry," he told them. "We are friends, then."

The man in front bowed. "Chanchai say to find you here. He say one is called Charlie. Which one is called Charlie please?"

"That's what they call me," Prey said. "I'm Charlie."

"We come to rescue you, but you already rescued, hey?" The man laughed.

"There aren't many of you for a rescue attempt," Prey said. "And you don't have any weapons."

"Many more far away, hiding with weapons."

"I see. How did you know where to find us?"

The man crossed his arms. "The devil drug come from here. They use it on us, make us smuggle guns across borders, give to criminals and spies. We know long time where you are."

"Is there a safe place we can go to hide from the Chinese?"

"We take you to Chanchai now. He take you to the dinosaur lady."

Li Ling felt like the situation was spiraling out of her control. "Hang on," she said. "You were looking for the dinosaurs? How did you know they were here?"

"The dinosaur lady told us. She is their friend."

"I don't understand. Who is that?"

"She is from America," the Hani leader said. "Her name is—"

"Samira?" Charlie cut in. "Samira is here?"

"She is far away," the Hani man said. "Long journey."

"Can you take us?" Charlie took several quick steps toward the man, who didn't flinch.

"We will take you."

Li Ling looked back and forth between them, baffled. The maniraptors were a tightly-held national secret, but these tribesmen seemed to know more about them than she did. "We have a truck," she said, pointing at it unnecessarily. "If you know a safe place for them, we can take them there."

The Hani man looked scornfully at the truck. "That truck can not take the mountain paths. We will take them where they need to go."

"Let's go then," Charlie said. "Quickly. More humans will come."

The Hani men turned toward the forest. The maniraptors seemed ready to join them. Were they all going to walk off together, just like that?

"Take me, too," Li Ling said.

"What?" Keju took her arm. "You can't go with them. This is crazy."

He was right, of course. This whole thing was crazy. She had broken dinosaurs out of a government facility, who had then killed her boss. The State Security Ministry would be after her. If they caught her, she would go down for treason, if not murder. She suddenly realized just how bad her situation was. She couldn't stay in China. Her "plan" had been a half-baked idea to rent a cabin in the hills until she could figure out something better to do, but that was ludicrous. She had no plan, not really. She had acted because what they were doing to these creatures was wrong. That didn't mean she wouldn't suffer for it.

"I have to," she said. "I'm sorry, Keju. I shouldn't have dragged you into this. Return the truck. Go back to your job. None of this was your doing."

"No! I can't just leave you."

"I'm a state criminal now," she said. "If you come with me, you'll lose everything. Stay. Go back to your life. I'll contact you when I can."

"Where are you even going? Will you live in the jungle? Eat off the land?" He looked up at the maniraptors. "What even are those things? How can they talk?"

She started to cry. "I wish I could explain. They were being tortured, and I rescued them. But more men will be here soon. The military will scour this whole area looking for them. You have to leave before they find you. Before they block all the roads."

He clung to her. "I'll leave the truck. I'll come with you."

"No! Please, Keju, I couldn't bear it. You can't destroy your life for me. Besides, if you run away, who would take care of our parents? When I can, I'll let you know I'm safe. I'll explain everything."

He began crying, too. "I was supposed to protect you, little phoenix."

"You have," she said. "Lao Zhou is gone now. I don't think I'll ever see him again. Now go. Please. Go right now."

He backed away. "I love you," he said.

"I love you, too. Go!"

He climbed into the truck and started the engine. Li Ling wondered if she would ever see him again either. Then he drove away.

THE HANI SPREAD OUT AS THEY MOVED INTO THE FOREST. They made their way quickly, but silently, accustomed to the uneven footing and dense undergrowth. The maniraptors too, big as they were, slipped through the trees like water flowing around the pilings of a bridge. Li Ling, however, seemed to trip over every root, step in every hole, and get tangled in every plant along the way. This was not her natural habitat.

She also tired much more easily. She was a woman of trains and elevators. She had a gym membership like most people her age, but her busy schedule rarely afforded her the chance to get there. Since she'd started working with the maniraptors, she hadn't even been once. After a few kilometers, she was soaked with sweat, wheezing, and longing for a drink of water.

At last, they came to a stream. The maniraptors splashed right in, shoving their faces into the water for a drink. The

Hani gathered around the edge, filling modern plastic water bottles manufactured for hiking. One man gave one to her, and she drank from it greedily.

"Where are we going?" she asked. "How far is it?"

"We go to Thailand."

"What? It's hundreds of miles to Thailand, through impassable jungle!"

The older man who had looked derisively at her truck now looked much the same way at her. "Chinese think it is impassable because they cannot drive through it. But we know the way. As China knows well." He worked his jaws a few times and then spat on the ground in front of her.

"Father!" A younger man put his hand on the older man's shoulder. "She's not part of that." He looked to her, as if for confirmation.

"Part of what?" she asked.

"Men from the facility you came out of have been forcing our people to smuggle a drug to Thailand for months now. They use the drug themselves to give us no choice. We call it the devil drug. Our people can enter Thailand without going through customs, so they use us instead of doing it themselves."

"That's awful," Li Ling said. "I didn't know."

She had been complicit, of course. But it made her more certain she had done the right thing by rescuing the maniraptors. She had thought that at least the maniraptors had been tortured for a good cause, to make China safe from her enemies. Now she saw that the cruelty extended farther than she had realized. She couldn't imagine that her life would ever recover from this—probably she would end up dead—but neither would she have chosen to do anything differently.

The chop of a helicopter sounded from above. The men ran for cover, and Li Ling ran with them. They stood quietly close to the trunks of trees, trying to maximize the foliage over their heads, while the helicopter grew closer. It approached and hovered directly over the stream, the wash from its rotors kicking up little waves and blowing back Li Ling's hair.

After what seemed like an eternity, the helicopter pulled up and away, its clatter fading into the distance.

"Do you think they saw us?" she asked.

The younger man from before said, "Probably. If they had infrared scopes, they could see that there were people here, but they wouldn't know who we are. Just bright shapes."

"What if they could see the bright shapes of the maniraptors?"

He shrugged. "They didn't shoot at us. Even so, there are probably soldiers heading our way to check. The forest near the facility must be swarming with soldiers by now, looking for some sign of us."

"They won't stop looking," Li Ling said. "These creatures represent a lot of power. They'll use as many people and as much time as it takes to track us down."

"Then we'll just have to stay ahead of them."

They walked for what felt like forever. This was the kind of landscape they called *tiankeng*, or karst topography, full of steep rocky cliffs, caves, and sinkholes that fell suddenly away, dropping sections of solid-looking ground into the empty spaces lurking beneath. The tortured landscape was caused by rainwater that wormed its way underground, slowly dissolving the chalky layers of calcium carbonate underneath their feet and turning the forest's foundations into a crumbling labyrinth. Eerie limestone towers loomed overhead like forests of stone, the ruins of collapses from centuries before. Sometimes, their path would skirt the edges of giant sinkholes, where Li Ling could gaze straight down, fascinated, at the tops of trees growing up from the hidden world below.

Not that there was any path to speak of. The Hani walked through this bewildering world confidently, following no markers she could see to tell them they were headed in the right direction. It occurred to her with a chill that if she lost her guides, she could die here. She had no idea how to find her way back. She would probably end up walking in circles until she fell into a sinkhole or simply collapsed from exhaustion and hunger.

Unnerved, she jogged a few steps to catch up to the young man who had spoken to her before.

"Do you live in this forest all the time?" she asked.

He laughed. "No. I live in an apartment outside Puer."

Her startlement must have been obvious, because he laughed again. "I'm sorry," she said. "I just thought—"

"You thought of the hill tribes stereotypes from stories you heard as a child."

"I guess. Sorry."

"Don't worry about it. My father fits those stereotypes better. He lives in a tourist village, the same one he grew up in, though he's lucky it still exists, given how often the Chinese government takes the land they want without any regard for who lives there."

"What do you do for a living?"

"I'm a computer programmer."

Surprised again, she bit back a laugh, not wanting to offend him. "I'm Li Ling. Thank you for helping us. What's your name?"

"Wen A-Zhu."

"Wen? That's a Mandarin name."

"My father wanted me to fit in."

"Can I ask: If you live in Puer, why are you here?"

He gestured to the older man farther ahead through the trees. "Helping my father."

"Yes, but why is he here? What were you doing that allowed you to show up when you did, right when I escaped with the maniraptors? You couldn't possibly have known I was going to do that. I didn't even know I was going to do that."

"We've been watching the facility. I told you how the government men have been treating people like my father.

That drug of theirs practically turns them into slaves. They made my father walk all the way to Thailand to deliver the drug to their agents there, and he couldn't resist. He knew what he was doing, and he remembered doing it afterwards, but at the time, he couldn't disobey them. Ever since, I've been trying to find out where the drug is coming from and what to do about it. We all have."

"Who is this 'dinosaur lady?' You said she's an American woman?"

"Yes, a scientist. One of the dinosaurs was taken from her."

"The male? It came from America?"

He shrugged. "So I hear. I didn't actually meet her."

"But you're bringing the maniraptors to her?"

"She cares about them, at least according to my father. She's the one who taught the male to speak English. Personally, I don't care where they go, as long as my father and my people aren't forced to be slaves."

She watched the two maniraptors loping easily through the undergrowth. "What must it be like for them?" she said.

"The maniraptors?"

"Yes. It's like that tale of the woodcutter who watched two immortals playing Go, and then went home to find that everyone he ever knew was long since dead," she said. "Can you imagine? Waking up to find humanity gone? I wonder what they make of all this?"

Prey didn't recognize anything. He thought that once he got away from human habitation, the land might at least look or smell familiar. This was the region of the world where he'd grown up, but it might as well have been a different planet. He smelled loam and moss and the chemical signals of a million tiny forms of life, but nothing he recognized. The thick leafy foliage around them was completely unfamiliar. The whole shape and character of the land had changed.

His wound hurt where the bullet had struck him, but the work they had done to close the wound was holding. The pain wasn't more than he could bear. He did wonder how far they would have to travel, though. His various confinements had given him little opportunity for exercise, and his muscles felt weak. As long as Samira was at the end of this trek, he would persist. She would know how to help.

Distant Rain was less confident. She wanted to leave these humans behind and make their own way in the forest.

We should kill them, she sent to him by scent. *They are our enemies.*

They're helping us, Prey responded.

When it suits them. When it doesn't, they'll hurt us, just like the others. You can't trust them.

They're bringing us to a friend. She'll know how to help us.

Rain's scent was tinged with frustration and anger. *Why do we need help? Let's kill them and go. We have everything we need here. A rough life, living off the land, but there should be food enough. All the humans will ever do is lock us in a cage.*

The whole world belongs to them now. We could never be safe here.

We could try.

The two of them ranged out from the humans, close enough to smell them, but far enough to catch and devour the occasional small mammal. Rain disagreed with him, but remarkably, she didn't force him to do things her way. She could have dominated him as easily as he dominated humans, but she was willing to trust him.

As they made their silent way through the forest, Prey told her by scent about the virus killing the humans and his ideas for how a cure might be created.

Let them all die, she said. *As long as they live, our kind is threatened.*

Our kind? Prey said. *It's just you and me. There are billions of humans, and they think and reason and hurt and love just as we do.* He sent her a glimpse, just a reminder of what he had shown her before: Paula throwing herself into the line of fire to save him.

Distant Rain snarled and released a stink of revulsion mixed with a little fear. *They are not like us.*

The humans leading them through the forest smelled different than other humans Prey had encountered, but their large animal stink was still unmistakeable from a great distance away. He detected the gathering of humans ahead long before he saw them. They smelled like the others who were traveling with them, though, not like the Chinese soldiers, so he didn't fear them. Eventually, their group forded a stream and met the others at what Prey guessed was a temporary settlement. Instead of hard, straight walls with square edges, rectangles of cloth had been strung from tree branches. A fire burned in a pit, surrounded by rocks, and meat of some kind cooked over it.

More humans who looked and smelled like the forest men tended the fire or worked to assemble more cloth shelters. "Come," one of the men said, beckoning Prey and Rain with a hand. When they followed, the man showed them an animal similar to the deer he had been given to eat in Samira's lab. It had a similar shape and size, but its hair was bristly and its horns curved back over its head.

"For you," the man said.

Prey didn't need to be told twice. He would have preferred to have hunted it himself, but it was fresh, and he was starving. He tore its throat out and tossed a steaming chunk toward the back of his mouth, swallowing it whole. Rain made no objection, either, ripping into its belly and licking the blood off of her jaws. Prey still had little idea of where they were headed or the shape of this mysterious new world ruled by humans, but he felt more optimistic with a full belly. He curled up underneath a tree to rest.

Just after nightfall, the helicopter returned.

CHAPTER NINETEEN

The dig site felt empty and exposed with the military gone. Most of the Thai students left, too, and Samira didn't blame them. Their country was under siege, and no one would protect them here. They wanted to be with their families.

That left nine of them to work the site: Samira and Beth, Arinya, Alex, Gabby and Arun, Brook, and two of Kit's students, Channarong and Kanokwan, who had decided to stay. Samira's parents didn't have the skills to help, and besides, her father's health had started to deteriorate again. Whatever Charlie had done to slow the progress of Julian, the virus was apparently catching up to him. They stayed in a tent by themselves, Mom caring for Dad as best she could, without much in the way of medical supplies, or even running water.

The villagers from Khai Nun offered tea and other remedies, but her mother wouldn't let them get close, for fear they would be infected as well. Samira felt bad not caring for him more herself, but she knew she couldn't really help. Their best chance, unlikely as it might be, was to find a solution somewhere in the memories of the maniraptors. Charlie had thought the disease might be curable. If only he were here.

They didn't have time to painstakingly scrape away the layers and document each piece of rock and bone as they encountered it. As Samira and Beth and Arinya smelled and experienced memory after memory, the others attacked the site with pickaxes, biting deeply into the rock, pulling up as much memory-infused sandstone as they could. They tried to steer clear of the chocolate brown ridges that indicated the presence of fossils, working around them to increase the chance they could later be dragged free without damage. Inevitably, though, dark chips of brown flew up with the rest of the stone. Samira nearly screamed at them to stop, but she knew scientific rigor couldn't be their priority right now. Any day at the site might be their last.

Without Charlie, though, what could she really hope to do? With a lab, and months to spend studying the chemicals they uncovered, and the expertise of molecular biologists and experts in infectious diseases, then *maybe* they could learn enough from the ancient knowledge of Charlie's people to design a cure. She was doing this to save the human race and to save her father. But what kind of chance did they actually have? Should she abandon the attempt and just sit with her father as he died?

She worried about Kit, too. There had been no sign of his whereabouts, and no word from the queen that he'd been found. That meant he was either dead, or the enemy had him. Knowing how he could be controlled, the second option almost seemed worse. There was nothing she could do about it, but that didn't stop her from running nightmare scenarios through her head.

After a day that felt more like destroying the past than uncovering it, she sat with the team in the near darkness around a low fire, eating a manioc mash flavored with chilis. An echoing boom sounded to the east.

Samira looked at the sky, which was stunningly clear, a

million stars blazing out from the black dome. "Was that thunder?"

Another boom sounded, louder than the first, and the eastern sky glowed briefly white.

"The war," Arun said. "The US will be trying to take out all the anti-aircraft sites along the coast."

The booms continued, some close and loud, some more distant. A little while later, they saw a bright flash, followed by a white, smoky trail that drifted across the sky, forking into two, three, and then four white smears until it passed out of sight.

THE NEXT DAY, SAMIRA'S MOM STARTED VOMITING BLOOD. THE day after that, first Arun and then Gabby did as well, and then Kit's two students. Samira knew it had been their choice to be here, and they could have gotten sick just staying home. But she couldn't help feeling like she'd condemned them to death by continuing the work. What was she doing? What did she think she could accomplish?

By then, they'd discovered eight different maniraptor skeletons, though they'd left them in the ground, not wanting to take the time needed to bring them out. They were fossilized bones, not the preserved maniraptors themselves, so they would never be revived like Charlie. Who knows what might be deeper, though. There were almost certainly a lot more skeletons they hadn't yet found, and maybe, just maybe, other pockets existed where exactly the right conditions had allowed another creature to be preserved enough to be revived.

It broke her heart to surrender them all to China. Their luck had already lasted longer than she expected, but she knew it couldn't be long before the Chinese army arrived in force. When they did, all of this knowledge and power would become theirs, and Samira and the others would become prisoners of war.

The sad thing was, she had known many Chinese paleontologists. They were brilliant men and women, at the top of their field. China had dominated the profession over the last decade, discovering more new species and making more landmark discoveries than any other nation. Where were those scientists now? Had they been pushed into secrecy and weapons development by their government, as she had? In past wars, it had been the chemists and physicists whose abilities were engaged by their governments in time of war. She supposed it was the paleontologists' turn now.

Samira sampled memory after memory, not even writing down what she saw. All she cared about was finding some clue about their technology that might be used to save the human race from extinction. Even if she couldn't replicate the technology herself—and realistically, how could she expect to with just the equipment they had in their lab?—maybe she could contact Evelyn Soderberg at the CDC and pass on the information. It would be too late for her parents and her friends and probably herself, but it might just save humanity.

She wondered if there was any way she could reach the Chinese equivalent of the CDC. Surely their disease specialists were working on the problem just as diligently. If she told them what was happening, maybe they could get their government to let Charlie come here. But no, not much hope of that. She didn't know how to get such a message through, and even if she could, how could she make them believe in the existence of a dinosaur with a realistic chance of curing the Julian virus? The story was ludicrous, and their own government would deny it.

It was up to them. Their chances seemed remote, but all they could do was try.

On the third night since the military left, as she lay looking up at the stars and listening to the distant explosions of the war, Samira wondered what was wrong with humanity. With the Julian virus, they faced what was possibly the greatest extinction threat they had ever known, but instead of working together to overcome it, they were expending their vast resources of ingenuity to kill each other even faster.

Had the maniraptors been the same? Was it a necessary consequence of individual consciousness and the drive to survive? Perhaps social creatures inevitably warred against those not part of their tribe, as did many primates and other mammals. Whether uniquely human or not, it was a failing that could cost them their survival.

A motion above her caught her eye. She thought at first it might be a bird, a crow perhaps. Had Cope and Marsh found her after all this time? Then she saw it again: a moving black circle that blocked out a patch of stars. She saw a second, and then a third. By the time she identified them as parachutes, Alex was standing next to her, staring up at them as well. Samira had never seen nor heard a plane.

"Which army?" she asked.

"Does it matter? They're coming for us."

Samira stood frozen, afraid. "It must be the Americans. China wouldn't have to come secretly by night."

Alex turned to her. "So Everson's been tracking us somehow?"

"I don't think so. At least, I don't know how he could. The US military knows this is a source of the domination chemical, and knows China will soon have control of it if they don't act fast. I don't think Everson or anyone else could know that we're here. Unless their satellite surveillance is good enough to identify people's faces from space."

"Well, whether they know we're here or not, they found us."

There was no point in trying to escape. Running would just get them shot. Samira and Alex woke the others, and they waited in the dark, trying to appear non-threatening. They didn't have to wait long. Soldiers in jungle camo and wearing gas masks materialized out of the darkness, surrounding them.

"We're CIA," Beth insisted to the special ops commander. She was half his size, but she looked like she could take him through sheer determination. "What's your name, soldier?"

"Captain Lucas Anderson," he said. "What's yours?"

"Beth Shannon, pleased to meet you. And before you ask, of course we don't have identification. We're working in country, undercover."

"Our instructions are to hold this site against enemy incursion until the full force arrives," Anderson said, "And to destroy it if that is not possible. No one told us to expect Americans on site."

"Typical Washington screw-up. *Our* mission is to extract the chemical that makes this site of strategic value. You can protect us while we do it."

Samira could tell that the man's confidence was wavering. It probably helped that Beth was a tiny, pretty blonde who appealed to his protective instincts. He unstrapped the gas mask from his face, and as soon as he did so, he was hers.

"Instruct your soldiers to remove their masks," she told him. The captain repeated her command, but the other soldiers didn't obey him. "Take them," one said.

One soldier grabbed Beth roughly and pulled her arms behind her back. He forced her to her knees and produced a zip tie, which he cinched around her wrists. Samira cried out as she was similarly pushed to her knees and tied. In moments, the soldiers had all of them restrained, including her parents and the Thai students helping them.

"They warned us," the captain said, his gas mask restored.

"I didn't believe it until I experienced it myself. That is quite a weapon."

"It also might be a cure for the Julian virus," Samira said. "That's really why we're here. We're scientists, not soldiers."

Captain Anderson tapped his mask. "Doesn't work when I'm wearing this."

"I'm serious! Look at these people—they're sick. We don't care about the war; we're trying to save the human race."

"Don't make me gag you," Anderson said. Then, to one of his men: "Set up a perimeter. Let's make sure we've got all the firing angles covered."

He turned back to his prisoners and his eyes focused on Beth. "Now," he said. "You're going to tell me how to create and use this weapon. If you lie to me, I will consider you enemy combatants and spies and treat you accordingly. Given that you just tried to make me your unwilling slave, I'm not inclined to be patient."

"We're not going to tell you that," Samira said.

His eyes swiveled to her. She was keenly aware of his taut muscles and the darkly oiled muzzle of his rifle, slung around his neck. "What was that?"

"This weapon's too easy to misuse. We won't help you."

"And making me your slave, that wasn't misusing it?"

"We wouldn't have hurt you. And maybe it was unethical, I don't know. But you're threatening us with big guns, and we're trying to save the human race from possible extinction. In balance, it seemed worth it."

"We're deep behind enemy lines here. How do we know you're not working for the Chinese?"

Dad coughed loudly, and bright red blood streamed down his chin. The soldiers nearest him jumped away. He kept coughing, trying to clear his throat, but with his hands tied behind his back, he couldn't even wipe the blood away.

"That's my dad!" Beth shouted. "Do you think we'd bring my sick father on some special spying mission for the Chinese?

The woman next to him is my mom. We're not part of the war. We're trying to do good here."

"Please," Mom said. "Untie me. Let me help him."

Anderson looked back and forth among them, his expression unreadable behind the gas mask. "Let her go," he said finally. "She can take care of him. Nobody takes their mask off, though."

"We need to continue our work," Samira said. "Seriously, who the enemy is won't matter when everyone on both sides is vomiting blood and dying by the millions."

"Explain to me, using small words, how letting you dig up this rock is going to make any difference to that."

"The chemical you think of as a weapon is just one part of a technology that can be used to alter genetics through carefully crafted viruses. I don't think our medical understanding is going to find a cure in time, but with this technology, we just might. I have a lead CDC researcher waiting for what we discover. The crucial information is right here, buried under these rocks."

Anderson maintained eye contact, weighing her words. Finally, he said, "Call him."

"What?"

"Call this CDC researcher. Let me talk to him."

"It's a her."

"Call her, then."

"I'll need my phone."

They retrieved her phone, but didn't untie her hands. Instead, they unlocked it with her fingerprint, and Anderson retrieved Evelyn Soderberg's contact information at Samira's direction. He pressed the button to call her. In Washington, D.C. it would be late morning.

"She's very busy," Samira said. "She might not—"

"Hello?" Dr. Soderberg's voice came over the speaker, audible despite being held in Anderson's hand.

He lifted it to his ear. "This is Captain Lucas Anderson of the United States Marines," he said. "Who is this?"

"This is Dr. Evelyn Soderberg of the CDC," she said, matching his tone of authority. "Why are you calling me from Samira Shannon's phone? Is she all right?"

"She's fine, doctor," Anderson said. "She's here next to me."

"Has she found something? Does she have any more information?"

Anderson hung up. He tapped the phone against his palm, eyeing Samira thoughtfully. "If this substance can be used to alter genetics, as you say, then it could be even worse in the hands of our enemies than we thought. I'll run your message up the command chain. But until then, I'm obeying orders."

"Captain—"

"Enough." He stood. "Sergeant? Let's get these civilians clear. Cut their bonds, but keep them together and away from the site. We don't want them in the way when the enemy shows up."

"I TOLD YOU SHE WAS WORKING FOR THE AMERICANS," ARINYA snarled.

The soldiers had escorted them into the large tent where they did most of their research and memory extraction.

"We are not," Samira said. "You saw how they treated us. Did that sound like we're friends?"

Arinya poked her chin at Beth. "She said you are CIA."

"I was *lying*," Beth said. "I was trying to get them to trust us long enough that we could control them."

"A lot of good that did us."

"They didn't even know we were here," Samira said. "It was a surprise to them, finding Americans. We're not working with them, and they didn't come because of us. They want the chemical, same as everyone else."

"So what do we do now?" Arinya asked.

The question was met with silence, save for Samira's father's labored coughs. Samira felt a wave of exhaustion as she realized how badly everything had gone wrong. They'd lost Charlie, they'd lost control of the site, and they had no idea how to stop the virus. World powers were intent on destroying each other and everything else, and there was nothing Samira or anyone else could do to stop them. The human race was going to die as they'd always lived, fighting each other to the end.

CHAPTER TWENTY

Li Ling had just climbed into a hammock, exhausted after the long walk, when the clatter of helicopters interrupted the quiet. At first just a distant thrum, it grew rapidly, until three helicopters loomed overhead, their deafening rotors rattling her brain. Blinding searchlights cut through the darkness. They had been discovered.

"Come out where we can see you," a voice called, artificially amplified to boom out over the noise. "Leave your weapons on the ground, and you will not be harmed."

A few of the Hani men carried rifles, but many carried only bows and arrows, or no weapons at all. The men sliding down ropes into the stream wore armor and carried military-grade weaponry. She couldn't make out their faces in the darkness, but she had no doubt they wore masks.

"Surrender and you will not be harmed," the bullhorn blared.

Li Ling thought they had little choice. What chance did a few tribesmen have against a troop of highly-trained Chinese special forces? She thought they would come out into the clearing with their hands up, surrendering their weapons. Instead, they scattered.

Startled, Li Ling found herself suddenly alone in the camp. The tribesmen had just run off, abandoning her! Not that they owed her anything—she had asked to come along—but somehow she hadn't expected them to just leave her.

The first wave of soldiers reached the ground. At the same time, she caught a strong scent in the air that loosened her locked muscles. *Run!* the scent said. *Flee!*

She ran.

THE FOREST WAS UTTERLY BLACK. SHE COULDN'T SEE THE undergrowth that scratched her clothes and whipped at her face. She couldn't see the roots she stumbled over or the trees her reaching hands fumbled into. She ran anyway, a panicked headlong flight, with no idea where she was going. She could have charged straight into a sinkhole and never been seen again.

A scent drew her on, and she knew it came from Charlie. It urged hurry, but not fear. She could do this.

Beams of light stabbed through the darkness: the soldiers pursuing them. She heard shouts and a few gunshots. She stumbled on.

"Freeze!" A light beam caught her, suddenly illuminating her path and casting her warped shadow against a dozen trees. A shot whistled over her head. "Stop now or you die here!"

She stopped. She turned slowly to face her attacker, arms raised, but all she could see was the blinding light.

The beam swung suddenly upward. A scuffle, a flurry of motion, and the light went out. Li Ling held motionless, afraid to move. Out of the darkness, another scent came that spoke of safety, urgency, the need for action. She turned again and ran.

Rain killed the humans without remorse. Perhaps Prey was right, and there were differences among them, some who could be trusted while others just wanted to use her for their own purposes, no matter the pain they inflicted. The female human had helped her escape, after all. The human males they had traveled with smelled different than the violent ones. These, the ones with weapons that threw death, these she could kill and even Prey wouldn't try to stop her. All they wanted was to trap her and torture her again.

She circled the human female at a distance. The human made good hunting bait, thrashing about through the brush and attracting the attention of the soldiers. She could sense their presence long before they could sense hers, so it was easy to ambush them. As soon as they turned their lights and weapons on the human, Rain would attack from the side, catching them by surprise. They wore hard plating over their bodies, but Rain knew how to attack armored prey. She drove her jaws into the joint at their throats and found the softness underneath.

The third time, she grew more clever. Instead of killing the man outright, she tore off his mask, bloodying him, but not killing him. At the same moment, she sent a cloud of pheromones into his face. Then she sent him and his death-throwing machine to hunt down his fellows.

The human female ran in a different direction from the others, separating the group, but it didn't matter. Rain could smell them from a long way off. It would be easy to find them again, once the fight was over. She hoped Prey was unharmed. He was smaller than her, but had most of the same advantages. She caught no scent of his blood, so she thought he was probably safe.

Finally, the sounds of fighting faded, and the smells of the soldiers fell farther behind. Rain stepped into the human's path, startling her, then dominated her and commanded her to follow. Prey probably would want her to use a lighter touch, encouraging her to come instead of forcing compliance, but this was easier. It was for her own good, after all.

They met up with the others. Several of the human men hadn't survived the fight, and two were injured, though they could still walk. Prey was unharmed, and like her seemed exhilarated by the fight. The humans led them again, this time down a steep slope into thick foliage. It seemed like a good choice, given the flying machines their pursuers controlled.

As they walked, Rain found that she was almost…happy. The terrain they traveled through smelled more like home than any she had encountered since waking up on this alien future Earth. All the plants were different, the jungle vegetation thicker and more abundant than anything she'd encountered in her old life, but the warm temperatures and humid air felt comfortable, as did the aromas of earth and green growth.

Most of the human world she'd encountered was cold and stark, with hard surfaces and confining boxes. The air was sterile and silent. This place was noisy instead with the constant scent conversation of plants and animals attracting mates, warning or deceiving predators, claiming territory. Even though much of it was unfamiliar, she knew this world. She could navigate and understand it.

The humans here were easier to understand, too. They couldn't communicate through smell, of course, but neither did they mask their scent with manufactured odors. She could read their moods and track them from a distance much more readily.

As they traveled, more people joined their caravan. They kept distant, but traveled in the same direction, occasionally ducking in closer to catch a glimpse of the two dinosaurs walking through their forest.

The walk was long, and the humans tired, but Rain sent them feelings of loyalty and courage and endurance. As the humans breathed it in, it strengthened their resolve and ability to press on.

Should we manipulate them like this? Prey sent to her. *They don't know how to resist.*

She snorted her annoyance. He should be happy she wasn't trying to kill them anymore. *Do they not influence each other with their own language?* she said.

Yes. But our language is so much more powerful. Isn't there a difference between convincing someone and enslaving them?

I'm not telling them what to do, Rain said. *I'm giving them strength. For now, we are a roost, reliant on each other. They lead us toward safety. We help them endure.*

That's what society was, wasn't it? To live in a social group was to influence others and be influenced in return. Social animals learned to manipulate one another in countless ways, by asserting authority or a higher social class, by forming alliances, by offering to mate. Those manipulations could be performed for good or for evil, but whether they were communicated by speech or by smell seemed beside the point. The tribesmen were already invested in undermining the Chinese government by helping them. The scents Prey and Distant Rain transmitted simply helped them achieve those goals better.

Prey paused to consider, then joined in, weaving the emotions she was communicating into a story of heroism and great achievements. She sent him her pleasure. *They help us. We help them.*

Suddenly, the chemicals coming from Prey turned much more complex. Rain was startled. How had a male learned such craft? She had taught him some fundamentals of modification while they were building the pits together, but he was a member of a telescope by training, not a geneticist.

She studied the new scent. Instead of communicating emotion only, it gave instructions directly to their unconscious brains, altering the chemical makeup of their sweat depending on what they saw with their eyes. The sweat, as it evaporated, smelled subtly different, the changes detectable by Rain's exquisite sense of smell. Once her own brain learned to translate the changes, the result was that she could *smell* what each of the humans was *seeing*. It was a far cry from being able to see through their eyes, but the indicators in their sweat smell gave her visual cues about their surroundings beyond what she could see herself.

The molecule itself was remarkably complicated, something it would have taken her or her colleagues days to devise. She had been the chief technician in charge of a modification factory; an untutored male should not be able to accomplish something she could not.

How did you do that? she asked, amazed.

Do you like it? I derived it from the virus.

What virus?

The one killing the humans.

He explained how he had figured out how to tailor the virus in one of the humans, the father of the woman they now traveled to meet, to slow its spread and preserve his life. He described how, with her help, they might turn it back entirely, potentially saving millions of lives.

Let them die, Rain said. *They took our home from us. We can take it back.*

They didn't take it, Prey told her. *We died and they took our place. This is their world now.*

They will only keep hurting us, she said, but without conviction. She had seen enough by now to know that Prey was right. These humans were people. They were like her own kind, each of them different, some self-serving and some self-sacrificing, some wise and some foolish. They didn't all deserve to die.

She asked Prey to share the details of the virus with her, and for a time, while they walked, they talked shop, trading technical options and possibilities. What Prey dreamed of was more difficult than he realized. With a modification pit and a team of experts, it might be possible, but with no records, no equipment, no library of previously generated molecules to design from, it wasn't going to happen. She didn't want to crush his enthusiasm, though, so she played along, enjoying the thought experiment and the conversation. From what she saw of the virus, she wouldn't need to kill any humans herself to make the world safe for her and Prey to live in. The virus would kill all the humans for her.

PREY COULD TELL THAT RAIN DIDN'T REALLY THINK IT WOULD be possible to devise a cure for the Julian virus. He wasn't willing to give up, though, not yet. Look at the odds the two of them had beaten just to be alive right now. Maybe Samira's father was right about the God he talked about so much, and he and Rain had been preserved this long for a purpose. But wouldn't that mean that destroying the rest of his species had been God's purpose too?

Prey reached out to the Hani tribesmen around him. Their ranks had grown over time as they passed through villages and other men joined them. Thanks to the chemical cocktail he and Rain were spreading among them, their little army moved as one: not as slaves, but with a coordination centered on the two maniraptors. It was a heady experience for Prey, reminiscent of being part of the great telescope that had discovered the asteroid so many years ago.

They left Hani territory and entered land mostly inhabited by the Akha tribe. Distant Rain let a general call for help waft on the wind, and soon Akha men joined them, further swelling their ranks. Many of the men carried the sharp metal smell of their guns.

The distance they had to travel, Prey understood from the humans, was great, a ten or twelve day walk by an experienced traveler. Their army, however, unfazed by fatigue or discouragement, flew along at a greater pace. Hunters foraged miles ahead and brought down game for the army to eat, so that at regular intervals they came upon meat already cooked on fires, or in the case of Prey and Distant Rain, animals left tied to trees for them to kill and quickly consume.

The scouts also warned of flooding or downed bridges that might delay their passage. All this was coordinated through Prey's mind. He doubted the humans were entirely conscious of the arrangement, but they participated willingly and seemed to derive joy from the experience as he did. Distant Rain, once she understood what he was doing, contributed suggestions from her greater knowledge of chemical structure, but she allowed Prey to take the lead.

Prey began to wonder what it would be like if the humans could share their memories and emotions with each other as his people could. Sound waves, no matter how expertly wielded, just couldn't communicate at the same level. He wondered if such a modification would even be possible, and if it was, how drastically altered humanity would be by the change.

They rested when it proved too dark to make their way, and when the sun rose each morning, they set out again. Some of the weaker members of their army began to grow fatigued despite Prey's help, so he encouraged them to return to their homes and pressed on with the rest. The female scientist in particular had grown very tired, unable to keep up with the group and growing weaker. Finally, Prey let her ride on his back the way he had with Samira.

A large bird with red feathers around its neck and a heavy, striped bill perched on a tree nearby and regarded Prey with one eye. Samira had explained to him how all of these birds were maniraptors, descended from a line of near-cousins to his species. Prey's civilization, with all its knowledge of genetic change, had understood the evolution of creatures, had in fact assumed it from their earliest myths. But it still astonished him to see that it was only the birds that had survived from his once-proud lineage, and the mammals—tiny, cowering prey animals during his era—had risen to conquer the world. He wondered what changes might be wrought in another sixty million years, and if the Julian virus would be the means by which the mammals fell and made way for the rise of yet another family of creatures.

On the sixth day of travel, they met up with the man called Chanchai. Prey could tell he was troubled by the size of their army and their weapons. Prey produced a scent to put him at ease. He explained how the Chinese government meant to recapture and torture him and Distant Rain, and that to avoid that happening they needed protection. Chanchai reluctantly agreed, though he begged them not to fight if a fight could be avoided.

They traveled on at his direction into the region called Thailand. As they passed through more mountainous jungle terrain, more men heeded Distant Rain's call and joined their ranks. Lahu, Karen, Hmong, and Lisu people drifted from their homes and followed along in loose groups, bringing their weapons. Prey could also detect that some of them carried the Julian virus. Even in this remote area, the virus had found them, and soon these villages would be ravaged and full of the dead or dying.

Eventually, they passed out of the mountains and entered more open areas of fields and roads. The size of their scattered army, though already well known to Prey, would now be evident to any humans watching. But secrecy was not his goal. He needed to reach Samira and what was left of the modification pit to see if enough knowledge remained to craft a cure.

Prey knew that the humans had technology that could communicate across long distances. He anticipated that once they were seen, the Chinese would send a force to recapture him and Distant Rain, but the attack came more quickly than he expected.

The Chinese lurked in the undergrowth and sheltered in copses of trees, wearing clothing that broke up their outline in colors that matched the foliage. It was probably an effective camouflage for humans, but laughable to Prey, since their smells stood out from the surrounding countryside as clearly as if they had posted signs.

The Chinese had superior weaponry and training, too, but they couldn't coordinate troops across a battlefield as precisely and effectively as Prey and Rain could. The tribesmen ghosted through the fields and struck the Chinese ambush like a hundred-fingered hand, all working in tandem. It was like the herd of cattle and deer he had used on the ranch in Oregon, except that these were people, intelligent and capable as individuals, yet operating almost as a single organism. Prey might have convinced some of the Chinese to join them, too, but they all wore masks that blocked scent. He was forced to kill them instead, until their leader called a retreat and they ran away. Prey let them go.

Next time, he knew, they would come in greater numbers, and his soldiers were starting to tire. The help he was giving them could only go so far. They could not exceed their bodies' natural limits. There was nothing else to do except stop to eat and rest and then press on as best they could.

Prey tore out the throat of a deer that was brought to him still alive. He had to make it to Samira. Nothing else mattered.

CHAPTER TWENTY-ONE

Kit lost all track of time. Most of the time, he was left in the cellar in the dark, hearing the skittering of what was probably rats, falling into delirious waking dreams more than any actual sleep. His arms hurt from where they had been lashed for days. His face hurt from where the colonel had kicked him, and blood had dried in his nose, preventing him from breathing through it.

The soldiers assigned to guard him gave him food and water, enough to keep him alive, but not enough to relieve the gnawing in his belly or his dry, chapped lips. The colonel hadn't returned. Kit hoped that meant there was some crisis, that things were not going well for him, or even that he was dead. More likely, though, he was just too busy supplying the domination chemical to the Chinese war effort to have time to play with his captive pet.

He hoped Mai was still in charge and would have people looking for him, but he didn't have much hope they would find him. He was in a nondescript cellar that could have been anywhere in the country, or maybe not in Thailand at all. No one had witnessed his capture. They would have no idea where to look.

The door crashed open, letting in a beam of harsh light. Kit cringed. It was probably the soldiers with his next allotment of food and water, but eventually it would be the colonel, and then no matter how bad things felt now, they would get worse.

It wasn't the colonel, but it was some of his men. They cut his bonds and ordered him to get up. Kit tried, but his legs were too weak and stiff. They kicked him, shouted at him some more, and then eventually picked him up and carried him up the stairs. The light in the building was bright, but when they carried him outside, it was blinding. He could barely open his eyes. Before he could get his bearings, they tied a blindfold around his face and tossed him into the open bed of a truck. Others rode in the truck with him, though from what he could hear, they seemed to be armed soldiers, not prisoners. The truck sounded like it was part of a caravan as well, presumably a military unit being moved from one location to another.

They drove for hours. Kit had no way of gauging the passage of time. Eventually, despite his discomfort and the oppressive heat, he fell asleep. When he jolted awake some time later, the caravan was still on the move.

No one offered him food or water. By the time the truck finally stopped, he could barely work any saliva into his dry mouth. There were shouts in Chinese, and the soldiers disembarked, their boots stomping noisily past his ears. His blindfold was ripped away, leaving him cringing in the glaring sunlight again. When his eyes adjusted, he could see the colonel standing over him, drinking from a bottle of water. "Hot, isn't it?" Zhanwei said.

Kit reached out for the water, but Zhanwei used the last of it to wash his hands and splash some on his face.

"Stand up," he said.

Forced to obey, Kit managed to put weight on his unsteady feet and followed Zhanwei. Soldiers were busy all around them, though Kit didn't know what they were doing. He didn't know where they were, either, until Zhanwei led him farther up the road, where a row of snipers sat looking out from behind a rocky outcropping.

They stood on a ridge overlooking the dig site. There were people down there, working the site, but he was too far away to see who they were. Too far away to be heard if he shouted, though with the colonel dominating him, he wouldn't be able to do that either.

Colonel Zhanwei approached one of the snipers. "Give me your weapon, soldier," he told him, and the sniper complied. Zhanwei handed the rifle to Kit. "Don't fire unless I tell you to," he said. Kit took the rifle and pointed it at Zhanwei, but of course, he couldn't pull the trigger.

Zhanwei laughed. "Take a look at who's down there," he said.

Obediently, Kit pointed the rifle down toward the site and looked through the scope. American soldiers surrounded it now, but near some tents, he saw the old team: Samira, Beth, Arun, and Gabby, all standing together. He focused the scope on Samira.

Zhanwei leaned in close to Kit's ear. "I could make you kill her, you know," he whispered. "It's not that hard from this distance. The gun practically does the work for you."

Kit took his eye away from the scope and looked at him. "Why am I here?"

"Tell me what you see. I want to understand what they're doing."

"They've been digging since I left."

"Don't mess with me," Zhanwei said. "You know I could make this a lot worse for you."

Kit cringed. "Yes, sir. They've been digging, and digging fast. But they aren't digging now, which is strange; you don't generally waste daylight hours on a site like that. The site itself looks like they've just been smashing away at it. I mean, not like a construction crew, but not really like paleontologists, either. They're been moving too fast for real scientific study. They're looking for something, and they don't care what gets destroyed along the way. Maybe they're just trying to extract as much of the chemical as possible, but my guess is, their goal is not domination, but finding a cure for the Julian virus. But if that's the case, I don't know why they've stopped."

"Our numbers are greater than the Americans'," Zhanwei said. "I've sent a team to take the site. I will interrogate your friends, of course, but if my team is not careful, and your friends die, I want you with me. You will examine the site closely and tell me exactly what they were doing."

Something at the edge of the site caught Kit's eye, and he moved the scope to see. A cloud of dust grew along the road in the distance. The American soldiers posted at the site saw it, too, and sprang into action, manning gun emplacements and taking positions by the blockades.

Kit watched a row of Chinese vehicles surge up the road. They were armored, with eight thick tires each and giant guns on the top. As they came into view, snipers from the hill next to Kit opened fire on the Americans from above and more vehicles appeared from the other direction. The Americans were outnumbered and outgunned. They had little cover and nowhere to run. As far as Kit could tell, this would be over quickly. He hoped his friends would surrender and not get themselves killed. Though becoming prisoners of Colonel Zhanwei might be worse than death.

A scream to his right: one of the Chinese snipers fell on the ground clutching at an *arrow* sticking out of his shoulder. *An arrow?* Gunshots fired from behind him. Kit whirled, confused, in time to see the most incredible thing he had ever seen or hoped to see in his life: a theropod dinosaur leaped down from the ridge above them and crossed the distance to the soldiers in a heartbeat, tearing a gun out of a Chinese soldier's hand and then burying its teeth in his neck. A second dinosaur followed it, and the two seemed to be everywhere at once, sowing mayhem and obliterating the row of snipers. Another force that looked like hill tribesmen ran among them, shooting mostly rifles and a handful of hunting bows. Despite their older technology and simple dress, they moved with precision, decimating the professional force they had taken by surprise.

"Back to the truck!" Zhanwei growled, and Kit had no choice but to obey.

PREY AND RAIN KNEW THE CHINESE ATTACK WAS COMING LONG before it arrived. Their forward scouts watched from the trees as the caravan gathered and followed the road toward the site where Samira and the others were gathered. Prey had wanted to go to her immediately, but Rain urged caution. They shouldn't show themselves until they knew the strength of the enemy. If they went to her immediately, they would be surrounded along with the others and lose the advantage of surprise.

Once the group on the ridge started pointing their guns down at the people below, Prey couldn't wait any longer. He attacked, the hill tribesmen covering him with their own guns and attacking from cover with the same precision and coordination as before. Prey himself felt the rage take him. These were the people who would capture and torture him if they could. He would not let them do it again, nor would he let them take Samira and Beth and Brook and Alex and the others.

He didn't force the tribesmen to attack, but they were willing, and he guided them to maximize the surprise and confusion of their enemy. Simultaneously, Rain attacked below, intercepting the caravan of vehicles and swarming over them. She cared less about the lives of the people she led, throwing them into harm's way in order to overwhelm the guns and tear off masks, dominating the enemy and converting them into allies.

Once the snipers on the ridge were dead, Prey left a few tribesmen who had the best guns and marksmanship to pick off enemies from above, then led the rest of his group screaming down the hill into the gunfire and smoke to attack the Chinese from both sides. The Chinese might be better armed and better trained, but they had never fought a foe like this. The close quarters neutralized their vehicles' big guns, and the maniraptors' coordination of their troops meant there were always hill tribesman where the Chinese soldiers least expected them, one drawing attention while another appeared to snatch away yet another mask. As one Chinese soldier after another was dominated into changing sides, the advantage of the battle shifted, until there was no one left to fight against anymore.

WHEN THE CHINESE ARMORED VEHICLES ROARED INTO SIGHT, Samira knew it was all over. Bullets whined through the air from the ridge above, and she saw one of the American soldiers fall. "On the ground!" Alex shouted, and they all dove for the dirt, trying to keep a tent between them and the source of the bullets. Not that a tent would stop a sniper's round, but if they couldn't be seen, then at least they couldn't be intentionally targeted. Of course, one of those armored trucks might just roll right over them, which would accomplish the same thing.

Samira's parents and the rest of the sick—Arun and Gabby and Kit's two students, Channarong and Kanokwan—were in a different tent, several rows down. Samira wanted to run to them, but she knew there was nothing she could do to protect them. All she could do was get herself killed.

The sound of automatic weapons was deafening. The air filled with smoke. She had no idea what was happening, except for the certainty that her side was going to lose. Either they would die here, or they would be captured.

Her body ached with tension, expecting at any moment to feel bullets tearing through her flesh. She wasn't ready to die. There was too much about the world she didn't understand. The universe was full of mysteries; how could she go off into oblivion without knowing the answers? It was impossible to imagine that the world could go on without her, that generations could keep on living, inventing new futures and uncovering new truths, and she would never know. She flinched yet again as the noise of an explosion assaulted her eardrums, sounding close enough to rip them all into shreds.

The noise and smoke seemed to last forever. Even when the clamor stopped, her ears kept ringing, covering over any sound with a distant shroud. It was a while before she recognized a familiar voice calling her name. A voice she'd thought she might never hear again.

HA-MEE-KAA!

She lifted her head, despite the danger. "Charlie?"

HA-MEE-KAA!

His pronunciation of her name had grown much better during the months they'd spent together, but she knew that screeching voice. In the heat of battle, she doubted proper pronunciation was the first thing on his mind.

"Charlie!" she shouted. "I'm over here!"

He skidded around the corner, his mouth dripping with blood. In that moment, she saw the predator and not her friend. She screamed and covered her head. Then she looked up again. "Charlie?"

He bared his teeth in an attempt at a human smile. It was terrifying to look at, all blood-stained teeth and lethal jaws, but she'd recovered from her initial shock. She scrambled to her feet and ran to him, embracing him around the neck. "I thought I'd never see you again."

The others gathered around just as a second maniraptor, much larger than Charlie, raced into view, its mouth similarly smeared with gore. Beth shrieked, and they all took a step back.

"This is friend," Charlie said. "Her name is Rain."

Samira could hardly tear her eyes away, despite the imminent danger. A second maniraptor, and a female. She was graceful and strong and one of the most beautiful things Samira had ever seen.

Finally, she noticed what was behind Charlie and Rain. The massive Chinese vehicles that had seemed poised to flatten the camp had halted. The ground around them was littered with bodies. The gunfire had stopped. Samira turned back to Charlie in astonishment. "You did this?"

Before he could answer, American soldiers approached from both sides, their rifles raised. They kept well back, having seen the maniraptors' speed and ferocity.

"Get back from them," Captain Anderson shouted. "We need a clear shot."

The soldiers raised their weapons. The maniraptors crouched and bared their teeth, ready to spring.

"No!" Samira stepped in front of them, quickly followed by Brook and Beth and Alex, each of them blocking the soldiers' sightlines. Even Arinya, who had never seen a living maniraptor outside of stored memories until that moment, joined them to stand between the soldiers and the dinosaurs.

"What are you doing?" Anderson said. "They're killers!"

"They were rescuing us," Samira said. "They're on our side."

"What even *are* those things?" Anderson demanded.

"Look around you," Samira shouted back, ignoring the question. "You would all be dead now if they hadn't showed up. It doesn't matter what they are. They were fighting your enemies."

Anderson shook his head in confusion. "I don't know what just happened. It was like we were attacked by two groups at once, only they were both fighting each other."

"Trust me. They're my friends. Look—" She held out her hand without turning around, and Charlie came up to her and nuzzled it. "Lower your guns."

Anderson hesitated. "You can control them?"

She laughed. "Control them? Not a chance. But I trust them. And so should you."

CHAPTER TWENTY-TWO

The confusion around the battle started to sort itself out. They had been attacked by the Chinese just as Charlie and Rain and their army of hill tribesmen arrived to rescue them. The hill tribesmen had since melted away, taking their dead and their injured with them, not wanting to stay where the great government powers were fighting each other. They had done what they could to stop the devil drug trade, but they had no desire to get caught up in the war.

Except for one: not a tribesman at all, but a young woman from China who had apparently traveled with the maniraptors. She looked like a shipwreck victim, her dark hair hopelessly tangled, her once professional outfit now stained with blood and torn. While the American soldiers were busy securing the site again, she approached the group of scientists shyly. She looked like she might fall over.

"Hello? My name is Li Ling."

"Chinese?" Samira asked suspiciously. She didn't know this woman's story, but she wasn't in the mood to be trusting. What was she doing here? Where did her loyalties lie?

Li Ling nodded. "I worked in the facility that studied Rain and Charlie."

"The facility that stole him, you mean," Samira said. "What have you been doing there? Harvesting his pheromones for the war effort?"

The young woman winced. "Some of that, yes. Mostly I studied how the pheromones worked. I wasn't even there very long."

"Oh, so it's not your fault, that's what you're saying?"

"I broke them out of that facility," Li Ling said, eyes blazing. "They wouldn't be here if it weren't for me. I risked my life to get them out, and left everything behind—my job, my family. So don't you dare judge me. I had to run away through hundreds of kilometers of jungle, getting shot at and nearly killed, all to get Charlie back to *you*. I'm a traitor now. I can never go back to China. I'll never see my family—" Her voice broke, and she started to cry.

Beth smacked Samira on the arm. "You monster. Don't you get it? She's you!" Beth wrapped her arms around Li Ling and led her toward a tent. "Come on, come with me. Let's get you cleaned up."

"Wait," Samira said. "I'm sorry. You really brought them here from China?"

"They brought themselves," Li Ling said. "I just tried to keep up and not die on the way."

Beth glared at them all over her shoulder as she led Li Ling away. "Don't tell Anderson and his goons that she's here. They'll want to interrogate her or something."

"They're going to know she's here," Alex said.

"She's a Thai researcher, then. One of Kit's students. She left when the others did, but now she came back to help."

Samira couldn't wait to show the maniraptors the dig site. She pointed out the long staircase as Kit had shown it to her, and how the slope into the ravine had shifted over the vast stretch of time. Rain became agitated, scratching in the dirt with her claws and emitting a strong scent that Samira couldn't interpret.

"She can see it," Charlie said. "But it much sad. Very sad? Seeing our home gone so long. Nothing left."

"There's not *nothing* left," she said. "Look at all of this. This is what we wanted. This is what we've been trying to do all this time, to get you to this place so you can make a cure."

Charlie was grim. "Much is lost. Liquid long gone. Not pit, not anymore."

"But you said it was possible! You said if you came here, if you could get to this place, then you could do it!" Samira felt the desperation of the last few weeks closing around her throat. She had left her parents and friends sitting in a tent to die while she hunted through this site for a cure, and now Charlie was going to give up without even trying?

"What about your friend?" Samira demanded. "Does she think it's possible? As a female, she would have more education, right? Didn't you say she was a specialist in this stuff?"

"She think worse I do," Charlie said. "She think—" he growled, struggling with his limited vocabulary. "She know more, yes. But she think no good."

"Tell her it's important," Samira pleaded. "Say everyone I love will die if we can't find a cure."

Samira couldn't tell if Charlie relayed her message, but soon the scent coming from Rain grew stronger, and Samira knew what was coming. She had experienced these shared memories often enough now to recognize the signs. Her first impulse was to resist losing control, but no—this was Rain's way of communicating with her. She had to let it come. She willed herself to relax.

The scene around her shifted. As if she were traveling

backward in time, Samira recognized the very same spot of land where she was currently standing, though a very different version of it, one from sixty-six million years earlier.

FIVE DAYS UNTIL IMPACT.

Perhaps five days left to live. Rain spent most of the day side by side with Prey, working together, teaching him what she could of the science behind the liquid she was preparing for them. She hadn't told Prey about their child that might have been. She had finally halted its development inside her body, though it had broken her heart to do so. She knew it would have been worse if she had allowed herself to lay the egg, knowing that it would never hatch. Ultimately, it was the desire to spare Prey grief that had motivated her to stop the process from progressing any further.

She focused instead on the work. The green liquid might look like a single compound, but it was an incredibly complicated stew of complex chemicals, its molecules organized to store the knowledge of a civilization. She and Fear Stink spent hours sitting in it, immersed to their nostrils, writing the molecular code that determined how protein chains would combine and react to the presence of living maniraptors.

Prey sat with them, not able to contribute, but Rain had found that explaining what she was doing to him helped her organize her thoughts. She stepped him through each chain in the algorithm, demonstrating how the donated memories were automatically cataloged in the movement of the liquid, how the request to retrieve memories on particular topics were parsed and delivered, and how, once the capability was activated, the cells of anyone immersed in the liquid would be infused and preserved. The vital dynamic chemicals of life were stored symbolically as data, saved in molecules less subject to deterioration and loss. Processes in the liquid could also sample the chemical environment, poised to reverse the process when outside conditions were once again conducive to life.

She tried to concentrate on the details of the work, but every once in a while, a sense of helplessness and fury would overwhelm her. How could the universe collaborate over millions of years to produce her and her people—the only creatures that had ever lived who could contemplate their own existence—and then wipe them from the face of the Earth with such callous randomness? If they didn't survive, would there ever be such a creature again? Or would the universe spin on, anonymous and unseen, unaffected by the loss of the only self-conscious beings ever to inhabit it?

Because to be honest, she didn't think they would survive. It was the most ambitious project of biological modification ever attempted, but she didn't have the time to do it carefully, nor the resources to save more than a tiny percentage. And what would the world look like again once they emerged? Would there be food? If the herds of prey animals they subsisted on were all destroyed, then survival might be a worse fate than death. Still, all they could do was try.

The memory lasted only a moment, but Samira surfaced from the vision as if from a vivid dream whose emotion and sense of reality she couldn't shake. The bright and arid emptiness of the Khorat Plateau felt wrong, like an alien landscape. She blinked her eyes and took a deep breath, trying to clear her mind, and saw the other humans doing the same.

Charlie, too, seemed strongly affected. She smelled pheromones from him and tensed, expecting another memory episode, but the smell was simpler than that. *Regret. Sadness. Love.* She watched him briefly nuzzle Rain, and realized that *he* had just learned of the egg that Rain had carried and lost. She hadn't told him at the time. She marveled that he could learn this truth that Rain had hidden from him, and at the same time feel her motivation and emotions in doing so. Humans might have felt hurt or angry, and would have had a harder time understanding each other's perspectives, but Charlie's response was to comfort her and share in the sadness of loss.

How much humans might benefit from that ability! But Rain hadn't primarily been communicating to Charlie. She'd been communicating to Samira, and Samira understood her message clearly.

All we can do is try.

The sentiment was fixed in her mind, along with the emotions of powerlessness and anticipated tragedy, and she knew that Rain had *spoken* to her in the way of her people. Samira marveled that this was how these maniraptors had communicated as a matter of course. In that moment of memory, Rain had related so much: empathy for the plight of their species, understanding of Samira's desperation, an acknowledgement that despite the fact that Rain didn't think a cure was likely, she would try.

And more than that as well: Samira now understood, in a way she couldn't possibly have comprehended before, how miniscule the scraps of memory they had excavated from the site were. The modification pit wasn't organized from the top down by topic or concept. It held a loose collection of a billion personal memories, networked together by links that could be traversed through chemical interaction, a design more like the internet than a dictionary or textbook. Organic processes formed the links by identifying chemical similarity and referencing it symbolically with complex protein chains. A maniraptor could use the protein chains to traverse the links and learn related information about a topic, inextricably connected to the emotions and experiences of the individuals who had formed those memories to begin with. It was a method of learning more akin to acquiring life experiences than to reading facts from a book.

If she had the whole pit at her disposal, Rain could have drawn from libraries of biological algorithms developed over centuries for the altering of organic life. She could have used them as building blocks to construct an attack on the virus or a modification to it that would have allowed humans to survive. Without those libraries, though, the job was impossible. It was the difference between constructing a flashlight given a battery, lightbulb, and lengths of wire, and trying to construct one by reinventing and manufacturing a battery and lightbulb from scratch.

The few, random slices of memory the team had extracted from the site might be fascinating from a scientific perspective, opening a window onto maniraptor culture and late Cretaceous ecosystems. As a tool for obtaining specific knowledge and biological control, however, it was a pale shadow of what it once had been. To have any hope of success, they would need much, much more.

Samira took a deep breath and blew it out slowly between pursed lips. Was that it then? Were they doomed? Should she give up hope and spend the rest of her life in the tent with her parents and friends, holding their hands and watching them die, until she too succumbed to the virus?

She thought of the maniraptors from so long ago and their vibrant culture, the millennia of growth and discovery and civilization they could have had if not for the asteroid. The lives cut off with no recourse, and the millions of other lives that could have existed but never had the chance. They, too, had thought extinction impossible. Was this now the fate of the human race as well? Was the Julian virus simply their version of an asteroid they could see coming but were powerless to stop?

No. That was listening to only half of Rain's message. True, the task seemed impossible, but Rain's task had seemed impossible too, and here they were: two maniraptors, living and breathing after sixty-six million years in the ground. Of course, she hoped for a higher survival rate for humans, but the point was, they could still try. They may not be able to see the end, but they could still attempt everything possible.

"All right then," Samira said. "We'll do what we can, or we'll die trying."

She strode back toward the tents, the other humans and maniraptors following her. It was a miracle that individuals of their two species might meet across the eons and communicate. Surely it wouldn't end here with just another extinction? She thought of her parents' belief in God and a universe in which everything had a purpose. She hoped it did have a purpose. But the problem with that way of thinking was it encouraged people to sit back and wait for deliverance, while the universe crushed them under its grinding wheels. Samira didn't want to just sit back and accept. She wanted to jam a spike into the wheels of the universe and stop them in their tracks.

At the edge of the site, she saw a soldier walking backwards with a spool, trailing wire. At first, she thought it was some kind of communication wire, strung to avoid wireless communications that could be jammed or spoofed. Then she realized the obvious. The last time American soldiers had come to a Thai dig site, they had wired it to explode when they left. Kit and Arinya had nearly been killed in the blast. They were doing it again.

"Hey!" Samira shouted, all of her disappointment and fear boiling up into rage. "Stop that. Put that wire down, right now."

The soldier looked up at her, but didn't stop. "Captain's orders, ma'am."

"For heavens' sake, don't call me ma'am, like I'm some little lady with quaint ideas you can dismiss. I know what you're doing. You're getting ready to blow up the last chance we have to defeat this virus."

"Best talk to the captain about that," the soldier said. She could see him start to form the word "ma'am" again but think better of it.

Captain Anderson strode up to them, his lips pursed in a frown. "Is there a problem here?"

"Please don't do this," she said. "If you destroy this site, then nothing else matters. Certainly not the outcome of this stupid war."

He narrowed his eyes at her. "I'm not telling you how to do your science. Don't tell me how to protect this site."

"Protect it? You're getting ready to blow it up!"

"And if the Chinese know we can blow it up, they'll think twice about attacking us again."

"Right. And if they attack anyway?"

Anderson held his fingers out taut, like he was trying to keep himself from crushing her in his hands. "This is not up for debate. If they attack again, and we don't get reinforcements here by that time, then you will be dead or captured, and the Chinese will gain control of a critical resource for this war. I will not let that happen. If it comes to a fight, we leave nothing for the Chinese to use against us. First sign of enemy engagement, we blow it all." He considered the maniraptors. "Honestly, we should wire them up as well."

"Try it, and they'll rip your arm off," Samira said.

"Fair enough. And they're good in a fight, I'll give them that. But understand me clearly: I will destroy this site completely before I give it to our enemy."

Samira threw up her hands. "That's ridiculous. Our enemy isn't the Chinese; it's the virus. You're preparing to destroy the human race's best chance for survival."

"The other option was to bomb it from the air," Anderson continued, implacable. "This option is more precise, and leaves the possibility that we may be able to hold back until the good guys arrive, thus not destroying it at all. You should be happy. If the brass had gone with the other option instead of sending us, you would have been blown to pieces along with the rest of it when the bombs started falling."

"And just what is the end game?" Samira demanded. "Your side gets to preside over the hospitals and graveyards for the last weeks of humanity's existence?"

Anger flashed in the captain's eyes. "*Those* bastards are the ones who started this fight, not us. Hundreds of my brothers, dead. Why? Were they attacking anyone? No. Because China wanted them out of the way. The *Ronald Reagan* was there for one reason: to prevent them from invading Taiwan. Which is exactly what the bastards did the moment the *Reagan* was gone. Took them all of three days to conquer it, too. Now they're rolling their way through Vietnam, Thailand, the Philippines. What's next, Australia? And you think we should just leave well enough alone?"

"I'm not saying that. What I'm saying is—"

"Did you know they still arrest people in China for telling the truth about Tiananmen Square? Their government censors books, blocks websites, and sends the police to arrest people who make memorials for the students who died. Thousands of unarmed protestors killed, and a whole generation of Chinese young people have grown up not even knowing it happened. They just erased it from history. Is that the kind of regime you want ruling the world?"

"Of course not. But it won't much matter if everyone dies!"

Anderson glared, holding her gaze. Samira glared back, until she felt Beth touch her arm. "Sami, this isn't helping."

"Fine," Samira said. "I guess I can't stop you. But let us do our work in the meantime. Maybe we'll find the answer before you destroy it all."

Anderson shook his head. "Sorry. I can't let you in there anymore. I will absolutely blow this place if I have to, and I don't want your blood on my hands."

Samira stood as tall as she could and looked at him defiantly. "But my parents' blood, that's okay? And my friends'? Because without the work I'm trying to do, they'll die for sure."

Anderson wavered. She knew he had seen how sick the others were, and no doubt he had friends or family who had died from the virus as well. "Okay," he said finally.

"Okay?"

"Okay, I'll let you in and any of your team who's willing to join you. Do your research. But I'm putting the explosives on a five minute timer. When I warn you to get out of there, it means the timer's counting down. It means you get out immediately, as fast as you can, because it's going off in five minutes whether you're in there or not."

CHAPTER TWENTY-THREE

Samira, Beth, Alex, Brook, Li Ling, and Arinya worked all day and through the night, digging in desperate hope for something that might change Rain and Charlie's analysis of the situation. Samira ducked into the sick tent just once. Her mother stroked her father's head with a cloth, despite her own sickness, trying to keep him cooler in the brutal heat. Charlie and Rain did what they could to slow the sickness, much as Charlie had done for Samira's dad before. The virus was more advanced now, though, and had evolved to resist their changes. Samira couldn't handle staying. She had to be *doing* something. She felt guilty for leaving, but her parents practically shooed her out the door, saying her time was better spent on research than on sympathy.

They believed in her. They thought she and the maniraptors could find a cure. Which just made Samira feel even worse, because they probably couldn't.

Even so, she poured herself into the work, uncovering every bit of green chemical she could scrape out of the rock. Now instead of reliving the memories herself, she could pass them over to Rain and Charlie, who could glean the information much more efficiently.

It was, Samira knew, a faint hope. The technology of a whole species had been lost. If she and Beth were stranded in the future, there was precious little of human technology they would have been able to reproduce, even as highly educated products of their civilization. Replicating even what Rain understood in a usable form might be the work of years, not an afternoon. Further applying that knowledge to the problem of the Julian virus might be the work of a lifetime. She kept working anyway, barely sleeping. She just couldn't stand the idea of sitting back and doing nothing.

The rock crumbled under the blows of her pickaxe, a breakneck pace compared to the careful sanding and sweeping involved in a proper dig. Most of the samples she retrieved were tiny, mere scrapings. According to Charlie, there would have been hundreds of liters of the stuff originally, but most of that was lost to the geological pressures and temperature changes of sixty-six million years. Until she cracked apart one layer of rock and hit the jackpot.

When she brushed the debris away, she saw the chocolate brown ridges of another maniraptor skeleton: the skull, neck, and shoulders visible before the rest disappeared beneath the rock. She almost cried at the beauty of its perfect preservation, longing to take the weeks of careful study such a find deserved. Alongside the fossil, a vein of rich green marked the rock, tracing the lines of skull and jaw and vertebrae and filling the interior of the skull, then beyond into a deep, unbroken reservoir, like an underground crystal pool.

It was more of the chemical than she had ever seen in one place. Most of what they'd found at this site had been infused into the rock, requiring a laborious process of extraction, but this was pristine: no longer liquid, but chemically perhaps not all that different from its original form. The surface became slick at once, the crystal pulling in moisture from the air and starting to turn back to liquid.

She called Charlie and Rain, who released chemicals Samira recognized as pleasure and excitement.

"We can work with," Charlie said. "This is good, much information here."

"It's enough to build on?" she asked. "Enough to reproduce your tools and create a cure?"

"Not know," Charlie said. "Must explore."

"Tell the others," Samira said. "We'll need all hands to get this out."

As the maniraptors loped away, Samira scored the edges of the find with her chisel, planning out her approach. They had to extract it fast, but carefully, so they wouldn't lose it. The liquid around the edge would start to evaporate. They had to get it inside and into containers as quickly as they could.

A series of sharp reports echoed against the rock. Gunshots. Samira was all too familiar now with the sound. She saw a cloud of dust in the distance, the growl of engines. *Not now!* She just needed a few more hours. Couldn't they stop fighting each other for that long?

The radio that Anderson had given her sprang to staticky life. "Get out of there now," his voice said. "This is your five minute warning. This is not a drill."

SAMIRA THUMBED THE RESPONSE BUTTON. "I NEED MORE time."

"No can do, doctor. The Chinese are here and I'm not taking any chances."

"I just found what we've been looking for. We're talking about saving the entire human race here. I'm looking at the cure for the Julian virus." It was an exaggeration; for all she knew, this trove of liquid held the maniraptors' zoning permit records. But it was the only chance they had.

"The explosives are armed and counting down," Anderson said. "Stop talking and get out of there."

The radio went dead. The rattle of machine gun fire cut through the air, and she could hear what sounded like approaching helicopters. Without American reinforcements, they weren't likely to win this one. Which meant they would all be dead or Chinese captives by the time the smoke cleared.

Five minutes wasn't very long, and she didn't know how far away she needed to get to be safe from the explosives, but still she hesitated. The salvation of billions might be right there in front of her. She grabbed her pickaxe and slammed it down into the rock, sweeping the chips of brown and green into a bucket. She did it again and again, heedless of the fossil, just trying to collect as much green as possible.

Beth saw her from the edge of the site. "Come on!" she screamed. "Get out of there!"

Samira ignored her, chipping again and again at the rock, trying to save what she could. She lost all sense of time. Had one minute passed? Two? Surely she could get one more swing in before she had to run.

She saw Anderson only moments before his body hit her, yanking her off her feet and lifting her into the air. The bucket slipped from her hand. She was not a small woman, but Anderson managed her weight anyway, taking long strides while carrying her away from the dig site. The slight slope helped him, but the rocky terrain made his footing treacherous.

"Put me down!" she shouted. "The bucket—"

The explosion threw her out of his grasp. She felt a moment of helplessness, flailing for purchase, until she hit the ground and the world disappeared.

THE BLAST RIPPED THE SITE APART. FOR A MOMENT, PREY thought he was back home, racing for the pits while the ground shook and the air above him turned to fire. Tons of earth and rock catapulted high into the air and spread out in a cloud, enveloping Samira and the other human who had been trying to carry her to safety. A concussion impacted his ears like a slap, followed by the choking smell of dust and pulverized rock.

He ran away from it, knowing Rain was right behind, even though he could smell nothing but dust and fire. He burst out of the cloud to find a battle already underway. Through the haze of the explosion, humans fired weapons at each other in a deafening chatter, both sides in helmets and gas masks. It wasn't easy for Prey to distinguish one side from the other, but he could see Li Ling and Beth and the others flat on the ground, trying to take shelter behind a hump of rock while a team of soldiers fought around them.

Their side seemed to be badly outnumbered and dying quickly. Prey had no gun, but he was a born predator. He launched himself at the nearest enemy soldier and took him down with a slash across his throat, then buried his teeth in a second man. Bullets whizzed past him, but he ignored them, using his speed to come at each soldier from an unexpected direction. By then, the soldiers protecting the site had rallied, shooting from behind barricades and using the low visibility to their advantage.

The last time, Prey and Rain had taken the Chinese by surprise, the tribesmen attacking their unprotected flank while he maniraptors controlled them like a single unit. The enemy soldiers hadn't been prepared to face predators from their distant past, and their fear had turned the attack into a rout.

This time, however, they had come prepared. The soldiers didn't panic or break ranks, clearly knowing they would face the maniraptors. In the sky, a machine like the one that had attacked them in the forest hovered and swooped like an insect, even though it was immense and made of metal. Prey saw humans riding inside it, their legs dangling out. The thing dove at him. He ran to evade, but it was faster than he was and could change direction as easily.

A soldier sitting in the doorway aimed a gun with a large barrel like a cone. Prey dodged, but the man fired, and suddenly Prey was down, thrashing and tumbling. Instead of a bullet, the gun had fired a net at him. The net was rimmed with metal weights that snapped together as he struggled to get free, tangling him further. He couldn't run, and he couldn't get up. He was caught.

Rain, twice his size, mowed through the human soldiers like they were the tiny mammals from their own era, but she couldn't escape the aerial predator machine either. As it bore down on her, she charged to meet it, leaping in the air to bring it down, but she fell short. The net caught her in the air, and she fell in a thrashing pile of limbs and feathers.

They were both out of the fight. Without their help, the Americans were badly outmatched. With the smoke and detritus from the explosion still clogging the air, Prey couldn't even communicate with Rain. He couldn't smell the people around him. He laid his head on the grass. Samira hadn't emerged from the cloud of smoke. He couldn't see her or smell her. Was she even alive? He cried out her name.

HA-MEE-KAA!

SAMIRA REGAINED CONSCIOUSNESS TO THE SOUND OF BULLETS and screams. Captain Anderson crouched over her, firing his rifle, a deafening chatter that she felt as a physical assault on her eardrums. The world was full of smoke and vague, running forms.

She tried to get up, but the captain roughly shoved her back down. He shouted something, but she couldn't hear it.

His body jerked and rocked backwards. He dropped the gun and fell, blood soaking through his shirt. *No!* Samira climbed up and tried to apply pressure to his wound, but the blood kept flowing out around her fingers. It covered her hands. She pressed her whole weight against it, screaming, though she could barely hear the sound of her own voice.

Finally, the weapons fell silent. Someone dragged her to her feet and forced her down to her knees. They zip tied her bloody hands behind her back, so tight it cut into her skin.

As the smoke cleared, she saw Charlie, sprawled in the grass and tangled in a net. His feathers were wet and damaged, his jaw smeared with blood. Beyond him, in a similar state, lay Rain. They had lost. The site, destroyed. Whatever mysteries it might have revealed, gone forever. They would never find a cure now. The fate of the human race was up to Evelyn Soderberg and the CDC and other organizations like it. She hoped they would succeed, but she feared it was too late.

Certainly it was too late for her family. She saw Chinese soldiers dragging her parents out of the tent, both of them too weak to stand. They would be dead by morning, she thought. And maybe that was a mercy. She didn't imagine that their treatment as Chinese prisoners of war would be pleasant.

A stab of guilt and grief split her open. Her parents had followed her to the end of the Earth. When she called, they'd dropped everything, risked infection, and defied governments: not for God or for a good cause or for hungry children on another continent. For *her*. Despite all the times she'd ignored their calls, her irritability, and her rejection of the faith they valued, they loved her. Not just Beth. Her.

She watched, helpless, as soldiers shouted at her parents and tried to pull them to their feet. She had dragged them into this. All the ways they annoyed her seemed petty now. She had taken advantage of their love to run after her own goals, and now here they were, alone and dying in a foreign country. She should never have brought them here. She had thought it was worth throwing away everything to save Charlie and pursue a cure. And what did she have to show for it? Nothing. She should have done what so many others in the world were doing: come together with family to spend their last days in love and mutual care. That's what Beth would have done, without Samira's constant prodding. Why did she always have to fight?

Prey lay with his face in the dirt and waited to be killed or dragged off to a cell. They had broken free only to fall right back into their enemies' hands. There was no way their captors would let them escape again. They would chain them to the wall, muzzle them, blind them: whatever it took to keep them trapped and terrified and producing the chemical they wanted.

He considered taking his own life. He knew how to do it. He could even do it in such a way as to kill all those around him. He would produce a toxic gas that would erode the seals in their gas masks and then react with the moisture in their airways, causing both their lungs and his to swell shut and suffocate them. There was no way to do it without killing himself and Rain and his human friends, though, and he wasn't willing to go that far.

He thrashed uselessly, trying to escape the net that held him, but he was too tightly tangled, and the effort hurt. He lay still again, breathing hard, as men with long sticks cautiously approached him. The grass smelled wet and burned, coated with ash from the explosion.

Wait.

Gradually, Prey realized he was smelling more than grass. There was ash, of course, singed particles from the site that had been burned and still floated and swirled around him. But there were unburned particles, too, pulverized and thrown up by the blast. The air was filled with millions of molecules, and most of them had been crafted by his people. The memories of generations were there, spinning through the air around him, passing through his nostrils with every breath.

He steadily inhaled and exhaled, drawing in the particles and sorting the information in his mind as quickly as he could. He sent a quick scent to Distant Rain, who confirmed that she, too, had noticed. The explosion had done what days of constant digging had not: it had blown the combined knowledge of his people into the air in mostly usable form. Somewhere in all of this information—just possibly—was the knowledge they needed to cure the Julian virus.

He sifted and sampled, experiencing scraps of countless lives. He felt a rush of emotion. He was breathing in his people's history. All of the people who made these memories were dead. His whole culture and people were gone and—except for him and Distant Rain—forgotten.

The soldiers leveled their guns at him, while others ran long poles through the holes in the net. Prey lay very still. They tied the poles to chains lowered from the flying machine and lifted the net in the air, turning him upside-down to dangle in the net like a caught fish. From there, he was lowered into the bed of a truck. Prey gave no resistance, concentrating instead on sifting as much of the information swirling through the air as he could.

An older soldier with glasses and no hair on his head pushed through the soldiers. When he saw Prey and Rain trussed and helpless, he laughed and clapped his hands and shouted something in a language Prey didn't recognize. A soldier approached with a large gun, shaped differently than some of the others, and pointed it at Prey.

We can do this, Prey sent to Rain. *The answer is here. We just need time.*

I don't think they plan to give us time, Rain sent back.

A dart buried its tip in Prey's neck, and he felt his consciousness fading away.

KIT COULDN'T BELIEVE THAT SAMIRA WAS STILL ALIVE. He had seen her standing in the middle of the dig site just minutes before it was vaporized in a giant explosion. Yet there she was with all the others, on their knees with their hands tied behind their backs while soldiers leveled rifles at them.

His gaze dropped to the miraculous creatures in the nets. Real, live maniraptors, moving and breathing in front of him. He had seen them briefly before, racing across the ridge, in terrible motion as they tore out soldiers' throats, killing with the grace of born predators. Now, though, he could examine them in detail. He could see their intelligent eyes, every elegant curve of claw, every filament of their protofeathers rising and falling with every breath. They were lethal and beautiful. A creature from another time. He hoped the nets wouldn't injure them.

Zhanwei was almost dancing with joy. This victory would mean even more power for him, and probably the supremacy of his faction over others. He would be a general now, though Kit wasn't sure if "colonel" had ever been his true rank, or just his undercover status when he had posed as an officer in the Royal Army. Who knows, maybe he would take over China and from there, rule the world. Emperor Zhanwei. He had all the power now, after all. He had won. Which didn't mean he wouldn't still sentence Kit to a horrible death or to some kind of sadistic, self-inflicted torture for his own enjoyment.

But Zhanwei, gleeful over the recapture of the maniraptors, seemed to have forgotten about Kit, at least for the moment. Could he take advantage of his distraction? Zhanwei was not currently commanding him, and although Kit wouldn't be able to hurt the colonel directly, he had a brief moment of relative freedom to act according to his own desires. It might be the only chance he ever got. Could he run away? Was there anywhere to run?

He could steal a vehicle. He knew the area and had contacts in Khorat. He might be able to get away and either find someone willing to hide him or simply escape to another country. But the chance of him making it to a vehicle and actually getting away were pretty small. Besides, that would mean abandoning Arinya and Samira and Beth and the others, not to mention the only Cretaceous dinosaurs in existence.

When he saw a soldier, off to one side, loading a tranquilizer gun, he knew what to do. He strode up to the man, marshaling the air of authority he used as a professor. "Hey there, what do you think you're doing?" A look back at Zhanwei showed him still admiring his new sources of power, not paying any attention to Kit.

The soldier glanced at Kit's shoulders and shirt, looking for an indication of rank, and found none. "Following my orders," he replied curtly.

"Were your orders to kill the dinosaur? It's a *bird*, not an elephant. It's all hollow bones and feathers. You need half of that dose, maybe less."

The soldier's confident air faltered a little. "You think so?"

"Listen, I've done wildlife capture for years. That's ketamine, right? Birds always weigh a lot less than you think they do, and they take fewer milligrams per pound. Trust me, you can always give it a little more, but you can't bring it back to life once you've killed it dead."

The soldier looked relieved. "Thanks," he said. "The colonel would kill *me* if I got it wrong."

Don't fight it, Prey sent to Rain. *Pretend to be unconscious.*

The dart had contained a chemical that was meant to knock him out, but they'd made a mistake. Not only was it not nearly enough to do the job, the natural ability of Prey's body to forge custom chemicals allowed him to counteract it, at least in part. He barely even felt drowsy.

If he let them see he was still awake, however, they'd just pump him full of more, and eventually, his body would succumb. He couldn't move—or even open his eyes—without giving away the game, but that didn't mean he couldn't act. It might give him just the time he needed.

Prey breathed deeply and captured the tiny particles of memory still floating through the air, experiencing each one in turn, gleaning its knowledge. He examined the molecules themselves to divine how they were put together. He realized that between his study of the Julian virus and the experience coordinating the hill tribes, he'd already learned a lot. The memory molecules were complex, but compared to the virus, they were straightforward, and he could understand them.

Then, with a dazzling burst of insight, Prey knew how to do it. It was so obvious, he didn't know why he hadn't thought of it before. They didn't have to invent something entirely new. They just had to repurpose what they already had at hand. Best of all, his idea required skills that he and Rain had between them. That and a sample of the virus currently raging through Samira's father's body.

He shared the idea with Rain, who confirmed his understanding. It could work. She suggested some refinements from her experience as to how the design might be made more efficient, but the core idea remained. It was exactly what was needed and the only hope for the humans' survival. But there was a cost. And he wasn't sure the humans were going to like it.

CHAPTER TWENTY-FOUR

Li Ling was terrified. She had recognized Colonel Zhanwei instantly as the site commander who had chosen her to work with the maniraptors. She kept close to the two Thai students, trying to stay out of sight, hoping with no real hope that she might be overlooked. She knew it was futile. Even if Zhanwei didn't remember her face, she was the criminal wanted for stealing the maniraptors. They would expect to find her with them, and here she was.

The Chinese brought a five-ton military truck with high metal sides wrapped in canvas, which lumbered over the rocky terrain and scrub grass as effortlessly as if it were a highway. Using rods pushed through the netting connected to chains, the helicopter lifted each of the maniraptors in turn onto the truck bed, preventing anyone from having to get close enough to them to touch. The maniraptors were thoroughly trapped, but to be safe, they shot them full of tranquilizers as well. Any hope Li Ling had for a last minute miracle began to fade.

They started to load the human prisoners into the truck bed. She went willingly, keeping her head down, but it didn't matter. Zhanwei stopped her, leering, and her faint hopes of being overlooked vanished. Worse, she could smell the domination chemical on him, and knew his power over her was complete.

"*Li xiaojie,*" he said. *Miss Li.* An echo of their first meeting, when he had used the same term, an old mode of address which in modern usage implied prostitution.

She said nothing in reply, just continued to look at her feet.

"You do not correct me?" he said. "Where is the fire? You were so proud. Look at you now, *Li yisheng.*" He spat the term. *Doctor* Li.

"They deserved to be free," she said, still looking down.

"Did they now." Zhanwei put his hand under her chin. She flinched, but found she couldn't pull away, not with the chemical working in her brain to please him. He lifted her chin until she was looking in his eyes.

"Why such a beauty would want to waste her time studying science, I will never understand," Zhanwei said. "But we can fix that. You will be my *xiaojie* from now on. Would you like that?"

Her stomach roiled at the implication, but she felt the chemical's hold on her, making her want to please him, and she knew that whatever he asked of her, she would do. This was worse even than she had feared. This evil old man would have her completely in his power.

He brushed his hand against her cheek, down her neck to her collarbone, then back up her throat until he rested two fingers against her lips. She couldn't pull away, couldn't do anything but what he desired.

"You can get in the truck now," he said. "I'll see you again tonight."

She didn't want to. She wanted to run away from this horrible man, even if the soldiers shot her down, but she couldn't. Her mutinous legs carried her toward the truck, even as angry tears of helpless fury rolled down her cheeks.

Samira kneeled in the brutal heat, sweat running into her eyes, feeling Captain Anderson's blood drying on her bound hands. The man had died saving her life. She had delayed for the faint hope that something could be salvaged of this disaster, and he had run into his own ticking bomb to pull her out. Then he'd stood over her and protected her to the last.

Perhaps he would have died anyway. The rest of the special ops team had, after all. If she had never come, they would have defended the site, blown it up when the Chinese came, and died. But she couldn't help feeling like his blood was—figuratively as well as literally—on her hands.

She saw Kit, standing there behind the colonel. The only person without a mask, he was clearly a slave. They had torn her mask off as well, and she could smell that horrible sweet petroleum smell coming from Zhanwei. She knew she would do whatever he told her to do as well. Maybe for the rest of her life, as short as that was now likely to be.

She heard the exchange between Zhanwei and Li Ling, and her stomach turned. She understood then that this man planned to torture them, physically and psychologically. He wasn't just interested in preserving his country's power. He needed to prop up his own personal sense of pride and control. He would take any interference with his power as a personal affront, and would make them pay for that affront until his pride was satisfied.

Prodded by soldiers to climb into the truck bed, she had no choice but to follow along with the others. The interior was like an oven, open to the blazing sun above, but with little airflow through the high metal sides. The soldiers tied the human prisoners to rings attached to the chassis of the vehicle, and the maniraptors, though unconscious, were similarly tied around their wrists and ankles. Her father looked deathly pale and seemed barely lucid. Her mother could barely walk.

Samira leaned her head back against the metal interior of the truck and tried not to cry.

It wasn't hard to imagine that none of them would ever be free of Chinese custody. Her parents would die soon, followed shortly by Arun and Gabby and the two Thai students. It was a wonder that she and Beth and Alex and Brook and Arinya and Li Ling hadn't yet contracted the virus, but they probably would. It was just a matter of time for the whole human race, anyway. Even if a tiny percentage of humans survived, she didn't like her chances in a post-apocalyptic scenario. The human race's profound capability for self-destruction was finally going to finish the job, and there was nothing she could do about it.

The truck roared and started to move. In the near darkness, Samira studied the four Chinese men who had been left in the back of the truck to guard them. In English, she asked them what their names were and where they were being taken, but they gave no sign that they heard or understood. It didn't matter. What did she think, she was going to talk her way out of this? Convince some Chinese soldiers that the fate of the human race rested on their freedom? She could barely convince anyone from her own country, never mind theirs.

Besides which, the site was gone. Obliterated by her own government to keep it away from anyone else. Even before the virus, she had once dreamed that this chemical would be the salvation of humanity, the means by which everyone could set aside their differences and work together without hatred. She'd thought that if people could truly experience what it was like to be another person, the prejudice of the self would erode. Humans would know that other people, even those of a different race or religion or gender or class, were just like them. They would remember having been those others, at least for a time, and so they would understand.

She'd been naive. Humans did with this technology what they'd done with every other technology since they'd learned to make fire and knap stone. They'd turned it into a weapon of war.

Even when they lifted him into the truck, Prey continued to pretend he was unconscious. He and Distant Rain communicated freely, working on the cure without the knowledge of their captors or even their friends. Prey's epiphany had been that there was a reason their species was immune to the Julian virus. It was because the virus was already part of their genetic code. In fact, the virus seemed to be the very mechanism that had given their species the ability to craft organic chemicals. In the distant past, their ancestors had incorporated it into their biology instead of dying from it, and repurposed it toward their own evolutionary fitness.

Perhaps all the creatures who had survived the Permian Extinction had done something similar. Most of those would have shed that portion of their genetics when it no longer provided a survival advantage, but Prey's species had found a way to use it to greater advantage. It was still a part of them now.

That meant that in order to make the humans immune to the virus, Prey and Rain had to do the same to them. The cure was not to destroy the virus, but to incorporate it into human genetics. The humans had to make the virus part of themselves.

But that had far-reaching implications. The virus could be used to alter human genetic code, but it wasn't as simple as crafting a scent chemical. Prey couldn't just snip out the code for the virus and slap it in somewhere else. Instead, he had to replicate large portions of his own genetic code and teach the virus to copy that code into the code of any host it infected. That's what the virus liked to do anyway—make copies of its genetic code—so that part was simple enough. But the changes needed to be consistent with the human's own genetic makeup, or it would kill them just as surely as the original.

It was difficult work. He and Distant Rain made progress as the truck bumped along the uneven ground and eventually turned onto a smoother road. They refined and refined the virus until finally, it was perfect.

Except. Except that it was more of a blunt hammer than a precise surgical tool. This would infuse maniraptor genetics into the human genetic code. It would change humanity forever and in dramatic ways, some of which he couldn't even predict. It would probably kill some of them. He couldn't guess how many—he hadn't met enough humans to be familiar enough with the variety of their genetics—but it should kill far fewer than the virus was doing by itself anyway. The deaths were less of a concern to him than the changes. If they did this, all humans would be different from that moment forward.

You could let it kill them all instead, Distant Rain sent. *We could even make it more lethal. It would be easy. Look, change this, and it will hide for longer in their bodies before affecting them. That means they can spread it more, and it will kill them all the more thoroughly.* She showed him how.

That's murder, he sent back. *Mass murder on a large scale. These humans are people.* He had shared with her his memories of Samira and the others. Surely she understood?

They are dying anyway. It will be better for us if we let it happen. We can't survive in this world, except as their slaves.

Do you want to survive in a world littered with their dead? In the crumbling ruins of a civilization we destroyed?

Save them, then, if you must, she replied. *There's nothing left for us.*

But still he hesitated. *If I make them a different species, have I saved them or killed them?*

What are you going to do, ask their permission? They're dying. This is the only way they can live.

Prey considered that. It was true that he couldn't ask all of them. But he could ask at least one.

THE WALLS OF THE TRUCK BED WERE TOO HIGH. SAMIRA couldn't see outside, so she had no idea where the truck was driving them. Not that it mattered. Any destination would just mean slavery and death. She wanted to hold Beth's hand, but their hands were still zip tied behind their backs and uncomfortably attached to rings in the truck bed. She settled for meeting Beth's eyes from time to time, trying to project courage and hope, even though she felt none herself. She had tried to speak to her, but the attempt had earned her a painful blow to the mouth from the rifle butt of one of the four guards assigned to ride with them.

Her parents slumped against each other, eyes closed and unmoving. Samira was terrified they were already dead, and kept studying their chests for signs of breathing. Gabby didn't look much better, though her eyes fluttered every now and then. Arun looked only at her, as if he could pour health into her body through sheer force of will.

The maniraptors didn't move. They lay utterly still, like dead creatures found on the side of the road. She wondered if she would ever see their lithe grace again, ever hear Charlie squawk her name or witness his keen intelligence solving a problem. His eyes rolled briefly under his eyelids. Was he dreaming? Then suddenly, he moved.

One moment, the four guards were there; the next moment, they weren't. In a coordinated attack almost too fast for Samira to follow, the maniraptors sprang from apparent unconsciousness into life and leaped on their abductors. The net came apart like paper, and she realized only later that they must have produced some kind of chemical that degraded the rope's molecular structure, weakening the bonds enough for the maniraptors to tear free.

The guards weren't expecting it. The maniraptors had been utterly still, apparently both drugged and immobilized, with no sign of communicating or preparing to attack. Before any of the soldiers could even raise their guns, they were dead.

Samira stared, shocked, her heart hammering wildly. Charlie turned to her, his jaws dripping blood. "I have the cure," he said.

AS CHARLIE EXPLAINED TO SAMIRA WHAT HE WANTED TO DO, the moment became more and more surreal. A year ago, she'd been an ordinary paleontologist, with reasonable expectations of where her life might take her and what sacrifices it might demand. Now, she was a prisoner of war, talking to a sixty-six million year old dinosaur about the genetic future of the human race. Assuming Charlie could really do what he said, she was being asked to make a choice that would dramatically affect billions. Either way, the human race would never be the same.

In some ways, the choice seemed obvious. Any option was better than death. But what if she had been overestimating the danger? What if the Julian virus didn't mean mass extinction, like it had in the Permian? It might kill only a few million before it ran its course, like the other terrible diseases of human history. Evelyn Soderberg or some other bright virologist might discover a cure with less of a cost.

She didn't know how certain Charlie was about his cure, either. What if his alteration of the virus just produced a different strain that killed just as effectively as the original? Then releasing it would make it that much harder for anyone to develop a cure, since there would be multiple versions of it out there. The maniraptors had just come up with this in their heads. It wasn't like they'd tested it in a lab or taken it through a medical review board. It only existed in their minds and the amazing chemical factories of their bodies.

There was so much she didn't know, and yet she was expected to choose for everyone?

She looked to those of her friends and family who were still conscious, but they had nothing more to offer. Charlie was presenting the choice to her, and they were willing to let her make it. And she knew what her choice had to be. In the end, it had little to do with the fate of billions. She just couldn't think that big. Her parents and her friends were dying, and she had the ability, just maybe, to change that. The possible cost to the human race at large didn't matter, not compared to her parents' lives. The best choice for humanity would just have to be judged by what was the best choice for the humans closest to her. If the rest of the world didn't like it, well, at least they would be alive to complain. Probably.

After everything they'd been through to get this cure, there was really no possibility she was going to decline it, no matter the cost. She wasn't going to sit by and do nothing while her species died. She would take the chance and hope for the best.

"I choose the cure," Samira said. "Do it."

"It travels through the air," Charlie said. "It will happen fast."

CHAPTER TWENTY-FIVE

Kit rode with the colonel in his staff car. He had no way of knowing if his trick with the soldier wielding the tranquilizer gun had accomplished anything. Maybe the soldier had ignored him after all. Maybe even the smaller dose was sufficient to knock the maniraptors out. They had certainly behaved as if they'd been thoroughly tranquilized. If they weren't, then they'd been faking it pretty convincingly.

Maybe he should have stolen a car and tried to run after all. He knew his chances would have been low. He would have been seen and shot before he even reached the vehicle. Even if he had gotten away, he would have been followed. The helicopter could have tracked him easily and shot him from the sky. He harbored little delusion that, having gotten what he wanted, the colonel would have just let him go. Zhanwei's petty desire to take revenge for his humiliation was too strong.

Kit wasn't even sure that he could have defied his master that much. It was possible he didn't choose that option because the idea was too clearly in defiance of Zhanwei's wishes. Certainly right now, sitting in a car reeking of the colonel's powerful scent, the idea seemed ludicrous. He could no more cross this man than he could fly to the moon.

As they drove south for hours, following the road that would eventually lead them to Bangkok, Kit could already see that the country had changed. Military checkpoints along major roads were manned by Thai Royal Army soldiers, but the soldiers saluted Zhanwei and made way for their caravan. As he had feared, the chain of command had been subverted. Whether by sheer military power or by chemical subversion, the Chinese controlled the country now. Was Queen Mai in prison, or was she once again a Chinese pawn? Was she even still alive?

The caravan finally pulled in through the gate of Korat Royal Thai Air Force Base near Nakhon Ratchasima, only ten kilometers from the university where Kit had taught before becoming Mai's Minister of Science and Technology. The guards at the gate saluted and lowered the barriers without question. Inside, they took several more roads and finally stopped by a building that Kit guessed was a command center.

Kit saw only Thai soldiers until two men stepped out of the command center wearing Chinese military uniforms encrusted with medals and bright colored rectangles. They saluted Zhanwei, who saluted them back.

They wore peonies in their lapels. Which meant they still relied on chemical compulsion for their control. That was good news, Kit supposed, since once the Chinese military machine rolled in, there would be no ousting them, domination chemical or not. Thailand would become a Chinese protectorate, with a government that answered directly to Beijing.

Kit followed the colonel and the other men as they circled to the back of the largest truck, where the maniraptors and other prisoners were kept. Zhanwei and the Chinese officers spoke rapidly. Kit knew the language, but he had to listen closely to understand around the masks they all wore. Apparently the plan was to transport the maniraptors by air back to the facility in Yunnan from which they had escaped. The ranking Chinese officers wanted to see this powerful weapon they had heard so much about.

One of the Thai soldiers in the caravan approached Zhanwei, speaking low. The soldiers inside the truck, he said, weren't responding to their radios. Zhanwei ordered a semicircle of men to stand around the truck with guns drawn and aimed at the doors, all wearing masks. At Zhanwei's signal, one of the other soldiers pressed a lever on the truck. With a steady beeping, the rear door started to lower, opening the back and creating a ramp.

The maniraptors lay crumpled in the center where they had been put, their bodies covered with nets. The humans all sat where they had been left as well, though they all seemed unconscious or dead, slumped against the sides of the truck. The guards at the back were facedown, as silent and still as the rest of the tableau. What had happened? Had the Julian virus taken them all that fast? Had they collapsed from heatstroke?

"You were meant to capture them alive," one of the Chinese officers growled. "Not kill them."

"They are only sedated," Zhanwei said. "They are just as alive and vital as they have ever been."

"You'd better hope so," the officer replied. "That screw-up in Yunnan could cost you your stripes. What happened to the people? Are they sedated as well?"

A rich, beautiful aroma wafted out of the truck. Kit realized that no one else could smell it, because their masks blocked the scent.

"Dr. Chongsuttanamanee, please climb into the truck and check to see if anyone inside is still alive," Colonel Zhanwei said through clenched teeth.

The smell from Zhanwei's peony was as compelling as ever, but the smell from the truck was stronger. Kit still wanted to obey the colonel, but...*everyone needs to smell this*, the aroma seemed to say. He stood for a moment, wavering between the two powerful ideas. The chemical scent from Zhanwei made Kit want to please him, but the smell from the truck made him want to share it with others. Perhaps he could do both? Surely, despite his command, the colonel would be *pleased* to smell something so beautiful. That would take precedence over simply obeying his command.

There was only one thing to do. Kit reached over and tore off Zhanwei's mask.

The colonel shouted and pushed the mask back toward his face, but it was too late. His expression changed, and he let the mask fall. He breathed in and out in great, satisfied gulps. Then: "Masks off!" he commanded.

The soldiers looked at one another, uncertain. They had seen Kit pull the colonel's mask off. Did that mean he was compromised? Should they ignore the order?

"You," Zhanwei bellowed, pointing at a nearby soldier. "Take your mask off."

"Don't do that," one of the Chinese officers said. "Zhanwei, what's going on here?"

"The situation has changed." Zhanwei approached the officer, smiling and looking apologetic. "For your own safety, I recommend you—" He reached out suddenly and pulled the other man's mask off.

The second officer, still wearing his mask, backed away. "Shoot anyone not wearing a mask," he shouted. "That's an order!"

The soldiers, wide-eyed, hesitated, reluctant to open fire on their own commanding officers.

"Ignore that order!" the first officer shouted. Zhanwei marched down the line of soldiers, shouting and pulling masks off until they were all breathing the scent freely.

Only then did the maniraptors hop, bird-like, out of the back of the truck and land among them, plumage gleaming in the overhead lights.

The remaining officer still wearing a mask turned to run, but Rain caught him quickly and knocked him down. With careful precision, she flicked his mask away with her teeth.

Kit wanted to check on those still in the truck, but he was feeling unsteady. The smell was everywhere, all around him; he was drowning in it. He was falling. *He panicked as he sank, the cold liquid soaking his feathers, but he willed himself to relax. The liquid was the most sophisticated technology his people had ever invented. He gave himself over to it, letting it fill his mouth, and told himself that all would be well.*

Another giant tremor made the world shake, undoing his calm. It was the end of everything. So many would die. Many were dying even now, and those might be the lucky ones, spared from the slow dying from cold and starvation.

He began to choke on the liquid filling his mouth. He couldn't breathe. His vision contracted. He groped with his hands, trying to reach a handhold, something to pull him out, but he sank deeper. He was going to drown.

No! This wasn't happening. Kit surfaced from the memory for a moment, gasping for breath, trying to hold on to his sense of self. He was on an Air Force Base. He was not a maniraptor. He was a human being. His name was Kit.

Then he was falling again.

He was in a classroom, at a desk—his desk. The teacher called his name. He stood, embarrassed to be singled out. His classmates stared at him, jealous because he earned better marks than they did and scored higher on all of the government tests. They took every chance to ridicule him, and now they would get another.

"You have not paid your class fees," the teacher snapped. "There are overdue fees as well, and you have not paid them either."

"No, lao shi," Kit replied.

"Why should I continue to teach a student who doesn't pay his fees?"

"I don't know, lao shi."

"Get out of my classroom. Come back when you can pay your fees."

Kit's face burned and his eyes watered. Never before had he felt his poverty so clearly as a humiliation. The school fees weren't much, only about 90 renminbi, but it was more than his mother could easily spare.

He walked home. He hoped he would find his mother there, who would sympathize with his embarrassment and comfort him, but of course his mother was at work. He tried to sneak through the door, but his grandmother saw him.

"Why are you crying?" she demanded. He explained.

"Ah, your life is so easy," she said. "When I was little, it was war and killing and no food to eat. Stop your foolish tears and do some work around here for once, You think feeding you comes for free?"

"I have no money," Kit said.

"So get a job. Work and pay your own fees. And buy your own food, while you're at it."

"Maybe I'll join the army like my father," Kit said. "Then you won't have to feed me anymore."

His grandmother slapped him, not hard, but enough to sting. "Your father joined the army and came back dead. Is that how you will provide for your poor mother and grandmother?" She raised her hands. "How can someone so smart be so stupid? Nobody with scores like yours joins the army. You will finish school, go to university in the city, get a good job, and send money back to support your family. This is how it is. This is your duty."

Kit knew all this. But he didn't want to go to university. He wanted to be a warrior, to fight for China, like his father. He wouldn't be like all the other boys who joined up, the ones who burned out after two years and came back home to become dishwashers or menial laborers. He would show his merit, rise in the ranks, become an officer. He would do everything his father would have done if he had not died.

His grandmother slapped him again, just for good measure, and told him to fetch her some vegetables from the back garden. He wished his mother was home. She would have responded with kindness and understanding. She worked all day in a factory, but tired as she was, she always had time in the evening to listen to his troubles. She would find the money for his fees, and convince him to stay in school.

He was still outside pulling vegetables when the policeman came to the front door. Kit knew it was bad, even before he returned to the house to find his grandmother wailing and shaking her hands.

The policeman took him aside and confirmed what he already guessed. There had been an accident at the factory where his mother worked. She was dead.

KIT LURCHED BACK TO THE PRESENT, LYING ON THE FLOOR with tears running down his face. That was a *memory*. But it wasn't *his* memory. Just like when he had inhaled the chemical he'd salvaged from the maniraptor fossil, he'd experienced a memory that was not his own as if he were living it. But humans didn't have the biology to encode their memories in organic chemicals and communicate them via smell! What was going on?

Colonel Zhanwei lay sprawled on the ground next to him, eyes flicking to and fro. Kit had no doubt that what he had just seen was a memory from the colonel's childhood in rural China. Rather than live alone with his grandmother, he must have enlisted and then risen through the ranks. Did that mean that Zhanwei was now experiencing a memory of Kit's? Or someone else's?

Gradually, the vision faded, and Kit became more aware of his surroundings. The other Chinese soldiers were also on the ground in various states of trance, confusion, or panic. The scientists from the truck, however, who had seemed to be unconscious or dead, were now up and moving around, not only awake but free. Kit tried to stand, but a rush of dizziness overwhelmed him. That smell, strong and heady, still pervaded the air.

Samira appeared at his side, taking his arm. "Take it slowly," she said. "It takes some getting used to."

"What does?" he tried to say, but his mouth was so dry it came out in a croak. The smells in the air were different now; they were changing. He felt himself falling again...

The taste of orange soda on her tongue. Dust on her lips. Chanting from the nearby mosque and the sharp sound of dogs barking. Beth was holding her hand...her sister, Bethany, only ten years old. They had snuck out at night to go see the hyena man.

She accepted the glass bottle from Beth and took a swig, the syrupy orange sweetness coating her tongue. They laughed together, high on the illicit pleasure of this midnight adventure.

They knew the streets of Addis Ababa as natives, and the hyena man was not far. They passed a house where sweet incense was burning, and Beth coughed from the smoke. Beth's hand was damp and a little sticky from the soda, and Kit giggled and pulled her along through an alley, past a few bleating goats penned in a small yard. Their agile bare feet avoided the piles of dung and other hazards of the road.

They darted down another alley and emerged in a square between houses where the hyena man had already begun. Two big males appeared out of the dark, their tan, spiky fur glowing in the moonlight. The hyena man waited calmly for them. He tossed each of them a piece of meat, which they wolfed down with a toss of their heads.

The hyena man skewered more meat on a short stick and put the other end in his mouth. The biggest hyena loped forward, its mouth big enough to take the hyena man's head in its jaws, but it shuffled up to him almost daintily and snapped up the meat from the stick.

Kit and Beth clapped. A third hyena slid in out of the shadows, but the memory was fading...

Kit took a gulping breath as his mind surfaced again. That was Samira's memory, for certain. He pressed a hand to his forehead. The changes were doing violence to his sense of self and leaving him feeling psychologically unhinged. He wasn't sure if he could take another one.

Samira was still there, leading him toward the truck, helping him in. Beth was there, too, and Arun and Gabby, who seemed more alert than when he'd last seen them. Samira and Beth's parents, too, were sitting up on their own and breathing freely.

The smells were everywhere around him, though, and he felt himself sliding again, this time with the taste of spicy red pepper on his tongue... *No.* Kit wrenched his mind back to the present. His head spun a bit, like he was going to faint, but the memory didn't come.

Samira helped him sit down next to that Chinese woman, the one who had freed the dinosaurs from their prison in Yunnan. Li Ling, that was her name. Outside the truck, the soldiers lay on the ground or reeled about drunkenly. What was happening to all of them?

Another memory assaulted him, and he couldn't help it, he felt himself slipping under...

Pain. Her cheek stung from the unexpected blow. She knew how much Lao Zhou hated tears, but she couldn't help it, they just flooded from her eyes.

"Oh, fine, you're going to cry now," Lao Zhou said. "Why do women cry all the time? I thought you were better than that."

"You hurt me!"

"I did not. I barely touched you."

She reached up to her face gingerly; her fingers came away red. "I'm bleeding!"

Lao Zhou scowled. "What, now you're going to make this my fault?

You're the one too stupid to buy the right beer. You think I'm going to drink that swill you brought home? You're supposed to be the smart one. Is that what you think? Is it?"

Kit was about to apologize, as she had done so many times before, offer to go back to the store, soothe his temper, but no. Keju's words rang in her mind: If he ever strikes you, walk out. No second chances. A man who strikes you will just do it again, and you'll never escape.

It was the hardest thing she'd ever done, but Keju was her mirror self, her dragon phoenix twin. Nobody knew her like Keju. No one else had her back. It all came clear in that moment in a way that it never had before, not all the other times when Lao Zhou told her something was her fault, and she'd believed.

She walked into the bedroom without another word. Lao Zhou shouted at her, but she didn't turn around. She pulled her suitcase out from under the bed and started throwing things into it. Slacks, blouses, makeup, jewelry. It didn't all fit, but she didn't care. She could get the rest later, or he could keep it. She needed to leave right now, before she lost her nerve.

Lao Zhou finally followed her into the bedroom. "What do you think you're doing?"

"Leaving."

He scoffed. "Where would you go?"

"I don't care. Away from you."

"Look, I said I was sorry."

He hadn't, but she didn't point that out. She just kept packing.

"This is beneath you, Ling. Having a little hissy fit and storming out? Come on. This is what little girls do. You're acting like a child."

She felt the well-worn reaction to his words, the sense of guilt, wondering if maybe he was right. Was she overreacting? She wasn't that hurt, not really. Just a little cut. But no. This wasn't just her idea. Keju had told her what to do.

"Keju said if a man ever hit me, I should leave him," she said.

Lao Zhou's expression darkened. "Keju? Have you been talking to him?"

"He's my brother."

"I told you not to talk to him. He doesn't want you to be happy. He's just jealous of you, how smart you are, how much better you did on the tests. He wants to break us up, just to hurt you."

She flipped the suitcase lid on and pulled the zipper around.

"Please, Ling. Don't leave me like this. You know I'm sorry. Please."

She almost relented. He looked so earnest, and she knew he hadn't meant to hurt her. But something inside told her that if she didn't leave now, she never would. She would belong to him forever. She yanked the suitcase off the bed, hitting her leg, nearly falling over from the weight.

He laughed. "Look at you," he said. "You can't even carry your luggage. Where are you going to go, at this time of night? You're ridiculous."

She looked in his face, and suddenly, she saw him. All in a moment, she could see what a petty, insecure, vindictive, fragile boy he was. He had never been kind to her, not really, not in the entire year they'd been together. She'd made a million excuses for him, but he wasn't worth it. He had been right about one thing. She was better than this.

She dragged the suitcase out of the bedroom and to the small apartment's front door. She unlatched it and pulled it open, half expecting him to yank her back or grab the suitcase from her hand. When she turned around, he was standing in the bedroom doorway, looking at her with derision.

"You'll be back," he said.

"No," she told him. "I never will."

She walked out the door.

KIT STRUGGLED OUT OF THE MEMORY AGAIN LIKE BREAKING free of the surface of a pool. The truck was moving now, carrying him with it. Kit glanced at Li Ling, and then looked away, horrified. That had been her memory he had just experienced. He felt like he had violated her mind, seen things that he had no business seeing. They weren't friends. He barely knew her. He doubted she would have shared that memory willingly, perhaps not with anyone, but certainly not with him.

On the road, he saw more soldiers lying on the ground or stumbling along weakly. Kit's friends in the back of the truck mostly lay back with their eyes closed. Were they experiencing his memories too? Were his secrets, his embarrassing thoughts, all his private moments, now being witnessed by his friends, or even by total strangers?

Every time he took a breath, more memories threatened to drag him under. For the next few minutes, he just fought them off, hanging on to his own sense of identity and awareness of his surroundings. It took a while before he could think of anything else but controlling his own mind. Once the worst of the onslaught had passed, he finally realized what was happening. While the soldiers on the base were incapacitated, someone was driving this truck toward freedom.

THEY WERE TOO LATE. WHEN THEY REACHED THE GATE, THEY found that the barriers had been raised. Guns pointed at them from behind the barriers and from emplacements on both sides. The soldiers holding those guns wore gas masks.

"Come out of the vehicle with your hands up," boomed a voice in Thai through an amplifier. "Drop your weapons and come out or you will be fired on."

After a glance at each other, Kit and the others in the back of the truck climbed down. They had no weapons to drop, but they raised their hands to show they were unarmed. Samira and Alex climbed down from the cab of the truck, where they had apparently been driving it. Their escape attempt had been short lived.

They were pushed to their knees again, and their hands were zip tied again, with no attempt at gentleness. This time Kit was among them. He preferred that to being with the colonel, but he had no doubt Zhanwei would take control of him again shortly.

The officer in charge at the gate marched them all back into the truck bed again and drove them right back to where they'd started. Zhanwei stood there, his face a mask of fury, flanked by soldiers who, aside from their dirty uniforms, showed no lasting damage from having experienced that onslaught of memories. Kit realized it had just been a last ditch attempt on the maniraptors' part to distract their captors long enough to escape.

Then the obvious finally occurred to him: where were the maniraptors? They weren't in the truck, and they weren't here. Were they loose on the base, where they would eventually be recaptured or shot? Or had they actually escaped? This was a much more developed area than Khai Nun; even if they had escaped, Kit didn't know where they could find to go. They would be seen.

As they were all marched back down off of the truck, he wondered if he would ever even find out. Zhanwei looked ready to kill someone, maybe even to just kill them all. He stalked forward and took Samira by the throat.

"Where did they go?" he snarled.

She looked scared, but she met the colonel's eyes. "I wouldn't tell you even if I knew."

He stepped back and spat on the ground. "You are not in control here," he said. "I should have killed you when I had the chance, back when you first showed me such disrespect. Well, you will learn."

He grabbed Beth by the hair and yanked her forward. With her hands tied behind her back, she lost her balance and fell to the dirt. Zhanwei put his boot on her back. "This is your sister. You love her very much, yes?"

Now Samira looked truly terrified. Kit wanted to do something, to attack the colonel, anything, but there was nothing he could do. Zhanwei had been made to look weak, he had been *embarrassed*, and he wouldn't be satisfied until he had shown his strength again.

Zhanwei walked over to one of his soldiers and took his rifle. He walked back to Beth, who still lay prone on the ground.

"Stop," said Beth's father. "You don't have to do this. We'll do anything you want."

"Please," said her mother. "Please, if you have to, take me instead."

"Silence!" Zhanwei roared. "I will show you the true meaning of power." He turned. "Kit." Kit felt his blood run cold as Zhanwei approached him, the peony still attached to his lapel. The scent of sweet petroleum flooded Kit's nose. *No. No, no, no, please, no.*

Zhanwei thrust the rifle into Kit's hands and pointed to Beth, cowering in the dirt. "Kill her," he said. "Shoot her in the head. Do it now."

Kit took the gun. It was his worst nightmare. The colonel would finally get his full revenge. He knew from experience that he couldn't resist such an order, no matter how hard he tried. He would have to obey.

Except…he didn't. Despite the unmistakable reek of chemical in his nostrils, Kit felt no compulsion. He didn't have to do what the colonel told him to do. He was immune to the chemical's effects.

Kit hefted the rifle and flicked off the safety. He pointed it at the colonel's chest. "No," he said, and fired.

CHAPTER TWENTY-SIX

Samira stood frozen in horror. This was it. They were going to kill her little sister, and it would be all her fault. She had insisted on not playing by the rules, every step of the way. She had angered this colonel when he took their fossils, had bullied her way onto the American drop team that parachuted in to the first site, had defied the Director of the CIA to announce her concerns on national TV, and had dragged her whole family into a war zone. Beth had never asked for any of this. And now she would pay the price.

Only when the colonel gave the gun to Kit to force him to do the job did she realize just how sadistic a monster he was. Would he have her kill her own parents next? She was about to throw herself at Kit and try to wrest the gun from him, come what may, when he raised it not at Beth, but against the colonel. And fired.

The colonel grunted from the impact. His mouth gaped and his eyes flew wide, and then he collapsed onto the ground. Suddenly all the guns in the square were raised, with shouting on every side. Kit's voice boomed out above them all. "I am General Kittipoom Chongsuttanamanee of the Royal Thai

Army! The Chinese have no jurisdiction here. Take back this base for Thailand!"

The soldiers, no longer under compulsion, swiveled to point their weapons at the Chinese officers. The officers made the mistake of firing their own weapons, and were quickly cut down.

Samira rushed to Beth and threw her arms around her. Her parents were close behind. "Are you okay? You're not hurt?"

"I'm fine," Beth said.

Blood pooled around the colonel's body, and his eyes stared lifelessly upward. Li Ling walked forward and kicked him forcefully in the head, snapping his chin back and away. Then she spat on him. Samira didn't blame her for a moment.

"Who is the ranking officer here?" Kit demanded.

A young man snapped his heels together and gave Kit that unique Thai salute that included puffing out the chest with a deep breath. "Lieutenant Anchali, sir."

"Lieutenant, how many more Chinese soldiers are on this base?"

"Three, sir."

"Are they in the command center?"

"Yes, sir."

"Then take back this base for Thailand."

"Yes, sir!"

Samira shook her head, amazed. Five foreign agents with the domination chemical had commanded an entire base of thousands of soldiers, guns, tanks, planes, and helicopters, just by controlling those at the top of the chain of command. She knew the same thing was happening on the level of countries, as well. No need to dominate everyone. Just the people in charge.

But however Charlie and Rain had constructed the Julian cure now spreading from person to person, it apparently had the added benefit of making them immune to domination.

She didn't know if that would be enough to prevent the spread of Chinese conquest now that it had started, or to turn back the American-Chinese war underway in the Pacific. It had been enough to spare their lives for the moment, though, and for that she was grateful.

But there would be a cost. If the world found out that she was responsible for the changes about to come, they would surely judge her for it. She could become the most infamous character in human history: a name whispered to children to scare them or hurled as an insult on social media. The human race, though it might survive, would not be exactly human anymore, at least not as they had always defined it. Time would tell how history would judge her. Some might even claim that humanity had gone extinct after all.

THE NEXT MORNING, SAMIRA WOKE IN A ROYAL AIR FORCE barracks with her skin itching like mad. Her sister lay sleeping next to her. Her parents were awake, drinking coffee they must have purchased at the canteen. They clearly itched as well, scratching at their necks and arms.

Samira had known this part was coming, but she wasn't looking forward to it.

"Samira," her mom said when she saw that she was awake. "What is happening to us?"

"Charlie and Rain healed you," Samira said. "They created a new version of the Julian virus that would make us immune to the first one."

"I understand that. And it's miraculous. We were getting ready to meet our Savior, and then here we are, completely healthy. But all the rest—all the things we saw; were they real? It's not as strong now, but I keep getting flashes of other people's lives whenever I get near them."

"Those are real memories," Samira said. She realized her

parents had been asleep when Charlie had explained to her what they would have to change about humanity. "To make us immune, they had to alter our genetics, the way they used to do in their factories to build their technology, or to themselves to improve their species in some way. They had to make us more like them."

Arun and Gabby heard them talking and came over to join the conversation. Like her parents, Gabby looked completely cured. "But how does it work?" Arun asked. "The maniraptors communicate thoughts and memories with each other via scent. Human brains can do a lot with scent—we categorize and retrieve memories by smell all the time. But we can't communicate with others that way, because we don't have the scent glands. Maniraptors have little chemical factories in glands on their necks, and we—"

He cut off suddenly as he felt the side of his neck, just behind his ears, where they'd all been scratching. "You've got to be kidding me."

Samira ran her hands to the same place, where she had already discovered the unexpected bumps. They weren't huge, just a tiny puckering of the skin in several places. That tiny external change, however, required much more significant alterations under the surface in order to work.

"We're communicating the memories ourselves," she said. "We're doing it unconsciously, because we haven't learned how to control it yet. At first, it was an onslaught, both sending and receiving indiscriminately. Even since yesterday, our brains are adjusting to the new inputs and learning to regulate what we send out."

"Can we do it on purpose?" Beth asked.

Samira turned to see her awake and sitting up in bed. "I don't know," she said. "Let's try."

She closed her eyes and thought about something simple: the taste of chocolate ice cream. She added fudge sauce and whipped cream, and remembered a specific occasion when she and Beth had gone to a Sweet Cow ice cream parlor in Boulder and she'd chosen a hot fudge sundae.

"Wow, I can taste it," Gabby said.

"I don't even like chocolate, and it tastes good," Samira's mom said. "How does that work?"

Samira opened her eyes. "You're experiencing my memory of the taste, not tasting it yourself. I'm not sure how it works entirely, or what the balance is between your own reactions and the ones I'm communicating. With the maniraptors' memories, it was pretty immersive, but over time, maybe we can distance ourselves a little more. Sample a memory without being overwhelmed by it."

The itching grew worse. By mid-morning, they were all sweating and felt dizzy and sick to their stomachs. Samira was afraid something might have gone wrong. After all, their bodies were all dealing with a modified virus intended to alter their genetics in drastic ways. What if their physiology just couldn't handle it? What if it killed them all just as quickly as Julian would have done?

They stayed in their bunks all day, increasingly miserable. It was impossible to sleep. Every inch of Samira's skin itched like a million ants were crawling all over her. She tossed and turned, soaked with sweat and half-delirious, only faintly aware of Beth nearby experiencing the same thing. Occasionally she thought she *was* Beth.

The night wasn't much better, though she occasionally fell into a fitful sleep, dreaming she was someone else, or just that she was dying. Finally, daylight brightened the room, and she took a deep breath. She felt exhausted, but stronger, and her skin no longer itched. When she ran her hand across her arm, though…

Samira jumped out of bed, alarmed. Her arms were covered with what could only be described as a fine layer of dark feather fluff the same color as her skin. The barracks had no mirror, but she felt her face, where more fluff followed the curve of her cheekbones and rimmed her ears. Her legs and feet had some, too.

She turned, astonished, to see Beth looking at her in astonishment. Beth's face and arms were similarly covered, but her feather fluff was the palest blue.

"This is not happening," Samira said.

But it was. All of them had it. The sickness, it seemed, had passed, but with it came changes Samira had never expected and Charlie hadn't warned her about, whether because he hadn't known or because he hadn't thought it worth mentioning. Maybe he'd even thought of it as a benefit.

"How is this even possible?"

"This is their core technology," Arun said. "I'm sure our metals and plastics and rifles and helicopters seem like magic to them. They can do a lot more than we can even dream of, I bet."

"Samira," Beth said, wide-eyed. "Is this going to happen to everyone? In the world?"

As if in answer, the door banged open and Kit walked in, flanked by several high-ranking Thai military men. He looked the part, resplendent in a brigadier general's uniform, but the effect was spoiled somewhat by the fluff that dusted his face and hands, and the face and hands of the men following him.

"What is happening to us?" he demanded.

Beth stepped in to explain. "It was all to cure the Julian virus," she said. "The maniraptors tailored the virus to alter our bodies to survive it. It just…had a few side effects."

"It's amazing," Arun cut in. "Kit, we can send memories by scent, just like they can. Well, probably not nearly as well as they can, but we can do it. Have you tried it?"

Kit held up a hand for silence, and for a moment, he looked like a man who had gotten used to operating at the highest levels of national authority. Then he looked at his raised hand and a laugh escaped from his lips, and he was just their friend again. "A few side effects?" he said. "We look like baby chickens!"

Everyone laughed at that, a bit too loudly maybe, the stress of it bleeding in. "We do look ridiculous, don't we," said Gabby.

The laughter lasted a little too long, and then stopped awkwardly. "Seriously, though," Kit said. "This is crazy. I had no idea they had this kind of power. I mean, yeah, it seems to have worked, you are all healed, and that's fantastic. Maybe that just makes it all okay. But nobody asked for this. Half the people on this base are affected, maybe more. They didn't sign up for this; they don't even know what's happening or why."

"It's not just the base," Beth said. "They mounted the genetic factories to accomplish all this *on the Julian virus*. It's spreading just like the virus does. If the maniraptors made it off base—"

"They did," Kit said.

"Then they're spreading it as far and wide as they can. And it's contagious, probably just as unstoppably contagious as the original."

"Faster, maybe," Gabby said. "Since this version doesn't kill. Instead of dying, all the infected will still be out there infecting more people. This is going everywhere. I don't think anyone can stop it."

Kit scowled. "What gave them the right? To literally remake our whole species in their image?"

"They're rescuing us," Beth said, a touch of awe in her voice. "They're saving us from extinction."

"But at what cost? We survive, but we're no longer human?" He pulled up his sleeve, showing the soft feather down covering his arm. "Does it stop here? Or are we growing claws and dagger-sharp teeth next?"

"It's the only way," Beth said. "They couldn't stop it. The only way to make us immune was to use a piece of their own genetic code as a basis. We're changing, yes, but in small ways. We're still human."

Kit crossed his arms. "But that wasn't their choice to make. Who gave them permission to do this to us?"

It was meant as a rhetorical question, but Samira smiled sadly and answered it anyway. "I did."

CHAPTER TWENTY-SEVEN

Li Ling sat at the far end of the barracks room, distant from the rest. They were all speaking English, which she could read a lot better than she could speak, and she couldn't follow the rapid back and forth. She understood that the human race was changing, though, and that no one really knew exactly how, and that a lot of people were going to be angry and afraid.

And where did that leave her? She was a foreigner here. She was behind enemy lines in a world war between superpowers. Would they imprison her? Interrogate her? It wasn't like she could go home again; in China, she was a traitor. She had escaped the country with their most valuable war assets and delivered them to their enemies. They wouldn't bother with prison for her in China; she would just be shot. But that didn't mean she was a hero here.

She wondered what was happening to her brother and parents. They would almost certainly have been arrested by now, interrogated as to her whereabouts, and suspected as American sympathizers. Keju, of course, had been complicit in the maniraptor escape, even if he hadn't known it. They would know he had been in Yunnan; the rental truck records would show that much. He should have come with her instead of staying in China. At the time, she had expected to be captured or killed, but as it turned out, he would have been safer with her.

Her parents wouldn't understand what was happening. They barely understood what her doctoral dissertation was about, and of course they had no idea about the maniraptors. They would be arrested and questioned and all they would know was that their daughter was in terrible trouble. She was afraid of what might happen to them. She didn't think they would be jailed, but they might lose the small stipend the government gave them for forcibly relocating them from their home. It had never been enough anyway, considering the move had cost her father his livelihood, but it had been something. The rest had come from Keju, who might not now be in a position to help them.

She had thrown away her phone when she escaped with the maniraptors, so she had no way to reach any of her family or find out what was happening to them. Not that she was in a position to do anything about it anyway. Maybe her best option was to defect. But to what country? Even if Thailand fought off Chinese control, they might be reluctant to grant asylum to someone China wanted as badly as they probably wanted her. The American scientists seemed friendly enough; she could ask them to sponsor her or help her defect to America, but from what she understood, they couldn't go back to their country any more than she could go back to hers, and for much the same reason.

They were all exiles. Which left only Thailand. Which meant the status of Thailand as a sovereign country was of critical importance to all of their futures.

"Please," she said in English, stepping forward into the conversation. "Please, you speak Mandarin?"

"I do," Kit said. The man had been a scientist at the dig site, but suddenly now he was a general in the army. She didn't understand how that worked, or what kind of power he had, but he seemed to be pretty important.

"I am a traitor in my country," she said in Mandarin. "I want to defect. I helped the maniraptors escape China and come to your country. I wish to beg the queen to take these actions into account and accept my request to become a loyal subject of Thailand. Will you help me?"

Kit looked grim. "I don't even know if the queen is still alive," he said. "Information is thin and conflicting. I haven't been too overt, because if Beijing controls Bangkok, we don't want to let them know this base no longer answers to them. If there's a counter force resisting Chinese control, though, we want to join it. So I'm sorry. I have to focus on taking Thailand back before I know if there will be a Thailand left to consider your plea."

"I understand," Li Ling said.

"For what it's worth, I support you. Your actions have been of great value to Thailand and the world, and the fact that they have alienated you from your home means that, as far as I'm concerned, you are welcome here."

Li Ling attempted a *wai*, hoping to show respect. "Thank you, sir."

He chuckled. "It's just Kit," he said. He stretched out his arms, showing off the fluff on his hands and coming out of his sleeves. "You can't really take me too seriously when I seem to be growing feathers, can you? We're all in this together. Let's take it a day at a time."

LI LING WENT BACK TO HER CORNER AND SAT BY HERSELF until Dr. Gabriela Benitez came and sat next to her. They hadn't yet met properly; when Li Ling was working on the site, Gabby was sick in the tent with Arun and Samira and Beth's parents.

"Hi, I'm Gabby," she said.

Li Ling was a little awed: this woman had been trekking around paleontology digs since before Li Ling was born, and had published her first paper while Li Ling was still in primary school.

"I understand you're the hero of the hour," Gabby said.

"You speak Mandarin?" Li Ling said, surprised.

Gabby shrugged. "I spent a year with my parents on a dig in the Sichuan Basin when I was at an age where languages came easily. You were a scientist working in the facility that held Charlie and Rain?"

Li Ling nodded. "I didn't know what the work would be when I came there. It was just where I was assigned."

"That was a pretty brave thing you did. To break them out of a military facility, leaving your country and everything you know behind? It's nothing short of heroic. Since I personally would be dead if you hadn't, I wanted to thank you."

Li Ling blushed. "It's the same thing that Dr. Shannon did. And you too, for that matter. I guess we've all betrayed our countries for the maniraptors."

"Betrayed our governments, maybe. Not our countries," Gabby said. "There's a good chance what we did saved the human race."

"And they'll all probably hate us for it."

Gabby laughed and looked at the fluff on her arms. "Yes, I suppose they probably will."

Samira and Beth's parents came over next and offered more kindness. Neither of them spoke Mandarin, but they made do with her halting English. Before she knew it, she had been pulled in to the larger group, included in the conversation through a mix of languages—everyone there seemed to know several—and made to feel like she belonged. Made to feel like a hero even.

It didn't solve anything about her uncertain future, but it made her feel a little more hopeful.

Samira felt happy. It was a ridiculous way to feel, given their situation. She was a wanted felon in her home country and hiding in a country being attacked by a nation that probably wanted her dead. She didn't know where the maniraptors were, if they were free or even alive, and she was responsible for a genetic change to the human race that—if everything went as planned—would probably make her a hero to many but a villain to even more.

But her parents were alive. Gabby and Arun were alive, as were Kit's two students, and soon, perhaps billions more. Whether the world ultimately appreciated what she'd done or not, she had her family and friends, healthy and talking and laughing together, eating a lunch that Kit had brought in for them. That was enough, at least for the moment.

Samira looked at Beth and concentrated, trying to send her the emotion she was feeling. She remembered a moment from their childhood, toward the evening of a Timket festival. Both of them were still dressed in white, their bellies filled with delicious food from the celebration. They were playing jump rope with other kids from the neighborhood while their parents looked on, no longer concerned that they would dirty their holiday dresses. There was no story to the memory, just a moment of joy.

She saw Beth take a deep breath, then turn to her in surprise and grin. "Did you just send me that? Playing *chinu* after Timket?"

Samira nodded. The others in the circle smiled too. "You were adorable," Gabby said. "Was that a birthday?"

Beth shook her head. "It's Timket, a celebration of Epiphany. Religious holiday."

Samira marveled at this new skill, almost like a magic power. She remembered her arguments with Everson about whether the ability to share the experiences of others would reduce the conflict in the world. She was still hopeful. So much conflict came from one group seeing another group as less than human because their experiences were beyond the ability of the first group to imagine. If you knew why a person acted as they did, not just intellectually, but because you could experience it from their eyes, wouldn't that make you more likely to respond with compassion? It should be harder to marginalize people when you could feel the emotions and experiences that made them who they were.

Of course, this skill could be used to project discontent, too. She could just as easily have recalled an ugly memory when Beth had been unkind or when they had fought, and sent that out instead. Would projecting hatred and anger to others turn out to be more powerful than projecting cooperation and understanding? Would it become easier to start riots or stir up violence? Groupthink wasn't always a good thing. She imagined this talent as a way to create a sense of unity among people, but stirring people to all feel the same strong emotion together could turn out very badly as well.

She supposed they would just have to wait and see. She told the others what she was thinking, and their responses were mixed. Some hope and excitement, some fear for the future, depending on their personalities.

"Can you imagine what humanity could accomplish if we could get past these tribal instincts?" Samira said. "We spend half of our capacity as a planet either preparing to fight each other or destroying things that we've built. We're always defending our own interests to the detriment of others, divided up into these arbitrary groups. What could we do if we actually worked together?"

"The problem is deciding what to actually work together on," Alex pointed out.

She sighed. "I know. It's a pipe dream, I guess. But I'm holding out hope that this will be a net good for humanity."

Alex lifted one of the water bottles that Kit had provided

in the gesture of a toast. "Saving the race from extinction, I'd have to call that a net good, no matter what else comes of it."

"Hopefully it turns out that way," Samira said.

OVER THE FOLLOWING DAYS, THEY WATCHED IT TURN OUT that way on international news. Wherever the maniraptors had gone, they had clearly spread the tailored virus, which was now spreading as rapidly as the original had, if not more. From Thailand, it spread into Myanmar, Laos, Cambodia, and Malaysia, and then internationally, popping up in every major metropolis.

Everywhere it went, people were healed. It raced through overrun hospitals, turning prognoses of certain death into miraculous recoveries. It couldn't bring back the millions who had already died, but millions more who were sick came back from death's door, or never got sick in the first place. Before long, the world's scientists recognized the trend: a sweeping tide of immunity originating in Southeast Asia. They just didn't know why.

And everywhere it went, people were changed. The spreading terror of Julian turned into a new kind of terror, as what seemed to be a new virus spread as quickly as the cure for the last one. The news reported people overcome by delirious visions and eruptions of strange skin growths. No one on the news had yet connected the visions with the real-life memories of nearby people, or recognized it as something people could send on purpose. That would come.

And everywhere it went, people died. The death toll wasn't nearly what had been projected for Julian, but it happened faster. It seemed some people's bodies just couldn't withstand the drastic genetic change. Samira suspected these would turn out to be part of a group, people with certain genetic markers, perhaps, or those whose bodies were already weakened by other illness or disease.

That was the worst part. She told herself they all would have died anyway, eliminated by Julian, or if they were lucky enough to survive that, killed by the subsequent collapse of society. But of course she didn't *know*. She had made the best choice available to her, given the information she had, and it was hard to believe it had been the wrong one. The alternative was just too dire. But she had made a choice to allow something loose in the world that had killed some to save others, and if the news got out about her involvement, she knew some people would always blame her for making that choice. She might be one of them.

CHAPTER TWENTY-EIGHT

Pak had heard the gunfire over at the dig site, and knew his status as the bringer of money and prestige to Khai Nun would soon be over. His reputation had already started to tarnish when several people in the village got sick, including the *puyaiban* himself. The disease quickly spread to their families. Pak knew about the Julian virus from his time in Bangkok, but it was the first time it had reached out to Korat. The big men from the capital must have brought it with them. Which meant that just as he had received the credit for the money and prestige, Pak received the blame for the sickness.

He told everyone who was sick to quarantine in their homes, and mostly they listened, but it spread anyway. When the Thai military abandoned the site and it came under Chinese attack, Pak was blamed for that as well. The same neighbors who had praised him for bringing foreign attention now cursed him for it. Pak didn't mind too much. As long as Kwanjai could keep attending primary school in the district capital, he could put up with some scorn. He deserved it, after all, if not for the reason people thought.

He wondered what was happening way off in Bangkok, in

the palace where he had once staged a revolt to free the queen. Pak was practically a world traveler, compared to most of the farmers he knew. Not that he had any desire to return to Tachileik, or Bangkok either, for that matter.

The money started to dry up. With Kit gone, the government no longer paid for the use of what had been their cassava fields, nor did they buy food or souvenirs in the village, or hire the farmers for labor. With no income and no crops, the village would be in trouble by the time the rainy season came. Though there might not be a village at Khai Nun by that time, at the rate people were getting sick. The *puyaiban's* father, old Kasem Kaew, was the first to die.

A flash of memory came to Pak: he and Nikorn, chasing the uneven block as it toppled and tumbled down the hill. At the time, Pak had been angry at his brother-in-law, thinking only about the money he would lose if the fossil was damaged. But Nikorn hadn't wanted to come. It was Pak who had bullied him into it. Nikorn should have been home in bed with Boonsri, not smuggling fossils illegally in the dead of night. If not for Pak, he would still be alive.

Nothing Pak did ever seemed to turn out right. He'd wanted to sell that fossil to get money for Kwanjai's schooling, but then the chemical vision had terrified him into shooting poor Nikorn. He'd run away to Tachileik, only to be pressed into service with evil men smuggling not just fossils and drugs, but young girls as well. He'd marched to Bangkok with the queen, only to see her controlled by the Chinese. Now, when he was finally back home and taking care of his daughter the way she deserved, it was all falling apart again.

Then the Change came. Overnight, those who were sick got better, and they all started seeing the memories of their family and neighbors. The worst was how Pak's wife looked at him afterwards: she wouldn't tell him which of his memories she'd shared, but he knew there was plenty. Plenty of what he had seen and done in the time away that he had never told her and never wanted her to know. Some other secrets came out in the village that night too: affairs that spouses had never known about, stolen farming tools from neighbors, or just unkind words spoken when behind closed doors. No one was happy.

Pak started thinking about leaving again. He had no job and his money was gone. If he wanted Kwanjai to keep attending school, he had to come up with more, and that meant leaving Khai Nun. He didn't want to, but things seemed to be going from bad to worse. He didn't know where else to go but Bangkok, distant as it was, so one morning he said goodbye to his wife and daughter and hitched a ride with a passing trucker to the district capital, where he could get a bus traveling south. He would miss Kwanjai, especially, but he couldn't provide for her without work.

After six hours on the bus, he wasn't even halfway there. Pak drowsed and then fell asleep. He dreamed he was back in Bangkok and the queen was in trouble again. He woke, disoriented, still feeling a sense of urgency. Someone in front of him mentioned the queen. Then someone behind him did as well, adding that she was under siege by the Chinese military. What was going on? Had there been news?

Everyone on the bus started discussing it. The queen was in trouble. They had to do something about it. Pak felt a surge of emotion: patriotism, national pride, and fierce loyalty to the Chakri dynasty. He had been around the maniraptor chemicals long enough to be suspicious, but he didn't smell that distinctive sweet petroleum odor. What was happening?

He rode the wave of emotion all the way to Ayutthaya. By the time they arrived, everyone on the bus knew each other's names and were utterly unified in the belief that Queen Sirindhorn needed their help. They disembarked from the bus as a unit and headed for the express train into Bangkok.

The train was packed. The ticket taker had waved them all through without paying and without limiting them to the number of seats. Hundreds climbed on, filling all the available space, but despite the claustrophobic heat, nobody minded. If anything, the sense of brotherhood and a shared cause increased.

Everyone on the train had feathers. Not full feathers like a bird, but short little tufted shafts erupting from their skin. Despite his enthusiasm for what was happening, a part of Pak's mind was still questioning it. This was weird. What was causing them all to feel this way? Clearly something like the domination chemical was in play, though it didn't seem quite the same.

Eventually, it occurred to him that the chemical was coming from them. All of them. They were projecting their emotions to each other from the new glands on the sides of their necks. It wasn't something that would have occurred to him a year ago, but he'd come a long way since his days as a rural cassava farmer. He'd seen some incredible things.

Knowing what was happening didn't change much, though. If anything, it made him more devoted to the cause. He had adored the queen already, before the mass feeling had taken hold; his own emotions had probably contributed to the shared fervor everyone else was feeling. "For the queen!" he bellowed, and the cry was taken up throughout the train, deafening in the cramped space.

Finally they arrived and poured out into the station. Other trains and buses were arriving from all over, filled with other zealots. The crowds merged, bled out into the city, and joined with thousands more already flooding the streets. Pak remembered the day they'd marched with the queen up Prajadhipok Road into the city, how the army had joined them and shot the pretender General Wattana and presented the throne to its rightful queen. Emotions had run high that day, too, and there had been a sense of unity and shared purpose, but nothing like this. He felt like he and the thousands swarming toward the palace were a single mind with a thousand parts. They *were* Thailand.

He thought it would come to violence and blood. The Chinese soldiers weren't likely to swear allegiance to Queen Sirindhorn, no matter how much public support was behind her. Pak imagined wave upon wave of feathered humans dying to Chinese bullets until the soldiers were finally overwhelmed with the sheer mass of people.

In the end, though, a massacre wasn't necessary. Millions of people in China had marched on Beijing, too, demanding an end to the war and a change of leadership. The press of people filled the streets, stopped traffic, and drew thousands more to its cause daily, many of them high ranking government officials and military officers. The Chinese government was swept away as if in a flood. Faced with a similar onslaught in Bangkok, Taipei, Hanoi, Vientiane, and Manila, and with chaos at home, the occupying Chinese forces abandoned their conquests and returned to their own country. The new Chinese government, according to the news, was suing for peace with the United States.

Mai appeared on the Grand Palace balcony, her image transmitted by camera to every television and phone in the nation, and announced the Chinese retreat and her own full command of the government and the military. "Full control" seemed to be an understatement, as nearly every citizen in the country hailed her as a goddess and vowed their everlasting allegiance. It seemed that the new ability to communicate emotions had an amplifying effect, each person boosting the signal to those around them until everyone reached a fever pitch of strong feeling. It had done some good, Pak thought, in giving ordinary people more of a say in their government, but what would it mean in the long term? Greater understanding between people groups and nations? Or a tendency to flash mobs that could turn on others with sudden violence?

It was a new world, and only time would tell. A lot had

happened since that moment of terror when he had fired his shotgun at the maniraptor vision and hit his brother-and-law instead. Pak would have given any money to be able to reverse time to before that day, but that was a miracle too far. He would have to do his best with the miracles life had handed him instead.

He hitched a ride with a trucker heading north to pick up his next load. The trucker had been in the Bangkok march, too, and the two of them traded stories like old friends. Half an hour after they'd passed through Nakhon Ratchasima and out into a more rural stretch of road, the trucker suddenly pointed out the window, shouting in fear. When Pak saw why, his whole body went cold with fright. Two maniraptors ran through the trees to their left, the same kind of creature he'd seen in the vision that had started this whole adventure so long ago.

Were they real? Was this another hallucination, brought on by the changes in his mind and body? But the trucker saw them, too. They had to be real. They ran alongside the trucks, making no move to attack, as if they were headed back to Khai Nun, too. He marveled at their grace and power.

Suddenly, Pak knew what he had to do. He told the trucker to stop. He climbed out, wary of the maniraptors, who had circled around behind him. The truck was an open flatbed, with wooden sides about three feet high, currently empty except for a few stray cardboard boxes. Pak lowered the gate in the back, and without being told, the raptors leaped in, as if it had been their idea.

On a whim, astonished at his own bravery, he climbed up into the truck bed with them and called to the driver to head out again. As the truck started moving again, he held on to the wooden rail, the wind tousling his hair, the dinosaurs crouched next to him. He knew the world would never be the same again.

CHAPTER TWENTY-NINE

ONE YEAR LATER

The Julian monument stood in a grassy square next to Denver International Airport. Sprinklers irrigated the ground regularly so the grass would grow—without it, the dry heat would have left nothing but dirt and scrub. Samira figured the grass was a statement of sorts, a raised fist to nature that life could be preserved despite its best efforts. A sign told visitors that Denver had been the first US city to report infections of the original Julian strain.

In the center of the grass, surrounded by a walkway, a gently curving copper sculpture stretched up into the sky, approximating the shapes of the two viruses. Listing the names of just the Colorado dead would have required ten times the space of the Vietnam Wall, so instead of names, the worldwide casualties were represented with grains of sand lacquered into the base of the memorial. One grain for each person who died.

"I think this was a bad idea," Samira said. "I'm not ready for this."

Beth took her arm. "Yes, you are. You have to focus on how many you saved, not how many were lost. You couldn't save them all."

The death count for the second strain was smaller, but still numbered in the tens of thousands. Some people's bodies couldn't handle the alterations, and they died. Others couldn't handle the changes psychologically and committed suicide. It had been a time of shock and adjustment for every human on the globe: first the physical changes to their own bodies, then coming to terms with the fact that their memories were broadcast such that anyone nearby could see and experience them. Most people weren't aware of the final change: that it rendered them immune to the power of the green chemical to dominate and sway them.

"But my action took all those lives," Samira said. "If the virus had run its course, maybe a lot more people would have died, but at least it wouldn't have been my doing."

"It wasn't your doing anyway. The maniraptors did it. You just agreed that it was the best course of action. Which it clearly was."

The sun was bright and the air was dry. A breeze ruffled Samira's feather fluff. She was still getting used to caring for it. Many people shaved it off, but a dozen new fashions had sprung up around how to present it attractively.

The jury was still out on memory sharing. The news cycles had been filled with stories of secrets coming out in the early days before people learned to control it. Wives experienced their husband's affairs, children learned of secret half-siblings, bosses saw what their employees said behind their backs. The world was in chaos for the first two weeks as the virus swept the globe. No one knew where it had come from or why it was happening, though researchers soon identified it as a new strain of the Julian virus. Some saw Julian Two as miraculous: a gift from God to help humanity learn to get along. Others thought it was a curse for sins already committed.

And what was it really? The question kept Samira up nights. Was it a net good for the species? Those whose secrets had been brought to light hated it, of course, but even those with nothing particular to hide were horrified when their private memories and thoughts suddenly became public. A growing number, however, especially among the young, embraced it. An open culture meant everyone knew everyone else better. Dating couples swapped memories to appreciate one another's pasts and motivations. Memory clubs sprang up to promote understanding across racial, cultural, religious, and gender identity lines. Perhaps it *was* possible to base a society around trust and understanding.

Julian Two had created the vision Samira had first imagined in Paula's office what seemed like a lifetime ago now. A way to combat humanity's inherent tribalism by giving each person a chance to experience what it was like to be the other. Of course, understanding why someone acts the way they do isn't the same as peace, but Samira was hopeful that it would make a difference.

The ceasefire in the Chinese-American War was a shining example of that hope made real. With humanity immune to the effects of the domination drug, they had less to fight for, and with so many in both countries dead from the virus, the two countries had more pressing concerns. Peace didn't come easy once blood had been spilled, but it seemed possible they would find a way. Thailand's Queen Sirindhorn was serving as mediator in the peace talks, which included each country's representatives experiencing the memories of those who had been hurt by the crisis on either side. At the end of the day, China still might not be willing to back out of Taiwan, at least not without the blood of millions more being shed. Backing down wasn't a very human thing to do. But then, the people involved weren't quite human anymore, either.

Homo sapiens was all but extinct. A few isolated strongholds kept the world at bay and had managed to avoid the virus for now, but eventually they too would succumb. In its place, *Homo maniraptora* thrived. New babies born of infected parents demonstrated the same new traits. Children shared memories readily with each other, achieving a silent but powerful social interaction that their parents struggled to understand. In a generation, what new capabilities might humanity have?

"It eats away at me that nobody knows," Samira admitted. "The world has changed. People deserve to know why."

"So write a letter to be opened when you die," Beth said. "You can't tell them now."

They'd been over this ground: If they told the story, they —along with their family and friends—would become the most famous and probably also the most reviled people on Earth. Some might honor Samira for her role in preventing human extinction, but many more would hate her for changing them without their consent. She couldn't expect other people to forgive her when she could barely forgive herself.

"Ready to go?" Beth asked.

"I guess it's that time."

The two of them returned to the airport and boarded their flight to Rogue Valley International in Oregon. Once there, a friend of Brook's picked them up in the smallest plane Samira had ever seen and flew them to Wagontire, a tiny private strip in the middle of nowhere, only a handful of miles from the Waters Ranch.

Everyone else was there already. Gabby and Arun had married two weeks earlier in Argentina, where Gabby's extended family lived, but they had scheduled their honeymoon to finish at this reunion. Samira and Beth's parents were there, as was Alex, and Brook, of course.

Even Wallace, Samira's macaw, was there. He had been flying loose in the house after the raid that had sent them all racing to leave the country. He'd escaped through a window and lived wild until a neighbor had spotted him and lured him in with crackers. Samira ran to him with a cry of joy, but got a sharp peck on the head for a greeting.

"I know, I know, you're cross with me," she said. She held out some peanut butter crackers she had brought for this very purpose. "Will you forgive me?" Wallace squawked loud enough to break eardrums and turned his back on her, but he ate the crackers.

It was great to see everyone again, though Samira still hadn't grown entirely used to the fine layer of protofeathers that covered everyone's skin. Mom's was barely noticeable—just some soft touches of color around her neck. Dad, on the other hand, was practically avian, with great feathery cheeks and fine blue down on his arms and the backs of his hands.

Samira gave each of her parents a kiss and asked, "How's Camila?"

Mom beamed. She still loved to be asked about her sponsored Compassion International children. "She's just wonderful. The original virus never did make it to her village, and now with the second, she's even more beautiful than ever. Did you know we've actually had an increase in sponsorship since Julian Two?"

Arun and Gabby shared some scent memories of their wedding, which had been a beautiful event, outside and by the sea. After they'd all experienced it, Gabby asked, "Any word from Charlie and Distant Rain?"

"None," Samira said. "There were rumors running for months about giant birds spotted in Thailand. But that was a long time ago. As far as I know, nobody's seen or heard from them since."

"I hope they've found a place to be happy," Gabby said. "I hate the idea that maybe China recaptured them, despite the fact that the domination drug doesn't work anymore."

"Amen," Dad said. "Humanity didn't treat them very well,

on the whole, and in the end it was the two of them who saved us all." He said it seriously, but Samira caught the twinkle in his eye.

"You know something, don't you?" she demanded.

He shrugged. "I might have heard a little hint of something from Chanchai," he said. "But you have to promise not to tell a soul."

"Oh, don't keep them in suspense," Mom said. "Make the call."

Brook had a laptop set up already, connected to a TV standing on the big oak table in his spacious kitchen. He pressed a button, and the video conference software started to make a dialing sound.

"Who are we calling?" Samira asked. "Chanchai? Does he know where they are?"

"Wait and see," Dad said, his smile positively mischievous.

Samira checked her phone. Ten after seven in the evening there in Oregon meant ten after nine the next morning in Thailand. After a few rings, the software chimed, and the video conference sprang to life on both the laptop and the TV screen. Kit's face, his jaw covered with a mix of soft feather down and a dark beard, smiled at them from an awkward angle, the screen bouncing as he walked with his phone.

"Kit!" Samira exclaimed. Not counting a few social media interactions, she hadn't seen him since their return to the United States. Their fugitive status had been revoked after a change in CIA leadership and the officially unacknowledged recognition at high levels of government that they had all been instrumental in turning back the tide of the Julian virus. The intelligence services had wanted them home, both to keep them under control and to find out what had actually happened out there. The spooks had aggressively debriefed them all for weeks. Samira and the others had told them everything they knew, but they could honestly report that they had no idea where the maniraptors were.

In the end, they were permitted to return to their homes and lives in the US. Samira had worried that the information would leak and the public would find out their role in what happened, but so far, the spooks had done their jobs and kept it all under wraps.

"What's going on?" Beth said to the TV. "Kit, where are you?"

He pushed his way through undergrowth along a thin, meandering path. The trees on either side were thick and old, and he seemed to be climbing steeply and breathing hard.

"Can't tell you that," Kit said, panting. "Sorry—I've got to assume someone might be listening in, especially on your end."

Samira looked at Beth, then at the others around the room. Her father was smirking, and Brook was grinning like the proverbial cat.

"What is this? You all know what's going on, don't you?" Samira exclaimed.

"We don't," Arun said. "Kit, do you know something about Charlie and Rain?"

Kit gave a short laugh. "I'm sorry we couldn't tell you sooner. You've been under such scrutiny by your government, and given the history here, we just couldn't risk it. I'm a little worried about doing it now, to be honest, but I couldn't keep it from you any longer. It's time."

"They're with you, aren't they?" Samira said. "The maniraptors. You've been hiding them."

"Almost there," Kit said, grinning. "You can see for yourself."

"How long have you known about this?" Samira demanded of her father.

He shrugged, trying to look apologetic, but failing. "Just since this morning."

On screen, Kit topped a rise and started to descend. The path grew even steeper now, following sharp switchbacks on the edge of a vine-encrusted cliff. Samira realized this was a karst sinkhole, where the calcium carbonate underground had eroded away over millennia, leaving behind giant holes hundreds of meters deep. Samira knew about them because sometimes animals or plants thought extinct were found still thriving in these hidden kingdoms, largely cut off from the rest of the world. There were hundreds more unexplored, their locations not even mapped, in the vast, mostly-uninhabited jungle territories through and around the Thai Highlands and surrounding mountain ranges in Myanmar and Laos.

As Kit descended, weird rock formations towered up from the jungle, their tortured shapes carved by the erosion of water and wind. As he reached the valley floor, they could see the wooden stakes and colorful draped cloths of a Hmong village resolve itself through the trees. Samira wondered if the Thai government even knew it existed here. Though she supposed Kit *was* Thai government now.

"This place doesn't appear on any maps," Kit told them as he walked. "Your friend Chanchai arranged it with the people who live here. No planes fly over this spot, it's not a destination for hikers, and there's no easy way to get here. None of the villagers are going to tell anyone."

"But you have cell service?" Alex asked.

"Not even close. This is an Iridium satphone, government issue. Encrypted and cyber hardened." He passed the village and into a clearing beyond. "Theoretically someone could find this place via spy satellite," he said. "But they'd have to know where to look. Even then, they'd have to spot two fairly camouflaged maniraptors under thick foliage."

"It is them!" Samira said. "I knew it!"

"You've waited long enough," Kit said. He turned the phone around, and there they were, Charlie and Rain, looking healthy and strong. Li Ling, the Chinese woman who had risked her life to rescue them from her government, was there, too, grooming Rain's plumage with a detangling brush. Rain preened in pleasure.

"HA-MEE-KA!" Charlie cried, rivaling Wallace for piercing volume. He could pronounce her name better than that, now, but the squawking cry brought back memories of earlier days, when the two of them had learned to speak to each other. When Charlie had learned to speak to her, anyway. Earlier days, but perhaps not better days, especially for Charlie. He had been in a cage then, alone and grieving. Now he was free, and though his civilization was still gone, at least he had one other of his kind to share the rest of his life with.

"It's so good to see you, Charlie!" Samira said, pitching her voice loud to make sure it carried over the satphone and the distance.

"You as well," Charlie said. "But Rain has given me a new name."

"Really!"

"It's about time," Alex said. "'Easy Prey' is no fit name for anyone."

"When you come, I will tell you," Charlie said, and Samira laughed. No one had yet invented a way to digitize scent and reproduce it across distances, so there was no way for Charlie to express his name in its true sense. Given the demand, she imagined someone would invent something soon, though it was a hard technology problem. In the meantime, though, it had brought a new revival to in-person gatherings in American culture. Since online meetings had no scent component, they missed what was fast becoming a major component of human—or perhaps post-human—communication.

"I would describe his new name as something like, *Mountain Breeze Carrying Rich Warmth of New Life after Thunderstorm*," Li Ling said.

"Good to see you, Ling," Samira's father said. "How is your family? Are they safe?"

"They are, thank you, Mr. Shannon," she said. "I cannot go back to China, not yet anyway, but with the change of regime, they have not been mistreated. I speak with my brother every day."

"I'm glad to hear it."

"That name is quite a mouthful," Brook said. "Any way to shorten it?"

"It's not long when you just smell it," Li Ling said. "It's only long because I'm trying to describe what the scent is like. Besides, I'm not really capturing it. You have to be here to experience it correctly."

"I would love to be!" Samira said. "Kit? Can we come?"

The phone swiveled again, and Kit's face came back into view. He looked remorseful. "One step at a time," he said. "You know if you traveled here, the major governments of the world would be watching to see where you go. We'd have no way to keep this place secret then. We're risking enough with this call, but I couldn't bear it anymore for you all not to know."

"Thank you," Beth said. "It means a lot. And of course we won't tell anyone."

Kit walked around, showing them the building that the maniraptors and the villagers, working together, had constructed for them to live in. It was like one of the Hmong huts, but bigger, and designed for maniraptor bodies. Rain and Charlie had begun learning the Hmong language, and they and the villagers had been getting along well. The maniraptors hunted and brought meat for the village, and could heal some sicknesses. Mostly, though, they were just content to live off of the land in a similar way, and they respected each other's ways of life.

"It looks like a good place for them," Beth said. "As good a place as is possible in this world, anyway."

"It's sad, though," Samira said. "They're the only two left. Even though they survived, it's an extinction event. The end of an intelligent species."

Kit chuckled, then outright laughed. "About that," he said, smiling. "There's one more surprise for today."

CHAPTER THIRTY

Pak held his daughter Kwanjai's hands as they hiked up the mountain slope. She had grown so big, and he was so proud of her. It had been Pak who had contacted Kit to tell him about the maniraptors, and he'd collaborated with Kit to find them a place to hide. In his important government role, Kit had made sure Pak's family lacked for nothing, and Pak helped keep the secret and bring messages and requested supplies to the remote karst valley.

Moving away from Khai Nun hadn't been an easy adjustment. but they were getting by. Kwanjai lived in the district capital during the week to attend school, but on weekends, like today, she came home, and they took this long walk together to spend time with her new friends.

Kwanjai ran laughing up ahead, following the scent markers that she could detect more easily than he could. When Pak topped the rise, he found her embracing the smaller of the two maniraptors.

"Charlie's looking good, isn't he, father?" she crowed. She accompanied the words with a complex scent that captured the smell of Charlie's new name (something like what the ground smelled like after a thunderstorm?) and her own feelings of joy and love.

Pak greeted Charlie himself using English rather than scent, which he was still more comfortable with. The two of them relaxed for a while in the shade, Charlie sharing brief memory scents with him while Kwanjai ran on ahead calling "Auntie Ling, Auntie Ling!" Pak told Charlie news about Thailand and the outside world.

A few minutes later, Kwanjai came skipping out of the building that served the two maniraptors as a home. "Come see!" she called, clutching at Pak's arm.

"Okay, okay," he said, allowing her to lead him.

Inside, the dimness was broken by several organic lights, created by the maniraptors, that glowed with a faint pulse. Another organic machine in the corner wafted scents into the space that Pak knew was a form of music, though it held no meaning for him. Distant Rain greeted him warmly, and he detected a fierce pride in her welcome.

He could hear Li Ling's voice in another part of the building, saying, "Usually two wouldn't give you enough genetic diversity. You need a lot more members of a species, preferably from a wide selection of the gene pool, to have any hope of bringing back a population. The way the maniraptors can alter their own genetics, though, I don't think that will be a problem. They can create their own diversity."

Kwanjai tugged Pak toward the back of the building. He apologized to Rain and followed his daughter to a small back room. Kit stood there talking on a chunky satphone, while Li Ling leaned over his shoulder, resting a hand gently on his arm. There was a spark there, Pak thought. The two scientists got along very well and shared a secret obsession they couldn't talk to anyone else about. They would be sleeping together within the month, he guessed, if they weren't already.

Kwanjai kept pulling him farther into the room, which was roughly circular in shape, an enclave that had been decorated with circles of flowers surrounding a soft raised dais. She stopped and threw out her hands like a magician presenting the conclusion of his trick. On the dais sat what Pak thought might have been the most marvelous thing he had ever seen in his life.

It was an egg.

THIS IS THE END OF THE LIVING MEMORY TRILOGY, BY David Walton. If you enjoyed it, please consider leaving a review and trying more titles by this author.

OTHER BOOKS BY DAVID WALTON

The Genius Plague (Winner of the Campbell Award for Best SF Novel of the Year)

Three Laws Lethal (Wall Street Journal Best of SF List 2019)

Terminal Mind (Winner of the Philip K. Dick Award)

Superposition

Supersymmetry

ACKNOWLEDGMENTS

Many thanks to Nadim and Julia Nakhleh for reading this book in its unpolished form and making suggestions to improve it. Thanks to Alex Shvartsman for publishing advice and ebook formatting. Thanks to Dr. Michael Brett-Surman, formerly Museum Specialist for Dinosaurs, Fossil Reptiles, and Amphibians at the National Museum of Natural History of the Smithsonian Institution. This book has many flights of fancy which are not his fault, but he reviewed an earlier draft and helped me get the real paleontology right. Finally, thanks to you, dear reader, for taking a chance on this book when you had so many other options available. I hope you enjoyed it!

ABOUT THE AUTHOR

David Walton is an aerospace engineer and the father of eight children. His love for dinosaurs started as a boy, but it wasn't until his own young son's enthusiasm that he really started to learn about how they lived and what they were like. His research obsessions have also included fungus (The Genius Plague), self-driving cars (Three Laws Lethal), and quantum physics (Superposition). When he's not writing, he's reading, playing piano, watching dinosaurs through his binoculars, or laughing with his family around the dinner table.

Printed in the USA
CPSIA information can be obtained
at www.ICGtesting.com
LVHW090847081123
763310LV00006B/71

9 798868 909283